Love Finds You
in
LIBERTY
Indiana

Love Finds You
in
LIBERTY
Indiana

BY MELANIE DOBSON

summerside
PRESS

Love Finds You in Liberty, Indiana
© 2009 by Melanie Dobson

ISBN 978-1-934770-74-0

All scripture quotations are taken from the King James Version of the Bible.

The town depicted in this book is a real place, but all characters are fictional. Any resemblances to actual people or events are purely coincidental.

Cover and Interior Design by Müllerhaus Publishing Group
www.mullerhaus.net

Published by Summerside Press, Inc., 11024 Quebec Circle, Bloomington, Minnesota 55438 | **www.summersidepress.com**

Fall in love with Summerside.

Printed in the USA.

Dedication

....

To my daughter Karlyn Skye

Your courageous spirit and loving heart have blessed me and so
many others. May God continue to use your compassion and your
determination to protect and defend all those who need a friend.

Acknowledgments
....

In the 1800s, every Quaker Meeting had a clerk who would scribble down "minutes" as people conducted business or spoke out when the Spirit led. As I've worked on this novel, my role has been almost like that of a Quaker clerk, recording just a few accounts of the thousands of brave men, women, and children who risked their lives either to flee from slavery or to protect those who had run away. This work is fiction, but it is based on true stories about the courage and compassion of Quakers who harbored runaway slaves in their homes and escorted them to Canada along the "Liberty Line."

Many people supported and encouraged me during my research and writing, and I'm grateful to every one of them.

A huge thank-you to the amazing Karen Coffey, Liberty, Indiana's research librarian extraordinaire. Not only did she provide me with an incredible amount of information about the town, both past and present, but she gave me a personal tour of the area and opened up the doors for me to visit William Beard's home (a renowned conductor on the Underground Railroad). Karen's great-great-grandfather worked at a woolen mill outside Liberty, and a photo of the old Cockefair Mill is the backdrop for the book's cover. The accurate details in this book are the result of Karen's hard work in collecting and sending me scads of material about the area. All errors (and I'm sure there are plenty) are my fault.

Rachel Meisel at Summerside Press—thank you for believing in this idea from the beginning and helping me mold it into the story it is today. You've been a joy to work with!

Jason Rovenstine at Summerside Press—you've encouraged (and fed!) me throughout this project. Thank you for your wisdom and your hard work in getting this book out to so many.

Connie Troyer—an incredible editor. Thank you for sharing your Quaker heritage with me and for correcting my many mistakes. The best of this book is the result of your hard work.

A special thank-you to Kimberly Felton, who cheered on this book from the beginning, as well. Attending an unprogrammed Meeting with you was a highlight for me, and I really appreciate your helping me learn about the Religious Society of Friends, past and present. Thank you for your interest in this story and for your enthusiasm.

Thank you to my critique group who gave me invaluable input through this whole process—Sandra Bishop, Leslie Gould, Christa Sterkin, Kelly Chang, and Kimberly Felton. You ladies rock!

Thank you to all the amazing people in Liberty, Indiana, who welcomed me to their town, with a special thanks to Julian, Ruth, Stephen, and Vicky Logue for letting me crawl around your attic and explore the other hidden places in your home, as well as allowing me to borrow your family papers to learn about the house and the local Salem Meeting. It was a delight to meet all of you! Thank you also to Beverly Wiwi at the beautiful Carriage Lamp Bed & Breakfast for taking good care of me while I was away from home. If my readers visit Liberty, the Carriage Lamp B & B is definitely the place to stay.

Thank you to Karen Trent at the Huddleston Farmhouse and Saundra Jackson at the Levi Coffin House for giving me personal tours of these historic gems. I learned so much from each of you.

Thank you to the many other people who graciously answered my questions about Quaker history and the Underground Railroad, including Janet Wacker, Bev Hamilton, William Jolliff, Rebecca Ankeny, and Tom Hamm.

Thank you to my parents, Jim and Lyn Beroth, for continuing to root for me during the highs and lows of this writing journey, and thank you to Carolyn Dobson, Christina Nunn, Miralee Ferrell, Patti Lacy, Tosha Williams, Diane Comer, Patricia Pursley, Heather Cotton, Lynda Shields, and Brenna Darazs for your many words of encouragement.

Thank you to Karly and Kiki, who asked almost every day how many words I had written and then cheered when I told them. I am blessed beyond words to have you both as my daughters.

Another huge thank-you to my wonderful husband, Jon. Without you and your support, not to mention the many Saturdays you spent trying to work at the local indoor playground/pizza place, this book never would have been finished. You are amazing!

Most of all, thank you to my heavenly Father and His Son and the Holy Spirit for your light. I pray I will learn to listen as well as the Quakers did (and still do!) to your voice.

-Actual stop on the Underground Railroad (right)
-Salem Meetinghouse (left)
Liberty, Indiana

QUAKERS IN UNION COUNTY, INDIANA, were active participants of the Underground Railroad, harboring runaway slaves in hidden rooms of their homes and secretly transporting them north. The small town of Liberty was the county seat, and in 1850, this town of 370 people held 110 houses, two churches, a courthouse, a jail, multiple shops, and the first woolen mill west of the Alleghenies. Today, Liberty is a peaceful farming community of nearly 2,000 people and gateway to the beautiful Brookville Lake just south of town. The Salem Society of Friends still gathers in the same Meetinghouse where they met in 1850, and right down the road stands the home of well-known Underground Railroad conductor and stationmaster William Beard. The citizens of Liberty are friendly, hard-working people who are rightfully proud of their town's heritage. They are careful to preserve the memory of the many Quakers in their community who aided those attempting to escape slavery in Kentucky, just forty miles south of their town.

Chapter One

....

September 1850

A shadow grazed the moonlit yard and ducked into the regiment of pine trees blocking the western winds. Anna Brent pressed her nose against the cold pane and scanned the row of evergreens. Clusters of cones and needles bounced and swayed like the stuffed arms of a scarecrow in the breeze, and her mother's quilt fluttered on the clothesline beyond the porch. The shadow didn't reappear.

Boots tapped across the wood floor behind Anna, and she jumped.

"What is it?" Charlotte whispered.

Anna stumbled back from the parlor window and turned toward her housekeeper. Charlotte's hair was bundled under a net snood at the nape of her neck, and tight ringlets dangled at the sides of her face to hide the rugged scars left by her former owner's knife.

Charlotte smoothed her fingers over her lilac skirt. "Did someone knock?"

"No, but I saw something outside." Anna glanced out the window again, but the night was still. "Are we supposed to receive another shipment tonight?"

"I don't know. I haven't heard from Ben since Tuesday."

Their agent usually sent Charlotte a note before guiding runaways to their house, although some nights Ben himself was notified only hours before he had to deliver a shipment. On those nights, they would be surprised by a knock on the back door.

Anna nodded toward the hallway outside the parlor door. They had to be careful, for the sake of the others staying in their home. "You had best hide our friends."

Fear stole through the resolve in Charlotte's soft brown eyes, and Anna wished she could tell her that she didn't have to be afraid. "It's probably a bear rummaging for food."

"Of course," Charlotte replied. Then she lifted her skirt and rushed toward the steps.

Anna stared out the window and waited. Moonlight illuminated the clusters of deep purple-and-white calla lilies scattered around the front yard. Her father's wagon stood beside the porch—but her father was in Cincinnati for three days, ordering supplies for the mill.

She had been born in this house twenty-two years ago and had seen a bear only once, when she was riding a couple of miles north. The bear had bolted away from her and her horse, disappearing into the thorny bramble.

This time of year, though, bears weren't the only animals that pilfered food. Panthers hid in the craggy hills and wilderness, too, along with packs of wolves. She often heard the wolves, but she rarely saw one.

Whatever she had seen outside tonight hadn't darted into the trees like a panther or a wolf. It snuck through the yard, too big for a raccoon or skunk, yet too small to be a deer. And if it was a person, it was either a skittish guest or someone intent on trapping the men and women hidden upstairs.

Anna fidgeted with the bow on her bodice, her eyes fixed on the dark trees.

Slave hunters traveled north more often these days. Even though the scriptures commanded care of the poor and orphaned, many of her neighbors collaborated with the enemy and willingly betrayed runaways in their flight north. Instead of rescuing slaves, they swelled their pockets with blood rewards and reveled in the pleasure of their own freedom.

These days it was hard to know whom she could trust.

Something moved in the row of pine trees, and Anna strained her eyes to see if it was a person or an animal. The apparition darted toward the trees and then back again, hidden in a nest of needled branches.

Anna lifted the footstool from the entryway and carried it to the hearth. The fire crackled beside her, and heat permeated through her layered skirts as she stepped up onto the stool. She gathered her skirts with her left hand and reached above the mantel with the other to pull down her father's Kentucky rifle.

In the kitchen downstairs, she tugged open the drawer that her father kept stocked with cartridges. Edwin Brent prized this flintlock more than the two hunting rifles he kept stored in their barn, saying it was more accurate than any modern gun. He'd never harm a person with it, but he was a deadeye for deer and fowl.

She slid three cartridges and balls into her pocket and then ripped off the end of a fourth foil cartridge, shook the black powder into the long barrel, and rammed the cartridge and ball into the gun with the rod. It took some people three or four minutes to load a rifle like this one, but her father had taught her how to load his gun in under a minute. And then he'd taught her how to shoot it.

When she stepped out the front door, strands of hair stole away from her braid and blew across her eyes and neck, but she kept both hands clenched on the gun. Hundreds of cicadas sang out in the darkness. Down the hill, the wheel beside the woolen mill dumped buckets of water back into the river, which hummed and splashed in rhythm along Silver Creek.

A wolf cried out in the forest behind the house, and goose bumps prickled her arms when an entire pack answered the call with chilling howls. Either they were stalking dinner or the wolves sensed trouble.

Anna moved to the edge of the wide porch, the gun propped on her shoulder, and pointed the weapon toward the rolling hills and woods. A single hit on the lead wolf should scatter the rest of the pack, but if it didn't deter them, it should also give her enough time to load her next cartridge and ball.

Her gun honed on the forest, Anna watched the oak and sugar maple branches bat at the dark sky. The wolves didn't wander onto her property, but their cries escalated into a frenzy until, in an abrupt finale, they stopped.

The pine trees rustled to her right, and Anna swung toward the noise. She'd shoot to kill if it were a bear, but if it were a bounty hunter, she'd have to set the gun to her side.

Even though her father had taught her to shoot, he'd also taught her that the battle against slavery wasn't a fight against her fellow man. It was a silent, steady fight against evil. Instead of blasting her enemies with force, she and a few other members of the Religious Society of Friends relied on a quieter strategy of persuasion—and deception—to protect those runaways who couldn't protect themselves.

She wasn't afraid to die, but she'd never had a slave owner threaten her guests before. If one did, God help her, she didn't know what she would do.

Seconds passed in silence as a cloud blanketed the full moon. Her finger wrapped around the trigger, she called out, "Who goes there?"

When no one answered, she lifted her gun and blasted a warning shot in the air.

From the row of trees, a baby cried out in the darkness, and Anna pointed her gun toward the cry. Then she lowered the gun.

"Who goes there?" she shouted again into the darkness.

This time a faint voice answered. "A friend of a friend."

The gun clutched in her fingers, Anna cautiously moved off the porch. The voice could belong to a catcher baiting her away from the house, or it could be a fugitive who needed her help. She walked through the tall grass, past trees and the hidden door of the root cellar west of the house.

"Show yourself," she demanded, as the clouds swept past the moon.

A fifteen- or sixteen-year-old mulatto girl stepped out from the covering of trees, her head bowed. In her arms was a baby loosely swathed in a linsey-woolsey blanket. The child squirmed in the girl's arms and cried out again.

Anna set the gun on the ground. "Why didn't you knock on the back door?"

The girl looked up, and in the moonlight Anna saw a fresh wound on her forehead. Dirt smeared her caramel-colored cheeks, and her curly hair was matted to her head. Her voice trembled when she spoke. "I ain't knowin' if it the right place."

"What is your name?"

"Marie." The girl held up the baby, and Anna saw his fair skin. "And this is my chile, Peter."

"He's hungry?"

"Yessum."

The baby's cries calmed into a whimper.

"When did you and Peter eat last?"

Marie closed her eyes and then reopened them. "Yesterday mornin'."

"Your milk?"

Marie shook her head. "Ain't workin' no more."

Anna glanced around the yard and down the hill to see if anyone was watching them. It was one thing to house a runaway slave, but should she house a runaway who might have stolen a white child? She couldn't risk her anonymity or sacrifice the lives of her other guests if this girl was lying to her.

Another cloud passed over the moon, turning the yard black for a moment. When the light returned, Anna set her hand on the girl's shoulder, and Marie flinched.

"Are you alone?" she asked.

Marie nodded in response.

"How did you find our house?"

"Unca Ben done brought us up the river and showed me the way." Her fingers caressed the baby's head and then pointed toward the house. "He say look for a quilt, but I ain't seen no quilt."

Before Anna could tell her about the quilt by the door, the pounding of horse hooves broke through the quiet. Marie clutched the baby to her chest. "He comin' for me."

"Uncle Ben won't hurt you."

"Not Unca Ben." Marie pulled away from her. "Massa Owens."

Chapter Two
....

Anna shouted for her to stop, but Marie had already bolted for the back of the house with Peter in her arms. The horses would be at their house in two minutes, maybe less. Anna pulled her skirts above her knees and followed the girl into the darkness.

The rush of adrenaline might give Marie the strength to sprint a couple hundred yards, but she wouldn't have the strength to go much further. She and the baby needed to hide, not run.

She chased Marie toward the barn and watched the girl fidget with the clasp on the door and fling it open. Anna caught the door before it slammed shut. Hay crunched under Marie's feet as she fled across the floor. Goats bleated from their stalls.

Anna snatched a match from the top of the barrel and flicked it to light an oil lantern. Shadows danced over the mounds of hay at the far end of the barn. Even if Marie and the baby buried themselves in the straw, it wouldn't take long for a slave hunter with a pitchfork to find his prey. She had to catch Marie before a hunter did.

Marie dove into the hayrick, and Anna reached down for her arm. "They'll find you in here."

The girl trembled in Anna's grasp. "Massa's gonna kill me."

"We've got to get you into the house," Anna insisted. "It's warm upstairs, and safe."

Marie didn't move, but the baby cried out again.

"Please let me help you," Anna begged. "We've got fresh milk for Peter and plenty of food for you."

Anna stepped toward the barn door, no time left to linger. She needed to greet her visitors like a lady and offer them a place to rest.

Her stomach rolled as she started to close the door. If her guests were hunters and they found Marie and the child in the barn, she would have to feign ignorance to protect the lives of the other runaways hiding inside the house...and the lives of the dozens of other fugitives who would pass through their station this fall.

"If they catch you....," she started to say—but she stopped herself. Marie knew better than she did what they would do if they caught her. She had probably traveled hundreds of miles in search of freedom. Anna wouldn't try to force her into the house.

She turned and jogged away from the barn. The horses were no longer trotting up the path. Either they had passed her house or the riders were tying their animals on the post in the yard.

Had she said the wrong thing to Marie? Maybe she should have been gentler instead of rushing her to make a decision when the girl was already scared.

She couldn't imagine how many white people had betrayed Marie in the past. She probably thought that Anna was going to lead her right to the hunters who would drag her back to her former master.

Anna flung open the back door and scraped the mud off her heels before she crossed the hallway and hurried down the stairs into the basement kitchen. Charlotte stood at the table, carving a roasted ham. She looked up at Anna and pointed toward the front of the house with the knife. "Someone's here."

"Are the guests safe?"

Charlotte shook her head; then her eyes grew wide with shock as she stared over Anna's shoulder.

Anna turned, and at the landing of the stairs stood Marie and Peter, tears streaking through the dirt on their faces. Instead of explaining why she changed her mind, Marie shut the door behind her and rushed down the steps. She flung her knapsack onto the table and dug out a dirty glass bottle.

Anna quickly rinsed the bottle in a bucket of water while Charlotte went to the cold spring in the next room, where they kept their milk and cheeses. The housekeeper returned seconds later with a jar of goat's milk, water dripping off its sides.

"I didn't lock the front door," Anna whispered.

Charlotte filled the bottle and handed it to Marie, who pressed it into Peter's mouth. The instant he began sucking, heavy footsteps pounded above, across the hallway floor.

Charlotte grabbed Marie's arm and hissed, "Hurry, child."

She pushed Marie toward a second staircase off the back of the kitchen and pulled the door shut behind them.

Her father's rifle was still out in the grass, abandoned beside the pines. Even though she would never kill a slave hunter, she had nothing with which to defend the people upstairs. Glancing across the counter, she plucked up the knife that Charlotte had been using to cut the ham. It wasn't much, but maybe a crazy woman flailing a knife would scare them away.

Her fingers balled around the steel handle, but instead of feeling terrified, an unexplainable peace rushed over her heart. The Divine Presence was in her home, with her. The Spirit blanketed her soul with peace and soothed her fear.

Her fingers loosened their grip on the knife. Whatever happened, she would remain calm.

"Anna?" Her father called out from the top of the steps, and she collapsed back against the counter. He had returned early from his trip.

Finding Marie in her yard had unsettled her. She had nothing to fear. She had almost put down the knife when she caught a glimpse of black hair behind her father.

"Evenin', Anna," Matthew Nelson said with a wink. His grin turned quickly to concern when he saw her windblown hair and the knife in her fingers. "Are you okay?"

She glanced between Matthew and her father. "There was a wolf outside."

Matthew stepped toward her. "And you grabbed a knife?"

She shrugged; it was too late to change her story. "I wanted to check on the livestock."

The elder Nelson appeared on the landing and walked down the ten steps behind his son and into the kitchen. "What's this about a wolf?"

Henry Nelson was several inches shorter than Matthew, and twenty or so pounds heavier, but even in his fifties he was a handsome man with thick dark hair, trimmed sideburns, and sharp eyes. Matthew had his father's hazel eyes and black hair, though his smile was much warmer than Henry's—especially when he smiled at her.

Matthew took her right hand. "A wolf was threatening Anna, so she threatened it back."

She bowed her head, tugging her hand out of his grasp. "I was just trying to protect our animals."

"Did you see it?" Henry queried.

"I watched it run away."

He stared at the knife in her hand. "Well, it was a good thing it wasn't running toward you."

The knife clattered when she dropped it beside the ham. "What brings you out to Silver Creek tonight?"

"I needed to talk your father into upping his production of blankets for me. I've got people from here to Indianapolis ordering supplies so they can leave for California before the first snow."

Matthew nodded toward the stove. "Something smells good."

"Charlotte just fried potatoes."

He glanced toward the cold spring at the right of the kitchen. "Where is Charlotte?"

"She's working upstairs." Anna smiled at her father. "You aren't supposed to be home yet."

"I finished early." Her father kissed the top of her head. "And I missed my girl."

She spoke to the elder Nelson. "We have plenty of extra food if you'd like to stay for dinner."

"We'd be delighted."

She reached up to the shelf overhead for the china plates, but her father stopped her. "Were you taking laundry off the clothesline earlier?"

"No...," she began and then paused. She had to get the quilt off the line before another runaway arrived. "Yes, I suppose I was. I stopped when I saw the wolf."

"There was only a quilt left," Matthew said. "You can take it down later."

"Oh, I couldn't leave it up. It was my mother's."

"I'll go with you," Matthew said as he followed her up to the main floor. "In case the wolf returns."

She protested, but Matthew wouldn't listen to her. She retrieved her wool shawl from a peg in the front closet and wrapped it around her shoulders.

As they strolled into the cool night air, Matthew began telling her a story about fishing on the Whitewater, but she couldn't concentrate. Two floors above the porch was the attic, and hidden inside the attic was a tired and hungry baby. She could only hope that Peter would fall asleep after his stomach was filled with milk. He had to stay quiet if they were going to keep their presence a secret from the Nelsons.

And they had to keep it a secret.

Henry Nelson exported products like wool blankets from Union County to small and large towns around the country. He and her father had done business together for three decades, but about ten years ago Henry had become an outspoken advocate for slave owners' rights. He was vocal in his beliefs that those who harbored slaves were breaking the eighth commandment...and hurting their country's economy.

She and her father and many of the Friends believed differently. Instead of condemning the work on the Underground, they thought God wanted them to care for the slaves like the Samaritan who had rescued the wounded Jew in the Gospel of Luke.

Matthew had never taken sides on the slavery issue—at least, he'd never taken sides when he was around her. She suspected that he, too, believed that helping runaway slaves was akin to theft.

Matthew trotted down the steps and stopped at the edge of the grass. "Where did you see the wolf?"

She pointed to the forest on the east side of their house. "He disappeared into the trees."

"Did he hear you?"

"I screamed and threw a couple pieces of firewood at him."

He stopped and turned toward her, admiring her with his gaze. "You're fearless."

When he smiled at her, she tried to smile back. Four months ago, after she returned from Oberlin College, Matthew had asked her to marry him. She had refused him then, and if he asked again, her answer would be the same. Matthew didn't know about her work on the Underground...and if they married, it would be impossible for her to continue harboring runaways if her husband opposed abolition.

Matthew stepped toward her, and she skirted around him. "I have to get back inside to help with dinner."

He reached out and caught her arm. "They won't even miss us."

She drew back from him and reached up to the clothesline instead. With a quick pinch, she snapped off each pin and tucked them into her pocket; then she folded the quilt once in her arms.

He turned her shoulders, but instead of stepping toward him, she stepped back again.

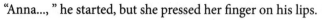

"Anna...," he started, but she pressed her finger on his lips. "Don't ask me again."

"Rachel and Luke are to be married in two weeks."

"I know."

He leaned close to her cheek and whispered, "What are we waiting for?"

He waited for her reply, but when she didn't speak, he dropped his hand. "Because you'll be disavowed?"

She folded the edges of the quilt again. "That's one of the reasons."

"If you say you'll marry me, Anna, I'll convert tomorrow." He slipped his hand under her chin, and she faced him in the dim light. "I've been saving my money, and I want to leave this place with you as my wife. I want us to go to California together, make our fortune in gold. Then we can come back here and live."

She shivered. "It's too cold to leave for California."

His hand dropped to his side. "We'll go the southern route, like everyone else."

She shook her head. "I don't want to go to California."

"We don't have to leave until spring...or we don't have to go at all."

She patted the calico on the quilt, her eyes focused on the trees beyond him. "We can never marry, Matthew."

He flung his hands up in frustration. "Why don't you want to get married?"

Her mind whirled, searching for words that made sense. Words that were kind but firm. She wanted him to know that she cared about him, but there were so many reasons she couldn't marry, especially him.

The words didn't come.

"You don't understand," she said softly.

"You're right, Anna." He turned toward the house. "I don't understand."

She wanted to reach out and take his elbow, but instead she tucked her fingers into the folds of calico. She felt guilty, letting him assume that she wouldn't marry him because of her faith or because he wanted to leave for California, but she couldn't possibly tell him everything.

It was more than the fact that she was a Quaker. She admired him, but she didn't love him like her friend Rachel loved Luke. Anna had known Matthew for years, but he couldn't be trusted with the secrets of her heart.

In the darkness above them, a muffled cry broke the silence, and Matthew stopped walking. Her breath caught in her throat. She glanced up at the windows and then at Matthew in front of her.

Her mind raced as she tried to concoct an answer to his expected question about why she had a baby in the house. She could say it was the child of a relative. A neighbor. He would ask more questions, of course, and she would have to answer them and then somehow inform her father and Charlotte of her story.

Perspiration beaded on her forehead when Peter cried again. If Charlotte were back downstairs, Matthew would want to know who was caring for the baby. And he would wonder why she hadn't mentioned earlier that she had a guest.

Matthew turned slowly back toward her, and she tried to smile at him.

"I told you there was a wolf," she said with a shrug.

He scanned the yard and then looked back at her. "It sounds like a pup."

She rushed around him and climbed the steps to the porch. "Which means the whole pack is nearby."

"I don't know...."

She shushed him. "Hurry, Matthew."

He followed her up the porch stairs and into the house. She bolted the door behind them.

Chapter Three

....

Anna shuffled around the kitchen, filling a basket with soda biscuits and a pitcher with fresh apple cider for the men upstairs in the dining room. The fire popped and blazed in front of her, but no sounds came from the attic. Either Peter had fallen asleep or his cries were insulated in his hiding place.

She had never been so grateful for the quiet.

Charlotte slipped down the back staircase moments later and reached for the knife to finish cutting the ham.

"I gave some paregoric to the wee one to help him sleep."

"Did it work?" Anna asked.

"For now."

Those who weren't sleeping were probably terrified.

Anna scooped the fried potatoes onto a platter alongside green beans. She didn't want to go upstairs to the dining room and serve Matthew, but she didn't have a choice. Both of their fathers would wonder why she was hiding. Matthew had stopped speaking to her when they walked through the door, and she doubted he would even attempt casual conversation over dinner.

She couldn't blame him for fuming, though she wished she could be completely honest with him. The truth would not only put her at risk, but it could threaten their entire network.

Walking into the spring room, Anna knelt by the cistern of icy water and pulled out a bottle of cream. Moving to the kitchen, she filled a bowl on the table with cream and added the blackberries that she and Charlotte had picked that afternoon for themselves and their hidden guests.

Even if she set aside her work on the Underground and married Matthew, they would never be compatible. He may convert, but he would always feel the pull of the world more than she did. And if he weren't careful, the elders would one day disavow both him and his wife.

When she was at Oberlin, Anna had read the journals of renowned Friends like Elizabeth Fry, who had helped revolutionize the prison system for women around the world. Elizabeth Fry, however, struggled at home with a complacent husband and almost a dozen children who chose to leave the Society of Friends. Anna would be devastated if she married a man who wasn't dedicated to his faith or if they raised children who turned their backs on the Friends.

Before she'd turned twenty, she had resolved herself to the fact that she would probably never marry. There was much more she could do as an independent Quaker woman than she could married to a man who was either pro-slavery or ambivalent to the sufferings of their friends down South.

But if she ever did marry, she hoped for a husband who was committed both to God and to the strict morals of the Friends. A man committed to helping her rescue those who had escaped slavery.

Charlotte placed the roasted ham, potatoes, and pitcher of cider into the dumbwaiter and yanked on the rope to propel it to the second floor. Anna slipped by her and went upstairs, biscuits in one hand and the bowl of blackberries in the other.

Matthew didn't look at her as she set the basket on the table. She turned toward the dumbwaiter to remove the rest of the food, but when she did, she saw the latest edition of the *Liberty Era* on the sideboard. She was supposed to burn that yesterday. How could she have forgotten?

While the men were eating tonight, she would feed it to the fire.

She reached for the paper, but before she touched it, Matthew swept it away. Turning to the dumbwaiter, she tried to ignore him and what he was reading. She'd already read the feature story so many times that she practically knew it by heart.

When she set the platter of potatoes on the table, she glanced up. Matthew was looking right back at her. "What is this?"

So much for not talking to her.

Edwin and Henry stopped their conversation as well, and Henry glanced over the shoulder of his son to read the front page. Minutes passed as she served the ham and the drinks. And she watched, almost in fascination, as Henry's eyes grew large like the harvest moon.

When he finally looked back up, his voice sounded like a growl. "Who is Daniel Stanton?"

Her father cut off a lump of butter with his knife before he spoke. "The new editor at the *Era*."

"He's turning the paper into propaganda!"

Her father smoothed the butter over a hot biscuit. "There's no crime against passion."

Henry pushed the paper away. "Rubbish! There's already enough animosity around here without an outsider coming in and infuriating everyone again."

Anna sat down across from Matthew and passed him the ham. Her father picked up the platter of potatoes and beans, but he didn't dish any onto his plate. "Isaac thinks he will help increase subscriptions."

"Isaac is a fool."

"Isaac is a good businessman," Edwin said as he handed over the platter. "And a friend."

"Well, the man he hired is trying to stir up sentiments."

Her father pulled the paper toward him. "It looks like the story of a fugitive slave."

Henry slapped the edge of the paper with his hand. "This Daniel Stanton claims that the slave's master was breaking moral law for retrieving his property instead of reminding readers that the slave was breaking our Union's law by running away."

"Did he discuss God's law?"

Henry didn't seem to hear him. "People like him don't realize that the end of slavery would mean the end of our Union."

"That's rubbish," Anna muttered, and then jerked her head up.

No one was looking at her, and she sighed. She had to mind herself and her temper before people like the Nelsons guessed where her and her father's sentiments lay. It was her actions, not her words, that defended the runaways. The lives of the six people upstairs were at the mercy of her tongue.

Henry continued ranting about the inane stunts of abolitionists, like it was the fault of abolitionists that the country was divided over this issue. How could he not be moved even a little by Daniel Stanton's story?

The new editor was a poor writer, yet he had captured the pain and despondency of an older slave named Bradley—a man apprehended near Bloomington by a notorious Negro slave hunter named Simon Mathers, whose profession was to betray other colored people in exchange for reward money. Bradley's owner had come all the way from St. Louis to retrieve his slave from Simon Mathers, and when he found him, he fitted an iron collar around Bradley's neck and made him walk the two hundred miles home. The owner had stated in public that he'd cushioned Bradley in the past, but now his Negro was going to find out what slavery was really like.

Runaway slaves like Bradley fought for a single breath of freedom like a drowning person fought for air, yet the catchers snatched away their last hope that liberty and justice was truly for all. And somehow the federal government justified this cruelty, ruling that slaves were property instead of people with rights. Their masters could do whatever they pleased with their property—sell them, beat them, kill them—as if these beloved children of God were hogs or cattle instead of souls enveloped in rugged flesh and blood.

The story had sickened Anna, as did every story about slaves who were abused by their owners. But Daniel Stanton had taken a stand and both condemned the owner for his cruelty and applauded Bradley for running north. Anyone courageous enough to write in opposition of slavery—and put their name on their articles—was a brave soul.

Henry didn't turn to the second page of the newspaper, but if he had, he would have read about Delia Wharton, a young woman in North Carolina who had been sentenced to death for helping five slaves escape. Henry probably would have applauded the courts for upholding the law.

She had never known anyone put to death by the courts or even jailed in Indiana for assisting a fugitive, although plenty of people had been tarred and feathered and run out of town for their work on the Underground Railroad. A few had even been killed by the opposition, but there had never been enough evidence to indict the killers for murder.

"Where did this Daniel Stanton come from?" Matthew asked.

"Isaac said he was a lawyer." Her father took a long sip of water. "From someplace in Ohio, I believe."

Henry set down his fork. "You'd better tell Isaac to be careful about what his new man writes."

A smile slipped across Edwin's face. "Why don't you tell Isaac yourself?"

Anna stifled her own smile. Henry may lambaste abolition around town, but he usually withheld his opinion from Isaac Barnes; the publisher of the *Liberty Era* was also the town banker and held the deed for the Nelsons' elegant home.

"You may think this is funny, Edwin, but there are serious repercussions for editors intent on riling up anger."

The smile on her father's face disappeared. "The press has freedom in our country."

"Didn't do much good for men like James Birney and Elijah Lovejoy."

Anna shivered at the mention of the two abolitionist editors—one whose printing press had been destroyed and dumped into the river and the other who had been murdered.

Her father didn't seem phased by the names. "I hope you don't start making threats, Henry."

The man waved his hand across his ham and beans. "I'm not threatening anyone, but someone has got to speak up for the truth and our country's laws."

Anna glanced over at Matthew, but his eyes were focused on his father. The opposition in their small town seemed mild in comparison to the bigger cities, though many people in their county hated abolition. They were afraid of slaves and of what would happen if the federal government decided to abolish the institution that imprisoned them.

"I've had a long journey," her father said as he pushed back his plate. "Let's leave the discussion of politics for another day."

Henry and Matthew both stood up, and Henry pointed back at the paper. "You might want to burn that."

Her father shook his head. "I'm not afraid of words."

Anna wasn't afraid of words either, but she had a powerful fear of *story*, especially stories that moved people to compassion or anger.

Her father may not burn the paper tonight, but *she* would pitch it into the fire.

* * * * *

Anna watched from the window ledge in the parlor to make sure the Nelsons left their property. Henry Nelson hopped on his horse first and then Matthew followed, both of them galloping back down the hill in the moonlight.

She drew the curtain over the front window and moved to the dining room. Her father was still sitting at the table, staring at the plate in front of him, but he didn't lift his fork again. Except for a couple of bites of ham and a biscuit, he hadn't eaten anything on his plate. Just a year ago her father had been a large man, but his clothes now hung on his body. His grey eyes were tired, and strands of white had woven themselves through his brown hair.

He may have aged a decade in the past twelve months, but she still well remembered the youthful man, the one who used to trot around the kitchen with her mother even though dancing was considered to be disorderly conduct. He had never failed to be kind to either her or her mother. Never failed to love her even when he was grieving for his wife.

Her father looked at her, and she savored the kindness that still played in his eyes. He may have lost his youth—and some of the sharp wit from his tongue—but she knew he loved her.

"How many are there?" he asked.

"Six. A girl arrived tonight with a newborn baby."

"Her child?"

"That's what she said, but his skin is as white as mine."

"You think she's lying?" Edwin asked.

It wasn't unheard of to have a white slave pass through the Underground homes of Indiana, but they had never hosted one in their house. As the female slaves in the South bore children for their masters, slaves were becoming lighter- and lighter-skinned. The color of skin—or the patronage—didn't matter to the state or the slave hunters. A white-looking child born to a slave woman was considered a slave for life.

Anna reached for the platter that contained potatoes and beans and slid it into the dumbwaiter. Marie had clung to Peter like any mother trying to protect her child, and then she had raced to hide him. "I believe she's telling the truth."

"Then we will send her and her baby up the line as soon as we're able."

Anna leaned down and hugged her father's shoulders. Even if Marie's story proved false, her father was erring on the side of compassion, and she loved him for it.

Edwin pushed back his chair and stood beside her. He picked up the bowl of blackberries and cream and put it on the dumbwaiter beside the rest of the food; then he heaved the small elevator upward until it stopped moving.

Together they walked up the main steps to the second floor and into the guest chamber at the end of the hallway. The room held a four-poster bed along with a rocking chair and a round table in one corner. Under the square window at the other side of the room was a built-in cupboard made of red oak. They usually stored blankets and pillows in the cupboard, but tonight the pillows and blankets were on the bed.

Edwin locked the door to the room, and Anna ducked down in front of the cupboard door. She crawled through the small enclosure and slid open a panel on the left side. On the other side of the panel was a tiny room with a ladder.

Slowly she climbed the ladder, toward the flickering light above. Her boot snagged the edge of her skirt, and she teetered on the rung as she tried to free herself.

A dark face peered through the opening above her and broke into a smile. "You okay, Miss Anna?"

"I am, George, but it would be a lot easier to climb ladders if I had a pair of trousers."

George reached out his hands to her, and she hoisted her skirt to climb the remaining three rungs with his help.

Inside the hiding place were two other middle-aged men named Roger and Paul, along with an elderly woman they called Auntie Rae. Charlotte sat beside Marie and Peter on the floor, showing the girl how to swaddle Peter in a blanket.

The room was only four feet across, but its brick walls stretched the length of the attic. A slave hunter could search every corner in the house for fugitives, but unless he cleaned out the pillows and crawled far back into the cupboard, he wouldn't find their guests. Not even his ax would penetrate the attic wall to this space.

Many nights, if they had only a guest or two, they would let their friends sleep in the guest room below with easy access to the ladder. But on nights like this, when people such as the Nelsons visited the house, it was safer to harbor their guests up here—especially if Matthew hadn't believed her ruse about the baby wolf.

Anna pulled the platters of food off the dumbwaiter and began setting them around on the floor. Edwin's head popped into the room, and he handed George a pitcher of milk before pulling himself up. "We're sorry dinner is so late."

"We're grateful for it anytime," George said as he plucked tin cups off hooks along the wall. The others left the talking to George, and he seemed to enjoy his role as spokesperson. "We heard you had a mite of company."

Her father poured milk into the cups. "It wasn't anyone you'd want to meet."

"I figured." George reached for a biscuit and devoured it. "There ain't many white folk I want to meet."

"It will be different when you get to Canada, my friend."

"I hope so, Massa Edwin. I sure hope so...."

Edwin placed his hand on the broad shoulder in front of him. "You follow the Light, George, and He will lead you to friends who know you are already free."

A timid voice spoke out from the other side of the room. "When can we go to Canada?"

Edwin squinted into the darkness, and Anna introduced her father to Marie and the baby.

"As soon as the moon begins to darken again."

"But when will that be?"

"In a little over a week."

She choked. "He'll come before then."

While the others ate, Anna crossed the floor with a plate of food and sat down beside Marie. Reaching out her arm, she tried to comfort the girl, but Marie scooted away. Anna handed Marie the plate and then folded her hands in her lap.

"You need to rest for now," she said softly. "We're going to protect you."

Marie devoured the food before she spoke again. "Ain't no one can protect me from him, Miss...."

"Please call me Anna," she said, smiling at the girl.

"I ain't never called a white girl anything but *Miss*."

"I know it seems strange, but we believe that all men and women should be addressed by the name their parents gave them."

Marie stumbled over her first name. "Miss Anna, Massa Owens is gonna find me here."

"No one knows where you are except us and Ben."

She fidgeted with a thread on Peter's blanket. "Somethin' else I gots ta tell you."

"You don't have to worry about telling me anything."

Marie hesitated. "Afore I got here's tonight, I knocked on 'nother door down the creek. Had a quilt on the line like Ben said."

Anna leaned closer. "Was anyone home?"

"Yessum. A man and his wife, seems to me. They was as surprised ta see me as I was ta see 'em." Marie smoothed her hand over Peter's chest. "I ran fast, knowin' they ain't gonna be kind ta me like some folks been."

Anna took a deep breath. There were five houses in the woods between their home and the river. She didn't know a single person in those homes who was sympathetic toward runaways.

"Did they get a good look at you?"

Marie bowed her head. "Yessum. And a good look at Peter, too."

If that family reported seeing fugitive slaves in their county, none of them would be able to travel right now.

"You'll still be safe here," Anna said as she unfolded two blankets for Marie. The girl collapsed on the wool with the baby at her side, but before she closed her eyes, Peter stirred. Then he began to cry again.

"Shut that baby up," one of the men barked from across the room.

Marie cuddled Peter close to her, but he didn't stop crying.

"I can take him downstairs and rock him," Anna offered.

"No..." Fear flashed through Marie's eyes, and she pulled Peter to her. "My baby should sleep with me."

She patted the floor beside Marie. "I could sit here, right beside you, and rock him while you sleep."

Charlotte walked over to Marie and handed her a gum ring, the end coated with sugar.

"Please..." Marie looked over at the four other runaways, gathered with Edwin around their meal. "Please don't be takin' him away from me."

"I won't," Anna replied as she reached for Peter.

Marie watched her and Peter from the floor until her body succumbed to exhaustion. The baby cradled in her arms, Anna let him suck on the gum ring until he began to rest as well. She rocked him gently for hours, late into the night.

Chapter Four

Fog draped over the shops in Liberty, and the scent of morning rain replaced the stench of manure on the streets. A pig brushed against Daniel Stanton's newly pressed trousers when he stepped out of his boardinghouse, and he shoved the wet animal away with his boot. The pig snorted in retort and then shuffled down the planks of the sidewalk in search of breakfast.

His own stomach rumbled as he turned off Main Street and onto the quieter one where his sister and brother-in-law lived. Orange and red leaves lined the dirt road, and fallen buckeyes were scattered across the street and wide lawns.

Daniel took his watch out of his pocket and checked the time. His sister didn't serve breakfast until precisely eight o'clock, and it was a quarter till.

He hopped up the steps to the veranda and sat down on the bench beside the Cooleys' front door. When he had first come to Liberty last month, his sister had invited him to breakfast on Seventh Day. He'd arrived a half hour early, and for the next thirty minutes, he'd listened to her rant while she and her poor housekeeper tried to follow a new gravy recipe from *Godey's Lady's Book*. He had told her he didn't need fancy gravy over his eggs and biscuits, didn't really need any gravy at all, but she had insisted on perfecting the sauce.

Every Seventh Day since, he had arrived fifteen minutes early and waited outside with his paper while Joseph dressed and the women fussed over the food.

Daniel blew into his hands and rubbed them together to ward off the chill from the morning air. Then he leaned forward and began to read the headlines of Union County's competing newspaper.

Unlike Daniel's paper, the editor of the *Union County News* didn't even mention the slave who had been chained in Bloomington and driven west like he was an animal. Instead, the editor spent the entire first page touting the benefits of the proposed law being debated right now in Congress—the Fugitive Slave Act.

In 1842, the U.S. Supreme Court had ruled that states did not have to aid in the hunting or recapturing of runaway slaves, but if this new law passed, it would repeal the Supreme Court's decision. A law that forced Yankees to hunt and capture slaves would turn Indiana and other Northern states into battlegrounds. Some people would comply. Others would rebel. And the rebellious ones would be tagged as criminals.

The fact that their Congress was even considering this type of law was unfathomable to him. If it passed, it would turn those who sacrificed to love their fellow man into lawbreakers. It would be a crime to even assist a wounded runaway.

Milton Kent, the editor of the *Union County News*, declared the law critical to uphold the Union of the States. It seemed as if that was what everyone was most concerned about—keeping the country together at all costs instead of actually protecting the people who lived within its borders.

Daniel quickly turned the page and skimmed the market reports and editorials. At the bottom of the page were boxed advertisements for stoves, shoes, and runaway slaves. The third advertisement caught his eye.

$1,000 REWARD. *Ran away from the subscriber, the fifteenth of June, living in Knoxville, Tennessee, my Negro girl,* **MARIE,** *about sixteen years of age, light complexion, pretty features, either pregnant or traveling with newborn. A red scar runs down the back of Marie's neck, approx. three inches long, two inches wide. She may be resistant if approached.*

Marie was last seen near Madison, Indiana, in August.
I will pay the above reward for both Marie and her child, or
five hundred dollars for either of them.

> *Noah Owens*
> *No. 45 Pearl Street*
> *Knoxville*

Daniel slumped back against the slats of the bench. Of course this girl would be resistant if a slave hunter approached her. Wouldn't most innocent people resist if they were forced into imprisonment for life?

Here was a young woman, pregnant, running north for almost three months, with her master on her trail. She had risked everything to get away from this Noah Owens and his family. Was she still pregnant, or had she birthed her baby along the way?

Traveling on foot with a newborn would be treacherous—for both her and the child. Especially with such a steep reward on their heads. Money like that might even set some of their more respectable citizens searching for the girl; a thousand dollars could buy someone a nice house in Liberty on a sizable piece of land.

He slammed the paper shut and set it on the bench beside him. How could men like Milton Kent fund their papers by selling advertisements like these? Kent was paying for his printing press by selling out innocent blood.

He would never agree to running advertisements for fugitive slaves in the *Liberty Era*. The only reason he had agreed to take on this newspaper was because Isaac personally paid for the printing costs and Daniel's salary. They received just a pittance from subscriptions, but they didn't need to rely on the blood money of slave owners to finance the news.

He leaned his head back against the window. In four hours, he was scheduled to debate Milton Kent on the steps of the courthouse—Daniel's introduction into gritty Hoosier politics. Kent's disciples may tar and feather him, but he'd speak the truth.

The front door creaked open, and Esther peaked her head outside. "It's freezing out here, Daniel."

He looked up at his sister. Her ribboned bonnet covered her light blond hair, and her face was freshly powdered. She wore a jacket trimmed with black braids and a lacy, hooped skirt he assumed was fashioned from a pattern in *Godey's Lady's Book*.

He folded his newspaper and tucked it under his arm. His sister didn't concern herself with stories about runaway slaves. Her every move was directed by a silly ladies' magazine she extolled as the crème de la crème of proper etiquette, fashion, and food. He'd never actually opened one of the magazines, but she had yet to discuss *Godey's* take on issues like poverty or slavery or abolition. How could anyone be concerned about the color and fit of their dress when there were thousands of people enslaved not forty miles away?

He stood slowly. He wished he could talk to his sister about slavery, but every time he broached the subject, she would pat him on the shoulder and ask him if he preferred plum cake or chocolate soufflé, like dessert would distract him from the horrors of slavery.

"We're having cream toast with peach compote for breakfast," Esther announced, like she was introducing breakfast for the president himself.

He followed her through the front door, into the warmth of the house. "How are you feeling this morning?"

Her hand rolled over her belly. "She kicked me all night long."

"Or he…"

"Oh, it's a girl, Daniel." Esther kissed his cheek and tugged him toward the kitchen. "A boy would stop and take a rest."

He tried to smile at his sister. Even as frail and simple as she was, he loved her. And he tried to forgive her fascination with worldly things.

"Is Joseph down yet?"

She motioned toward the dining room. "He already drank two cups of coffee."

"If there's any left..."

Esther scooted away. "I'll pour you a cup right now."

Walking by the kitchen doorway, Daniel peeked his head into the room. "Morning, Greta."

The housekeeper turned from the blazing fire and waved at Daniel. "Mornin', Mr. Stanton."

Greta Lawson was a pretty woman, her skin the color of creamed coffee. She was almost thirty and among the privileged colored people who had been born free.

"You know I don't call anyone by 'Mister' or 'Missus,' Greta, and I don't answer to it."

"Then I guess you won't be answering to me."

Esther laughed at the woman, and Daniel brushed off his sleeves like he was sweeping off her comment. "Is Ralph coming to the debate today?"

She grinned. "Depends who's debatin'."

"No one of consequence, I'm sure."

Esther hung the coffeepot on the crane by the fire, and Greta swung it over the flames. She wiped her hands on a cloth and turned back to Daniel. "He wouldn't miss it."

"You married a fine man, Greta."

"Lord knows I did!"

"How does he put up with you?"

She snapped the cloth at him. "You get out of my kitchen!"

He laughed. "Gladly."

"I'll bring your coffee out in a few minutes...." Esther's voice trailed off as he rounded the corner to the dining room.

Joseph Cooley sat at the head of the long table, his china cup pushed to the side as he scoured the *Union County News*.

Daniel tossed his paper onto the table. "You reading about the fugitive slave law?"

Joseph nodded. "Congress is going to pass it."

"It's unconstitutional."

"Now, Daniel..."

"You can't tell me that God meant for any of His children to live as slaves, especially in a free country like ours."

"It's a fallen world, Daniel, and not even you can change that." Joseph took a sip of coffee. "I don't believe that God meant anyone to live as slaves either, but I do believe that those who are already slaves should be subject to their masters."

"Even if it means being beaten or killed..."

"I am responsible for what God has entrusted to my household, Daniel. Slave owners are responsible to what God has entrusted to them. Yes, they should treat their slaves like family, but none of us have a right to interfere if they don't."

Daniel remembered the despair in Bradley's eyes, utterly broken in bitter disappointment and anguish, as the master who should be treating him like a son or brother fitted him with a collar and chained him to the wagon.

He had tried to talk Bradley's owner out of abusing the man, but anger and humiliation had overtaken any reason in the man's actions. Instead of rescuing Bradley, all Daniel could do was write his story, and he determined to write about every abused runaway that crossed his path.

Daniel stared at the paper on the table, the black print blurring into gray.

He wished he were better with his pen. He wished he could convince people like Joseph that slavery in every form was evil. If he could convince respected men and women to take a stand on this issue, others would follow.

Yet in spite of his words, his own brother-in-law still had more compassion for the slave owners than their slaves—while Daniel had no compassion for someone who would offer a thousand dollars for the return of a slave girl and her child.

"I've never met a slave who felt like he was part of the family," Daniel said.

Joseph sighed. "That's because you've only met the ones running away."

Daniel looked up from the paper into Joseph's face. "Have you ever talked to a slave?"

Joseph met his stare. "Have you ever talked to a slave owner?"

Esther slipped a china cup filled with coffee onto his place mat. Steam billowed up to his face, and he reached for the cup and took a long sip of the hot barley before he spoke again. "It doesn't matter if Fillmore and the others pass this law. I won't stop fighting for the slaves."

Esther sat down beside him. "You need to leave the fighting to someone else, Daniel."

He glanced back at his sister. "Surely you don't think we should ignore the runaways."

"Mrs. Gunther said that you and your paper are upsetting the whole town." She leaned toward him. "You have got to stop telling everyone that you hate slavery."

He stared at his sister, stunned that she, too, thought he needed to pacify his views. If he didn't speak out on behalf of slaves, who would speak for them?

Esther's hands moved to her hips. "If you aren't careful, you're going to lose this new job as well, and then who would hire you?"

"I am not going to lose my position," he insisted. Yet his words sounded empty. He'd lost two jobs because of his stance on abolition.

"Mrs. Gunther said that..."

Joseph interrupted his wife. "You will not repeat gossip in this house."

"But he is sacrificing his career for a bunch of..."

"He is not sacrificing his career," Joseph said, but Daniel stood and faced his sister.

"For a bunch of what, Esther?" he asked.

The word that came out of her mouth shocked both men.

"Esther!" Joseph exclaimed—but she continued, her fists clenched to her sides.

"People pay good money for slaves," she said. "They are supposed to do the work that God intended for them to do."

Anger surged inside him, and his voice shook. "What if someone came and put Greta in chains and hauled her away to work in the fields?"

"I think—"

He didn't let her finish. "What if you were born black, Essie? Would you be satisfied picking cotton or ironing for fourteen hours a day, every day, for the rest of your life?"

Joseph pounded his palms on the table. "Enough!"

Esther muttered something and then pursed her lips. Daniel looked away from his sister, grateful that Joseph had stopped them both before he shredded both her and her ridiculous notions.

Many Americans thought that colored people were part of an inferior race, that they existed for the sole purpose of serving and obeying their white masters, but Esther seemed to treat Greta so well. How could she believe these lies, too?

Esther patted her hair, and then smiled. "The peach compote is almost ready."

"Thank you, dear." Joseph glanced at his pocket watch and stood. "Unfortunately, I can't stay and eat with you this morning."

"Oh, Joseph, it's Saturday...."

"Illness has no respect for the calendar, my dear."

When Esther rushed into the kitchen, Daniel turned to him. "A house call?"

Joseph nodded. "Down near Roseburg."

Daniel pushed his chair back. "Do you want me to come with you?"

"Not today, thank you. It's a pneumonia case, and she's still contagious." He reached for the jacket on the back of his chair and pulled it over his shoulders. "Aren't you debating Milton Kent this afternoon?"

Daniel sat back down. He'd almost forgotten.

His sister returned from the kitchen and handed Joseph a cloth napkin filled with food. "You need to eat, Joseph, or you'll be the one sick in bed."

Joseph kissed his wife's forehead and took the napkin before she walked him to the front door.

Daniel stared down at the *Union County News*. He was ready to meet Milton Kent today. Ready to break through the propaganda and expose the underlying evils that so many in both the North and South sought to hide.

Esther and Gertrude Gunther and half the town of Liberty may not want to hear the truth about slavery, but God had created him to speak out for those whom their government had silenced.

No one could silence him.

Chapter Five

....

The path to Liberty was a rocky affair that cut through tree-covered hills and boggy swampland near the creeks. Ripe apples and blackberries sweetened the late morning air, and resounding bangs echoed across the fields as farmers harvested their corn by throwing the ears against wagon bang boards.

Anna's chaise sloshed over the narrow path like cream in a jug. One of her hands gripped Samara's reins, and her other hand clung to the bench. Usually she walked to town, but she didn't want to be gone from the house for so many hours. She would be of no help to Charlotte if she spent her day roaming through the wilds of Indiana.

The bumps, along with the two cups of coffee she'd drunk before she hitched the buggy, kept her awake and somewhat alert, although Samara knew this old road so well that she didn't need even the slightest nudge in direction.

Sleep hadn't come to Anna until four or five in the morning. She didn't remember exactly when Peter had fallen asleep. He had cried and moaned in her arms for hours before he finally succumbed. She had placed him beside Marie and then collapsed on a straw tick in the attic. With no windows in the hiding place, the morning light didn't wake her, and even when Charlotte came to invite the others down to the breakfast table, they didn't disturb her. She'd slept until almost nine.

Her father had promised he would rush Marie and the others to safety at the new moon, but Peter couldn't leave until he had warm clothes and booties for his journey. With the onset of autumn, the nights were getting colder. Snow wasn't supposed to arrive for another two months, yet with the cooler temperatures this year, it might come sooner.

After a mile of dodging downed logs and gopher holes, Anna's path broke onto a muddy road that traveled through a covered bridge and wound around Carter's cornfield. Then it dumped her right into Liberty's bustling downtown. She rode her horse past a row of shops first and then the county's towering courthouse, which had been hewn from a local stone quarry.

In a treed area beside the courthouse stood a jail with grated windows marking four small cells. A lone face in a window watched her ride by, and the man lifted his hand to her behind the glass. She looked away and then chastened herself. She should at least wave to the miserable soul who could see all the activity on Main Street but participate in none of it.

She shivered as she stopped her horse below the large sign reading Trumble & Co. There was no worse fate than to be chained inside a cramped room for weeks or months, locked away and alone.

Anna tied Samara to the post outside the mercantile and walked toward the door. The owner, Lyle Trumble, was an elder at the Salem Anti-Slavery Meeting, and even though her family didn't attend that Meeting, Lyle was a good friend of her father. His prices were higher than the other general-goods store in town, but Lyle did his best to purchase and sell items that weren't produced by slave labor. She always shopped at his store.

Bells rang overhead when she opened the door, and Lyle lifted his head from the ledger, shoving his wire-rimmed glasses up his steep nose. With a quill pen in hand, he waved at her. "Greetings, Friend Anna. Are you coming for tea or sugar today?"

"Neither." She lowered her voice as she stepped to the shiny wood counter. "I need to purchase a warm baby gown and shoes."

His eyes shifted across the room and then back to her, his voice falling to a whisper. "A baby gown?"

She nodded. "For a friend."

"Oh, I see." He set down his pen and scooted around the counter. "I've got the perfect gown for you."

"Thank you."

She followed Lyle past the dusty barrels of flour and stacks of boots and yards of gingham to the back of the store. Folded in neat rows were store-bought trousers, bonnets, and shirtwaists. Lyle pointed to the end of the row, and she picked up a long gown made with shiny white chintz. The chintz would be too fancy for Marie and Peter's long trek north, but underneath the white gown Anna discovered a rainbow of gowns, each of them dyed with gay colors like raspberry, moss green, and sky blue.

Lyle picked up a plum-colored gown. "This one is lined with flannel."

She ran her fingers over the soft material. "Is it free labor?"

He nodded. "I bought it a few weeks ago in Indianapolis."

She fingered the satin sash on another long gown. "They're all beautiful."

A Quaker baby would never wear such bright colors, but Marie wasn't Quaker. A fancy outfit on her white baby, along with a bonnet to hide Marie's face, would help them to escape notice during the rest of their journey. When they arrived in Canada, Peter might be the finest-dressed fugitive to reach its shores.

The bells rang again as the door of the shop opened, and Lyle excused himself. Anna draped the plum gown over her arm and decided to purchase it along with a white cap and sheepskin booties to keep Peter's toes warm. She and Marie could knit him an extra pair of booties to wear under the sheepskin.

A woman's voice rang out in the quiet shop. "What beautiful silk, Mr. Trumble!"

"The finest material on this side of the Alleghenies."

"I'd like to buy four yards, but I don't know in which color."

"I'm in no hurry."

The woman clapped her hands. "It'll make the prettiest gown and cap."

Anna didn't hear Lyle's reply, but the woman walked around the bolts of fabric and met her by the baby clothes. Anna recognized her immediately.

Esther Cooley was the wife of the town physician and an avid promoter of all things social in Liberty. She had ridden alongside their town's mayor, Frederick Gunther, and his wife, Gertrude, during the town's Independence Day parade last July. Even though Esther was dressed in a full skirt layered with ruffles and a tightly laced corset, neither the corset nor the yards of fabric could hide her condition. In a few months, she would be delivering a child.

Esther silently critiqued Anna's plain dove-colored dress and apron, but when she saw the items in Anna's hands, she smiled. "When are you expecting your event?"

"Oh, no," Anna protested. Gossip like that would spread like fire through their community until it reached the ears of the Ministry and Oversight Committee. She respected the men and women on the committee, but she didn't want to have them admonish her over this. "I'm purchasing these for a friend's baby."

Esther picked up a hand-crocheted rattle with white tassels. "Then you must get her a little toy as well."

Anna smiled back at the lady. "Are you working for Lyle?"

"He needs some help," Esther whispered. "He only buys free-labor materials, you know."

"I've heard...."

"It doesn't help business, but the quality at this store is so much better than what you can find at Perkins's."

Anna took the rattle from Esther's hands. "That's why I shop here."

"Me, too." Esther directed her to the bolts of material at the front of the store. "Do you think I should buy pink or white satin for my baby's gown?"

"White," Anna replied, "in case it's a boy."

Esther smiled again. "I'm sure it's a girl."

"You want to buy pink, don't you?"

Esther picked up the bolt and held the soft pink material toward the sunlight. "Just think how beautiful she'll look."

"Then I think pink is the right color for you."

Esther stepped toward the counter and handed Lyle the bolt of silk. As he scribed the price of the material onto her account, Esther turned back to Anna. "Are you from Liberty?"

"Just south of here," she replied. "My father owns the woolen mill on Silver Creek."

"The Brent Mill?"

Anna nodded, and Esther's face brightened into yet another smile. She wrapped her fingers around Anna's arm. "I've been wanting to purchase a special blanket embroidered with my baby's name."

"That would be a wonderful gift."

She patted Anna's arm. "Do you think your father could make it at his mill?"

"Maybe..."

"I'd pay top dollar for it."

"I'm sure he would be glad to talk to you about it," Anna said. "You could come out to the mill and discuss the design."

"Oh, I don't know."

"Or he could meet with you when he's in town."

Esther bounced on her toes like she couldn't contain the excitement bubbling inside her. "Could you talk to your father about it for me? Then you could come to tea at my house next week, and we could design it together."

The last thing Anna wanted to do was design a baby blanket, yet something in Esther's pleading eyes wouldn't let her refuse. The woman was desperate to welcome her child into the world...and maybe she was desperate for a friend.

"It depends," Anna said, though she didn't explain the reason.

Lyle wrapped the silk in brown paper and tied the package with twine. When he handed it over the counter to Esther, she clutched the paper package to her chest. "I do hope you can come! I will send you an invitation tomorrow."

The bells rang again over the door as Esther departed, and Anna glanced over her shoulder to make sure that no one else was coming into the store. A crowd was gathering outside, along the street, but no one moved toward Trumble's. She stepped to the counter and placed the baby garments on it.

"Should I put this on your father's account?" Lyle asked.

"I'm paying with cash today."

The register chimed when he rang up the total. "Two dollars and ten cents."

She pulled an envelope from her pocket and then stuck it back into her pocket quickly as she dug for her coin purse. She still needed to deliver the envelope to Isaac Barnes this morning, and then she would rush back to Silver Creek to help Charlotte prepare dinner for their guests.

"These are for a friend, Lyle," she repeated as she gave him the money.

"I know, Anna. I won't say a word."

"I thank you."

She turned toward the door and looked at all the people gathering in the dusty courtyard across the street. "What's happening at the courthouse?"

Lyle stepped to the window, his nose almost touching the glass. "Milton Kent is supposed to debate the town's newest editor today."

"About slavery?"

"And any other topic Milton feels compelled to expound upon."

"Maybe Milton has met his match."

Lyle stepped back from the window. "I just hope this man stays around a little longer than the last editor Isaac hired."

The crowd surrounding the courthouse had spilled out into the street, and Anna had to elbow her way through the mass to get to her chaise. She had heard many debates over the years, and most of them left people feeling more confident in their own opinions instead of swayed by another's. Talk was purely frivolous when it wasn't backed by some sort of action.

She hid the brown paper package under the seat of her chaise and then turned slowly toward the courthouse. She needed to find Isaac, but curiosity drove her closer to the podium.

Was Daniel Stanton a man of action as well as of words?

Chapter Six

························

"There is no liberty in America as long as there is slavery!" Daniel cried out to the hundreds of people in front of him. "We must set every one of them free."

Milton Kent let the words settle, almost as if he wanted the people of Union County to consider Daniel's words. Then he retorted with a booming voice that echoed across the crowd.

"But what will happen if we set all the Negroes free?" Milton paced the length of the portico, his voice growing louder. "Millions of them will swarm our countryside and town like the flies that plagued Egypt, and not even God Himself will be able to stop them."

He paused again like a tent preacher so his words would resonate, and then he leaned toward the people in the front rows. "If they are freed, like our young Friend here suggests, they will raid our fields. Steal our livestock." His fist hit the podium. "Hurt our women and children."

"Send 'em back!" a man yelled.

"That is one proposition that we should consider." Milton seemingly tempered his outrage as he pointed at the man with his hat. "By sending the slaves back to Africa, we could rid our country of slavery altogether and have honest white folk working the cotton fields instead."

"I ain't working them fields!" someone else shouted.

Daniel leaned into his podium. Milton was riling the crowd to anger instead of speaking sense.

"Most of the slaves that live on our soil were born in this country," Daniel responded. "It's deplorable to even consider shipping these people off to a continent where they have never lived. Half of them probably wouldn't survive the journey, and the other half may not survive after they arrive."

Milton disregarded Daniel's comments, focusing instead on the man in the crowd who had shouted out his refusal to pick cotton. "Someone has to be in the fields, working to get sugar and coffee and cotton. It's only a mite harder than the work in our cornfields up here in Indiana." He paused and wiped his forehead with a handkerchief. "And a mite hotter, too."

Daniel rolled his eyes at the drama as Milton continued to entice the crowd into his web of fear. He was like a charlatan, swaying emotions and tricking God-fearing men and women into supporting a despicable trade. These men and women would probably go out of their way to help a white person in need, but they were turning their backs on their colored neighbors.

Daniel intended to find out what would make the people of Liberty and across Union County fight against slavery instead of promote the popular views of people like Milton Kent. He needed people like his sister and brother-in-law and their respected associates to speak out against this evil practice in spite of the cost.

Daniel scanned the crowd for Friends. He saw businessmen dressed in long coats and top hats, intent on Milton's words. He saw farm boys slouching around the perimeter and shop owners who'd snuck outside to listen.

He didn't see many Friends in the ocean of faces until he spotted a pretty young woman with the familiar dove-colored bonnet. He stopped looking around. Instead of focusing on his opponent, the woman's eyes were on him.

Daniel cleared his throat and turned back toward Milton. "No one here is going to Mississippi or anywhere else to pick cotton. We farm just fine in Indiana without slave labor, and by improving the way they run their farms down South, they can operate without slaves as well."

* * * * *

Anna couldn't take her eyes off Daniel Stanton. It seemed like he was looking right at her, and she listened as he clearly refuted the silly notion that their country couldn't survive without slavery. He was a better speaker than he was a writer, which would help tremendously since Milton Kent liked to obliterate his opponents with both his voice and his pen. Few people agreed to debate him twice.

She moved through the crowd, closer to the portico where the men were speaking, so she could hear their words.

Daniel Stanton was younger than she'd imagined. He was tall and lanky and wore the plain coat of a Quaker. His skin was clean-shaven, and the tips of his brown hair curled over his ears. He was a handsome man, but it wasn't his features that caught her attention. It was his expression. In spite of the harsh rhetoric between Milton Kent and him, Daniel Stanton's face was calm.

Milton Kent's cheeks, in comparison, matched the deep red in the scarf that topped the copper buttons on his jacket. He was shorter than his opponent, but his loftiness made him appear almost six feet tall. She'd never known a more arrogant man in her life. Instead of observing and writing news, he often created it and then reported on what he had done.

The *Union County News* editor lived over in Brownsville, their neighboring town, but his subscribers resided in Liberty and across Union County. He probably sold at least twice as many papers, if not more, than Isaac Barnes, but she guessed people liked to read it more for entertainment than to get the news.

Milton's voice was escalating into a roar, but she didn't hear his words. Nor did she honor his rhetoric by turning her head. She focused on the courageous Quaker man who was slowly unnerving his opponent.

She couldn't help but admire him for taking a stand against Milton and facing the ridicule of at least half of Liberty. The last man who had scuffled with Milton had left the debate coated in eggshells.

"Slaves aren't property," Daniel insisted. "They are Americans who deserve a chance like the rest of us at life and liberty and the pursuit of happiness."

Milton motioned to someone in the crowd, and as if Moses himself was walking through, people parted on both sides. Anna pushed herself up on her toes like the rest of the crowd to watch the next act of Milton's performance.

"This here's Enoch Gardner," Milton said, pointing at the black man who was crossing the portico with his face held high. Instead of the torn, threadbare attire she had seen on most of the slaves passing through Liberty, he wore a clean, white jean shirt and denim trousers with suspenders. There were no chains in sight, though the man who escorted him had his hand secured around Enoch's elbow.

This man was the perfect example for Milton—subdued enough to seem content with slavery yet imposing enough to reiterate Milton's claims that the colored population might plunder the North if set free.

The crowd around Anna murmured with a mix of curiosity and anxiety until Milton spoke again and introduced the man at Enoch's side. "And this here is Enoch's owner, Whitney Johns, from Kentucky."

The slave owner shook Milton's hand before Milton continued. "My friend is a typical Southerner, owning thirty-six slaves on his horse farm in Kentucky. Yet unlike what Mr. Stanton here implied, Mr. Johns provides well for his slaves and treats them better than most employers around here."

Milton turned to the man at Whitney's side. "We're glad to have you visiting Indiana, Enoch. Are the fine people of our state treating you well?"

The man bowed his head. "Yessuh."

"How about your owner here? Has he been treating you well?"

Anna didn't hear his answer, but it must have been positive since Milton kept exalting this real-life example of slavery and how well it worked for Enoch and Whitney Johns and all the people in Union County who didn't want to destroy their fingers and backs picking cotton.

Apparently Enoch was treated well. Fed well. He had security for life in the Johns home. According to Milton, self-righteous people like Daniel Stanton were the real troublemakers, trying to stir up animosity when their Southern neighbors and slaves were content. Slavery may be a peculiar institution, but it was an institution that worked.

Anna wanted to march up onto the platform and shake both Enoch and his master—and then tell Enoch to run. She glanced over at Daniel, and it looked like he wanted to shake Milton instead.

Daniel stepped around his podium. "I'd like to ask Enoch a few questions, too."

Milton chuckled. "Oh, I don't think that's necessary. You might scare the fellow."

One hand resting on the front of his podium, Daniel seemed relaxed as he smiled back. "I don't think it's me he's scared of."

Several people around her snickered at his comment, and for the first time, nervousness washed over Milton's face. "Would you like to speak to Mr. Stanton, Enoch?"

The slave shook his head back and forth.

"I'm sorry, Stanton," Milton replied. "He doesn't want to talk to you."

"Oh, that's okay," Daniel said as strolled toward Milton and the other men. "I can understand why he'd be afraid. If he doesn't say what his owner here has instructed him to say, he's liable to get beaten."

"Now, that's not...," Milton started, but Daniel interrupted him.

"Because, my friends, Enoch is free to think, but he's not free to say what he really thinks. His owner tells him what to do and what he can eat and what he can say. Even his heartfelt declaration of how much he enjoys being a slave is proclaimed under the watchful eye of Whitney Johns."

"Here, here," Anna muttered, before clamping her mouth shut. Thankfully no one looked her way. All eyes were focused on the man who was stealing the reins from Milton Kent.

Milton flanked to the other side of Enoch, but Daniel managed to step in front of the colored man. He whispered something to Enoch and then looked at the crowd. "What I would really like to know is if Enoch would like to be free."

Milton stepped to the podium. "Enoch is not able to answer that question."

Daniel looked perplexed. "Why not?"

"Well...," Milton stumbled over his words.

"Because it is illegal for slaves to bear testimony in our country?" Daniel prodded.

Milton looked relieved for the moment, even if it was his opponent who had given him an out to the argument. "Exactly."

Daniel turned back to Milton. "Why is that?"

Milton's face turned red again. "I will not let you badger this man...."

Daniel didn't let him continue. "The reason is that the courts don't believe slaves always tell the truth."

Milton started to say something and then stopped when Whitney stepped forward and said something in Milton's ear. Milton addressed the crowd again, his voice not quite as strong as it had been minutes ago. "Even though this is unprecedented, I'm told that Enoch is willing to answer Daniel's question."

Daniel turned toward Enoch again, his voice loud enough for the people closest to the courthouse to hear. "Would you like to be free, Enoch?"

The crowd was silent as they waited for Enoch to answer.

"Nosuh," he finally said, but there wasn't even a hint of fervor in his tone.

Milton nodded like he had won the point, but the damage had been done. No one in the courtyard believed that Enoch desired to remain in bondage to Whitney Johns or anyone else.

Someone tapped Anna's shoulder, and she twirled around to see Isaac Barnes. She greeted him with a smile, but he didn't smile back at her.

"You shouldn't linger here, Anna."

"I was looking for you." She glanced around her, and then she retrieved the envelope from her side. Without looking at it, she stuffed it into Isaac's coat pocket.

He patted his jacket. "Go home now."

Her gaze wandered back to Daniel, and he seemed to be looking at her again. Then she looked at the crowd and saw angry faces mixed in with the complacent ones...and the solemn ones.

Isaac was right. She couldn't stay. Most of the people were listening, but a few would be watching. Those people didn't need to know that Edwin Brent's daughter had been rooting for the newcomer.

Chapter Seven

....

Marie pushed her heels on the carpet to rock the chair. Peter lay in her arms, dressed in the prettiest gown she'd ever seen on a baby, black or white. If her mama were still alive, she'd be so pleased to see her grandbaby draped in such finery.

She kissed the tender skin on Peter's nose and leaned her head back on the rocking chair to watch the pink glow of the sky outside the window as she softly sang one of the many songs her mama used to sing to her. "Your hands my heartstrings grabbin'; just lay your head upon my breast, just snuggle and rest and rest, my little colored chile."

Her mama was up in heaven tonight, probably rejoicing that her daughter was finally free from Master Owens and his angry wife. So many times during this journey she could almost feel her mama running along with her. On the darkest of nights, as she crouched in the swamp and listened to the snakes slithering through her hiding place, there was someone warm beside her. No matter how soaked she was—or how cold—it was like God Himself had given her the gift of His presence and He'd brought Mama with Him so she wouldn't be afraid.

So through the swamps and forests and farmland, she talked to her mama. And she kept running and stumbling and following the Drinking Gourd in the dark sky until she reached Indiana.

It wouldn't be long now before she reached the Promised Land.

The four other fugitives were downstairs helping Charlotte clean the dishes. She should be helping, too, but after dinner, Miss Anna had told her to go upstairs to the guest room and rest with her baby.

She gently patted Peter on the belly.

She'd never had anyone be so kind to her as the two women in this house. For the first time since she'd started her journey, it seemed like maybe she would make it all the way to Canada. There weren't many miles left now, especially with people helping them. Miss Anna had assured her that all of the stationmasters along the line would take good care of her and the other runaways.

When she was a child living in the main house, she'd heard Master Owens and his guests whisper about the slaves who'd been swept away overnight on a train that moved so quickly and so quietly that it seemed to pluck slaves out of their cabins and then disappear with them underground.

She hadn't known how to catch this invisible train. And she'd never have imagined that she would be a passenger on it. She'd only known that she had to leave the Owens house. The same day she realized she was expecting, Mrs. Owens had thrown Marie out of the house in shame. Marie had tried to explain to her that she didn't want to be pregnant, didn't want to have a baby. But even though Marie had spent the past nine years caring for Mrs. Owens, the woman refused to speak to her again.

Marie looked down at the light clump of hair on the top of Peter's head. She hadn't wanted him at first, but now she'd do anything to help him survive. She'd never had anything of her own in her entire life, and this baby was hers to love and hold and protect. She would never give him back, and she would never let Master Owens or anyone else take him away from her.

She knew exactly what would happen if she relinquished Peter to the Owens.

A few years ago, her mistress had found out that a house slave named Nelle was expecting, and just like with Marie, she had sent Nelle out to work in the plantation's grist mill until she began her laboring pains. Then she took Nelle into the house for the birthing.

Before Nelle even got to hold her son in her arms, Mrs. Owens stole that baby away. No one except the Owenses knew exactly what happened to the child, but Nelle was convinced that Master Owens had sold him to a neighbor. She grieved the loss of her son for weeks until their mistress insisted that Master Owens take Nelle to auction. Marie didn't know if the slave woman would ever completely recover from the not-knowin'.

Even though she had been only thirteen at the time, Marie had never believed that Nelle's baby made it outside the iron gates of the property. Their mistress didn't want anyone to know about the child. Even if they took the baby to the slave market, the neighbors would talk about the light-skinned slave.

When Marie discovered that she, too, was expecting, she knew she had to run.

She waited for months for an opportunity, and then one morning the slave driver had taken her and another girl out of the mill and sent them to collect ginseng for the very pregnant Mrs. Owens. As she wandered into the forest, the light summer rain turned into a violent thunderstorm. Lightning flashed around her and thunder crashed, but she kept on moving through the trees.

No one had anticipated that she, so soon to her event, would run away. Yet she did run—through the forest, across the river, and into the rugged mountains.

Master Owens and a few slaves from the plantation had come looking for her that night, but they never found her. When she heard the horses, she climbed a tree and hid in the branches. Master Owens rode right under her and never even looked up.

Marie ran all the way to the Ohio, and when she reached the border between slave and free, a white woman had mercy on her and helped her cross the grand river, into the free state of Indiana. This woman pointed her to the farmhouse of a colored couple near Madison, and Marie birthed Peter in their cellar so no one would hear her pains. Days after Peter was born, Master Owens caught up to her. Somehow he had found out where she was hiding, and he came knocking on the front door.

The colored man slipped her and Peter out the back while Master Owens was searching upstairs. The man gave her directions to the next station, and she'd been on this strange and wonderful railway ever since. Even when she got sick with the fever and her milk left her, people took care of her and Peter until she was healthy enough to journey north again. Marie looked into the face of her sleeping child. If she hadn't run away from her master's house, Peter would have met the same fate as Nelle's child. One look into his pure, white face would have removed any doubt as to his father. Their mistress would never let anyone upstage the birth of her own child.

Marie pulled her son to her chest and rocked him. Darkness slowly settled over the room, but she didn't want to lay Peter down for fear that they might have to run again. If she were too far away, she wouldn't be able to rescue him.

She'd been with the Brents for almost a week now, and part of her was anxious to head north, toward freedom. Another part of her, though, was content to stay here in the warmth and security of their home. Anna and Charlotte were both kind to her, and Peter had plenty of milk to soothe his cries.

She had watched Anna rock Peter in this very chair, watched her care for him when nothing seemed to stop his cries. Anna would be a good mother, never letting anything or anyone harm her child.

The idea struck her quickly. She could leave Peter here and continue on the journey alone. He would live a privileged life with a white family. He would never even know that he had been born a slave. Anna would care for him for the rest of his life.

But if she left him here, people would ask questions. They would want to know where Anna had gotten a baby. If anyone guessed that he was the son of a slave, he would be returned to Master Owens's plantation to do whatever the master and his wife pleased.

She suspected that they would dispose of him quickly, but if they didn't, Master Owens would sell him at the market, and Peter would be sent into the cruel world alone to be mistreated by his new owner. He would never know how much his mother had loved him.

She had to get him to Canada. It would be the only place where he could ever truly be free.

Peter squirmed in her grasp, and she settled him back in her lap.

After they crossed the great lake, she'd work as a house servant or in the fields or even in another mill. She'd do everything she could do so they could live together in freedom.

Someone knocked gently on the door, and Anna slipped into the room.

"I don't want to disturb you," Anna whispered. "I thought you might want some light."

"Yes...please," Marie said quietly. It unsettled her to have a white woman waiting on her, but Peter had fallen back asleep, and she didn't want to wake him.

Anna lit two candles on the candle stand, and soft light filled the room.

Marie's benefactor was dressed in gray, but in spite of her plain attire, Anna's face was one of the prettiest she had ever seen. So much prettier than that of Mrs. Owens. Even when she dressed in lace and finery, her mistress often had a cruel look in her eyes that frightened everyone in the house, including Master Owens.

Anna's kind eyes were the vibrant blue of the cornflowers Marie used to pick in Tennessee. And though Anna pinned her honey-colored hair back each morning, ringlets often fell to her shoulders and fluffed around her neck like ruffles. Marie wondered what it would be like to have such pretty hair.

After she lit the candles, Marie thought Anna would hurry back to the kitchen, but she sat down on the bed instead. "I will miss you and Peter."

Marie stopped rocking. "Is it time ta go?"

"In two more days."

Marie stared at the flickering candles. "I'll be sad ta leave."

"You will be safe in Canada."

"I don't care about my safety, Miss Anna." Marie looked over her. "You see, if I die, my mama's gonna meet me at them pearly gates."

"You're not going to die," Anna said gently.

"I will if they catch me, because I ain't goin' back ta the plantation alive."

Anna took a pillow and hugged it to her chest. "Was it that bad for you there?"

"They treated me okay, I guess, until...until they found out about the baby."

"They were angry?"

"My mistress, she was furious. If she ever got hold of Peter, she'd either starve him or sell him."

"I'm so sorry, Marie."

She slid forward in the rocking chair. "It ain't time for Peter ta go meet His Maker, Miss Anna. I want him ta live, and I want him ta be free."

"He's going to be okay."

Peter squirmed again, this time from her tight grasp of his legs. "They ain't gonna send him back."

"They won't..."

Marie turned to her, urgency pressing her to make Anna understand. "You gotta keep 'em from takin' him back. They'll do awful things ta my baby."

Anna reached out and took her hand. "We're not going to let him go back."

Marie nodded. Maybe she should leave Peter here with Anna for just a while. She could send for him in a month or two, once she got to Canada and found a home and a position to support her and her son.

"You're a good mother, Marie."

Marie's eyes filled with water, and she blinked. She hadn't asked for this child, but she tried to be the best mother she could to him.

"Am I doin' the right thing?" she asked, her eyes pleading with Anna for an honest answer.

"There's no greater gift you can give to Peter than freedom."

"I'm gonna do my best."

Anna squeezed her hand. "And I'll do everything I can to help you."

Chapter Eight

....

KENTUCKY BUSINESSMAN DESPONDENT OVER LOST SLAVE

Anna's hand flew to her lips when she read the headline, but she couldn't hide the grin.

The front-page story of the *Liberty Era* was devoted to the escape of one Enoch Gardner and the despondency and woes of his owner, Whitney Johns. Apparently Enoch hadn't been as contented in slavery as Whitney wanted everyone, including himself, to believe.

A fortnight ago, Daniel reported, Enoch had slipped out of the tavern in Richmond where he was staying with his master, and no one had seen him since. Anna could almost hear the stout owner hollering Enoch's name along the streets of Richmond like he was a dog that would come running home.

Whitney said his slave had "lost his way" in the new city. He'd sent a search party out to retrieve the man, convinced that Enoch was walking around the city in distress and searching for his master.

Run, Enoch! Anna whispered. If he kept pushing northward, he would be in Canada in a couple of weeks.

She doubted that Milton Kent's paper would cover the story, but Daniel covered it in detail. The racket at the tavern on the river after Enoch was reported missing. The astonishment of Whitney Johns when someone suggested that Enoch might have run. The intensity and anger of the six slave hunters and their bloodhounds as they tracked the man up to Newport and then lost his trail.

Had Daniel followed Whitney and Enoch after the debate and convinced Enoch to run? If he had urged Enoch to escape, he was *creating* news like Milton instead of just reporting it. Even so, a man brave enough to help a slave and write about it was the kind of person she wanted to support.

She closed the newspaper, took her pen from the stand, and dipped the nib into the glass inkwell. Words spilled out of her and onto the linen paper on the desktop. Marie's story was as powerful as any Anna had heard, and the former slave had given Anna permission to tell it as long as her name was changed, along with the name and location of her owner.

Anna had readily agreed.

Marie was a survivor and a fighter. She had survived her bitter introduction into womanhood when she went to live in her former master's house. When she'd found out she was expecting, she'd turned into a fighter to save her child.

Marie was more than a player in a story about escaping from slavery. She was a heroine who was risking her life for someone who couldn't help himself.

The door to the study creaked open, and Charlotte slid into the room.

"Ben just delivered a message," she whispered.

Anna glanced at the window to make sure it was closed and then refocused on Charlotte. "What did he say?"

"There's a gentleman from Tennessee wandering around Liberty and asking about a slave girl named Marie. Said she has a baby with her."

Her stomach clenched. "No one knows she's here."

"But they suspect she's close."

Had the man and woman down the creek contacted Marie's master? She wondered how much it was worth to them to turn over an innocent girl and her child.

"Father is supposed to take them to Newport tomorrow," Anna said.

"Ben said we don't have any time to lose. We need to take all of them west to the Sutters tonight to throw this man off the trail."

Anna checked the clock on the wall. "Father won't be home for at least two more hours."

"We can't wait that long," Charlotte insisted as she backed toward the doorway. "George and I can prepare the wagon and put in the horses right now."

Anna replaced her pen and stood. When she was home from college, she had ridden with her father a dozen or so times to make a delivery. She didn't know the route as well as he did, but she could take their friends to the Sutters' station.

She hid her papers inside a book and blew out the candle on the stand. "I can leave in twenty minutes."

* * * * *

Anna tied her wool cape across her shoulders and her bonnet around her head before she retrieved a flannel riding blanket from the trunk beside the front door. The night would be cold, but until she delivered her friends to the woods near the Sutter home, she wouldn't feel the temperature. When she accompanied her father on these trips, she was so nervous she didn't feel much of anything. Every time she heard a noise in the woods or the pound of horse hooves on the dirt, her heart seemed to stop beating entirely.

Four of her guests stood in the basement kitchen, quietly eating cold ham and cheese. Every leg of the trip had dangers of its own, but this trip would be especially dangerous since Marie's owner was searching the area for her.

Marie looked up from the table, and Anna could see both fear and determination in her eyes. She may be afraid of her former master, but Anna was certain that she would fight for her life. Peter was awake in her arms, drinking from a bottle of honeyed milk mixed with a few drops of paregoric to help him sleep on their journey. Before Anna asked to hold him one last time, Marie eased the blanket off Peter and held out her arms. Anna gently took the child.

Dressed in his cotton outfit and warm booties, with his golden hair hidden under his cap, he looked like any of the babies she'd seen pushed around in perambulators in Cincinnati or Indianapolis. His blue eyes focused on her face, and his lips moved into the slightest upturn that she knew in her heart was a smile. She pulled him to her cheek, and his long eyelashes brushed against her skin.

Almost every other week she said good-bye to the runaways who had stayed in her home. And almost every time, she wanted to cry. Usually she could hold back her tears until they were gone.

But this evening tears came unbidden, spilling over her cheeks before she realized she was crying. She turned her head away from her company and dried the wetness with the hem of her cape.

The back door opened, and Charlotte peeked inside the kitchen. "The horses are ready."

With knapsacks over their shoulders, each of the men and women moved toward the door. Even in the few days they had been at the Brents' home, they looked much better than when they had arrived. They were rested and fed and wore new clothes that had been hand-sewn by a small group of Quakeresses who donated their wares for people in need. The clothes the women made quickly disappeared from the meetinghouse storeroom, but they never asked questions about who benefited from their work. God called them to sew, and they simply answered.

Anna felt privileged to be able to see how God used their sewing to turn a downtrodden collection of slaves into a polished assembly. Only the color of their skin—and the heaviness in their hearts—differentiated them from the thousands of farmworkers and businesspeople who lived in Union County.

Peter still burrowed into her arm, Anna lifted the tin lantern from the table and clutched it in her hand. "May I take him?" she asked. Marie nodded, taking the tin lantern from her and carrying it outside.

Darkness clung to the trees and outbuildings like a thick black cloak. The air was cool and misty, and in the distance, Anna could hear the creek pounding over the rocks in the gorge and then pouring into the river.

Peter nudged his head against her cape, but he didn't make a sound as they crept across the stone path to the barn. With every step, she prayed for him and begged God to protect Peter from the evil trying to capture his body and his mind. She prayed he would grow into a free man who would relish the grace and love and proddings of his heavenly Father instead of growing bitter at the earthly father who had rejected him.

The Sutters owned the next safe house on the western line, but she didn't know whose house was after theirs. Only Ben and a handful of others knew the entire route up to Canada—for the protection of both the stationmasters and the runaways. When she said good-bye to Peter and his mother, she would never know what happened to them. Not knowing if her friends made it safely to freedom was almost more difficult than the fear of being caught. It wouldn't be safe for them to correspond, nor could she keep her work a secret if she journeyed up to Canada for a visit.

She prayed that God would reunite her and Marie and Peter in the next life, where they would all be free to worship Him together.

George and Charlotte were waiting inside the barn beside the farm wagon and two harnessed horses. Filled with mounds of wool blankets, the wagon was almost ready for a delivery to Connersville. All that remained was to load their friends.

On the floor behind the driver's seat, George and Charlotte had left a space of about three feet empty of blankets, though a wall of blankets towered on each side of it. In this empty space, a small latch opened a door, and under the door was a narrow crevice that ran the length of the wagon. Her father had hid up to eight fugitives under this floor, but today they had only five and a baby.

One at a time, her guests climbed up the step of the wagon, crawled over the driver's seat, and lowered their feet and then their bodies into the false bottom. In spite of the cool night, it would be a hot journey for them. Her father had driven tiny nail holes along the sides and bottom of the rig so they'd have enough fresh air to breathe, but they would be well-insulated with the blankets above them and the people on each side.

Marie was the last one to step over the seat and drop her feet into the hole. She held down her skirt, and as she lay on her back, she scooted her body as far as it would go.

"That's my head," Roger muttered, and she apologized to the man.

Anna kissed Peter's forehead and carefully handed him down to Marie.

Beside the driver's seat, Anna hung the lantern on the pole, and then she and Charlotte lifted the remaining blankets from the ground and threw them over the seat until the pile covering the trapdoor matched the surrounding piles on the wagon bed. If all went well, no one would suspect that she was doing anything except making an evening delivery for her father.

Anna stepped down from the wagon and reached for the cape she'd draped over the mahogany trunk along the wall—the beautiful piece her father had brought out to the barn a year ago, after her mother died. She supposed it reminded him too much of her to keep in the house. Anna's hands drifted over the wood. Nights like these she ached for her mother.

"She'll be with you in spirit, Anna," Charlotte said.

Anna tied the cloak around her neck. Sometimes it did seem as if she could feel her mother beside her, urging her on, like Marie's mother had done for her in the swamps.

Charlotte straightened her cape. "If you rush, they'll think you're hiding something."

Anna climbed up onto the seat. "I'll take it nice and slow."

"I'll be praying for all of you," Charlotte said.

Anna gave a quick flick of the reins and the horses walked forward, out of the barn and onto the dirt driveway. She drove the team down the hill and then west along the creek that supplied power to her father's mill.

Her lantern gave an eerie glow along the path and flickered every time they bumped over the ruts and logs embedded in the road. Stars covered the sky in a brilliant mantle of twinkling lights.

Anna turned north to follow Phenix Creek. An owl hooted in the trees beside her, but the fugitives were silent in their hiding place. Remarkably, even Peter was quiet—the opium tincture lulling him to sleep.

She couldn't imagine having to travel crammed together like sausage links under the low roof of the floor, but not one of them had complained when they climbed under the bed of the wagon. If nothing else, she surmised, their strength was a testament to how squalid their conditions were down South.

If only more people would speak out against these conditions.

Her mind wandered to the handsome, plain-coated man she had heard debating Milton in Liberty. Even though he had been in town for a month now, she had yet to see him at the Silver Creek Meeting. Perhaps he belonged to the other Orthodox Society of Friends, the Salem Meeting, on the other side of Liberty...or to the Salem Anti-Slavery Meeting.

She was interested in hearing more of what he had to say, but if he had joined the Salem Anti-Slavery Meeting, she would have to be careful. Quakers no longer owned slaves, but whether or not they should support abolition had been a bitter debate among the Indiana Yearly Meeting—they had split eight years ago after Levi Coffin and other abolitionists were disciplined for speaking out so adamantly against slavery and not adhering to the "quiet" and unified ways of Quakerism. As a result, the Salem Anti-Slavery Meeting had formed in 1843 because they believed that their members should fight slavery in spite of what their government mandated.

Some Orthodox Quakers believed that the Bible, as stated in 1 Peter 2:18, commanded colored men and women to be subject to their masters—both good and bad masters—while the new faction upheld Moses' words in Deuteronomy 23:15: "Thou shalt not deliver unto his master the servant which is escaped." Like Daniel Stanton, this group of Anti-Slavery Friends spoke out boldly, trying to convince others that they must abolish slavery, while many Orthodox Quakers worked quietly to help escaped slaves within the confines of their government's laws.

In spite of Anna's and her father's strong opposition to slavery, they'd never even considered joining Salem's Anti-Slavery Meeting. Their work on the Underground depended on secrecy, and everyone in the county knew who attended the Anti-Slavery Meeting. While those Quakers spoke out vehemently against slavery laws, few of them could actually host fugitives in their homes because bounty hunters knocked often at their doors.

The wagon hit a rut, and she pulled back on the reins to slow the horses.

Even if she never saw Daniel Stanton again, at least she could continue to read his words in the paper each week. Like this recent piece on Enoch's escape, she had read all of his stories and editorials, which were filled with more opinion than fact. Fortunately Isaac was a good editor. In no time, Daniel would be able to write as well as he spoke, if Milton and other opponents in town didn't drive him out of the county first.

The hill in front of her turned into a craggy trail of rocks, and Anna steered the horses west, following the wide path down toward the river she knew so well. A shallow, sandy bank rose from the water ahead, and she led her horses straight toward the bank and into the water.

Instead of an easy crossing, water splashed up below her, soaking her feet and the sides of the wagon. Thanks to her, her passengers were probably drenched. They had never gotten stuck in the river when her father was driving, nor did she remember him ever soaking their passengers.

Her father wasn't here tonight, so she pushed the horses through the water in spite of the splashing. The people below her may be wet, but she wouldn't jeopardize their lives by sinking the wheels into the sand. If the wagon got stuck, they would have to walk ten miles to the next station, near a busy road.

The wheels creaked and groaned, but the horses plodded faithfully through the water before clambering up the rocky path on the other side.

From under the wagon, Peter released a wail, and Marie shushed him. Anna turned her head toward the back. "Is everyone okay?"

A host of affirmatives responded: "Yessum." "Just fine, Miss Anna." "Thanks for askin."

She glanced in the woods around them to make sure no one was watching. "Is Peter okay, too?" she whispered.

"He's startin' to fall back asleep," Marie replied.

Anna breathed a sigh of relief as his cries tapered off. Then he was quiet again.

She drove the horses through the forest and then up another hill before they emerged on the smooth road between Liberty and Connersville. The next six miles, to the cutoff toward the Sutters' house, was the flattest portion of their journey. It was also the most dangerous with travelers and watchers on the road. Because of the secrecy of their network, she rarely knew the difference between friend and foe.

A buggy passed them on the other side of the road, and she ducked her head so they couldn't see her face. It was probably too dark to see who was driving anyway, but she didn't want to take any chances.

They rode for three miles or so without incident, until she heard a sound behind her that made her catch her breath. It was the steady pounding of hooves, galloping toward her. Her heart started pounding in sync with their beat.

Even as fear enveloped her, she resisted the temptation to speed. Just like her father would have done, she slowed her horses to let the rider pass.

The rider didn't pass.

Instead of riding by her, the rider reined in his horse, and she glanced over at him. In the lantern's light, she could see the man's cap ducking low over his eyes. His hunting shirt was stretched across broad shoulders that were more brick than muscles and blood, and the silver badge on his chest shimmered in the lantern's light.

When he lifted his hat, she saw who it was, and her heart lurched.

Will Denton. The deputy from Liberty.

Chapter Nine
....

Marie held her breath when the wagon stopped moving. A horse panted against the panel beside her face, but she couldn't see anything through the pinholes. A slave hunter could take all the blankets out of the wagon and not find them hiding under the false floor, but if he had an ax.... She shuddered to think about the blade chopping through the wood barely an inch above her face.

After the river crossing, they'd traveled for at least an hour without incident. Peter lay in the crux of her arm, sound asleep by the wagon's side, but she didn't know how much longer the medicine would last. Her fingers crept over to his body, and she felt his chest moving slowly up and down.

Roger had been angry about taking Peter with them tonight, but Charlotte assured him and the others that the paregoric would keep him quiet. Even so, Marie worried that the baby would cry or get agitated in the darkness or even smother to death in the cramped space. If he did cry out, she could cover his mouth for a few seconds or even a minute, but she'd have to stop and let him breathe. No matter what happened to her or the others, she wouldn't suffocate her son.

She clutched the gum ring in her fingers and took the slightest breath of air so she wouldn't wake him.

The man on the horse beside her greeted Anna, his voice friendly. "Evenin', Miss Brent."

"Hello, Will Denton," she replied. "How's your family?"

"My little one's got croup, but Doctor Cooley's caring for him."

"He's a good doctor."

"That he is." The man nudged his horse closer to the wagon. "What are you doing up this way?"

Auntie Rae reached over and took Marie's free hand, their fingers trembling together. Anna's voice was calm, but she must have been as scared as the rest of them. "I'm making a delivery to Connersville for my father."

"It's awful late for a delivery."

"It is," she agreed. "But Jacob Sutter sent a messenger down hours ago and said he needed these blankets before morning."

Marie waited for his response, but the man was quiet for the moment. Anna had told them that Jacob Sutter was a well-known merchant in eastern Indiana. Most people did what he asked, even if it meant delivering woolen blankets to his store well after most shops had closed their doors for the night. She could only hope this man believed it, too.

"I'm sorry to bother you." He spit on the ground. "Sheriff Zabel's got all of us out patrolling tonight."

Peter stirred beside her, and she nudged the gum ring into his mouth, wishing she could nuzzle him close to her chest and sing. All she could do was pull him closer to her side...and not say a word.

"What are you looking for?" Anna asked.

The man lowered his voice and leaned toward the wagon, so close that Marie could have petted his horse with her fingers if the holes beside her were a bit bigger. "A girl slave from Tennessee, supposed to be running away with a baby."

Marie sucked in her breath. Master Owens even had the local people searching for her.

"With her baby or someone else's?" Anna asked.

"No one bothered me with the details. Just told me to find her."

"I'm sorry I can't help you." The wagon crept forward a few inches. "But I can't keep Jacob waiting."

"Of course not."

He nudged his horse away from them, and when the wagon lurched forward, Peter whimpered. It wasn't a loud sound, but it was enough to make her jump. Her hand flew over Peter's mouth, but he jerked his head away.

"Hush him up!" Roger snarled.

It was too late.

* * * * *

Will yanked back on the reins of his horse as a wail sliced through the darkness. "By sugar...," he muttered.

The wool blankets muffled the cry behind Anna, but the sound was distinct. There was no way she could pretend that these were the cries of a wolf. She was obviously carrying a baby in her wagon, somewhere buried under these blankets. It would take only seconds for Will to find the baby and his mother and the other fugitives hidden underneath.

Anna opened her mouth to speak, but the words froze on her tongue. Nothing she could think of would explain away why she was hiding and transporting a baby so late in the evening.

She couldn't look at Will. It was as if she ignored the cries—cries that were escalating by the moment—they would go away along with the sheriff and any other slave hunters on their route.

Will bent his ear toward the wagon. "Sounds like a sheep or two snuck in with your blankets."

Her hands relaxed so fast that she almost dropped the reins. Her voice was steady, but her eyes pleaded with him. "My sheep aren't fond of the cold."

He scrutinized the stack of blankets. "Mine don't like the cold or the darkness either."

"I have one lamb onboard, a product most certainly of his mother's." She kept her words as calm as she could manage. "I'm trying to get him and his mother to a safe, warm place for the night before the wolves catch up to them."

"It's getting awfully late." Will checked over his shoulder before he turned back to her. "And there are a lot of critters on this path."

"I won't let them steal my sheep."

Will backed his horse away from the wagon's side slowly. "You'd better get your delivery up to Connersville in a hurry."

Her eyes softened. "May the Lord bless you and your family, Will."

He tipped his cap. "And Godspeed to you."

Then he turned his horse and galloped away. With a quick snap of the reins, Anna's horses began to trot again.

"Just a few more miles," she said to herself, barely loud enough for the men and women beneath her to hear.

Marie shushed Peter again and again, but he was inconsolable. Anna couldn't imagine how maddening it must feel to be trapped in the dark cranny below, unable to rock or stroll with her child to soothe him back to sleep. She'd heard horrible stories of children being smothered along the Underground Railroad while their mothers tried to quiet them.

Peter's cries overpowered the clip-clops of the hooves and the rustling of the wheels. There was no place she could turn off the road until he was quiet again. No place for them to hide.

Yet in spite of the cries, Anna could feel the presence of the Spirit. She knew He was guiding them to safety. Silently she thanked Him for allowing Will to be the man searching the road tonight and for Will's decision to allow God-inspired compassion to supersede his duty to uphold the law. He was only one of many who struggled to maintain the balance between love and the law, and she was grateful that he chose in his heart to love.

Ahead of them, a carriage rounded the corner, but instead of feeling panicked, Anna was empowered. She didn't know the lyrics to many songs, but in spite of the reigning edict against music in church, her mother had sung "Amazing Grace" to Anna each night when she was a child. As the years had gone by, Anna had guarded those lyrics in her heart as if they were a treasure, not permitting herself to sing them even in private. She hadn't allowed herself to forget the lyrics either.

Tonight she didn't think God would mind if she exhumed this treasure and used music to protect His children. At the top of her lungs and completely off-key, she belted out words about the sweet sound of grace, sounding a lot like she'd spent the evening drinking in the tavern instead of contemplating salvation.

Let the people coming toward her think she was drunk! She didn't care what they thought as long as they didn't hear Peter crying.

He wailed behind her, and she wailed even louder, shaking the heavens with her falsetto to squelch the sound of his cries. Everyone within a mile of her would know that there was a fool coming down the road, and they would probably pull over to let her pass.

Anna started giggling in spite of herself. It was ridiculous. Her, a birthright Quaker, singing and laughing like she was drunk to cover up her attempt to sneak slaves across enemy lines. It was utterly and completely ludicrous.

The road curved to the left, and she saw another buggy approaching. With a grand finale, she wrapped up the hymn and then began again, singing from the top. As long as Marie and Peter and the others spent the rest of the night at the Sutters' home instead of in jail, she would sing "Amazing Grace" a hundred times.

The carriage passed by on the other side without incident, and when Anna stopped singing, she realized that Peter had quieted as well.

Her singing, she was certain, didn't soothe him; it must have been the steady gait of the horses.

Anna leaned back. Wind ruffled the ribbons on her bonnet, but she didn't feel the chill. She was steady—alert—as the dark miles passed slowly under the wheels. Whenever another rig passed them, she braced herself, preparing to belt out yet another rendition of her mother's song if Peter cried again.

A mile before Connersville was a rundown cabin along the side of the road, and when they passed the cabin, she pulled back on the reins. The ears of the horses perked, and she listened with them. A frog croaked nearby, and she heard a fluttering of bat wings prowling the night, but she didn't hear voices or the tromping of other horses pursuing them.

She drove her team off the main road and onto a path that curved behind the cabin. The leaves that brushed against her face camouflaged both her and the wagon. Surrounded by darkness on every side, it was almost like she was driving through a cave instead of a forest.

A half mile off the main road was a placid stream that loped through the trees—the end of the line for her. The horses waded through the water, and then they stopped on the mossy bank where the path vanished into a mesh of branches and leaves. The only way to cut through the woods from here was by foot.

She listened one more time to the night's busy creatures before she turned and hoisted the first of the twenty or so heavy blankets off the hidden door. Sliding the blanket over the side of the wagon, it landed with a soft thump on the moss. She didn't hesitate. The instant one blanket left her fingers, she pulled the next one from the pile and pushed it over the side. One blanket at a time, as fast as she could, she threw off every blanket until the ground around the wagon had been carpeted with wool.

She leapt into the back of the wagon and unlatched the door so her passengers could crawl out. They emerged slowly, stopping to stretch their arms and legs before they climbed over the seat. Their new clothes were wrinkled and damp, their faces flushed.

Except for Auntie Rae, they all ignored Marie, apparently angry at her for not forcing Peter to be quiet.

Several of them rested on the pile of blankets while George and Roger paced back and forth by the creek, anxious to move on. Anna understood—the longer they stood out here unprotected, the more likely they would become prey.

Plopping a knapsack onto the driver's seat, she untied it and lifted out six candles. One at a time, she held the candles up to the lantern's flame and passed them down to the adults. Then she hopped off the seat, and her friends gathered around her.

"It wasn't Marie's fault that Peter cried," she said. "God protected all of us in spite of his cries, and I hope you will continue to care for her and each other during the rest of this journey."

She told them that she would miss them, and then she whispered the directions. "Follow the creek north for two miles until you reach a giant beech tree with an *S* carved into its trunk. Turn right at the beech tree and follow the path to a whitewashed farmhouse with a cupola."

George edged away from her, ready to start the journey, but she reached out and grabbed his arm so he would listen to all of the directions. The last part was the most important. "You mustn't knock on their back door unless the light in the cupola is lit."

An owl hooted beside them, and she caught her breath. The sooner they were on their way, the better it would be for all of them. "If the cupola lantern is dark, wait in the cornfield by their house until they give you the signal that it's safe."

She swallowed hard as she recognized the anxiety in each of their faces. "God bless each of you."

Auntie Rae held out her hand. "We hope to be seein' you in Canada someday."

Her fingers felt like worn leather when Anna shook them. "The next time I see you, you'll be as free as I am."

The elderly woman kissed her cheek. "And I'll be praisin' the Lord."

Marie stepped up and held Peter out to her for the last time. "I couldn't make him stop crying," she said, her own face as teary as her son's.

Anna reached for him and clutched him to her chest. "It's not your fault."

"I near killed him."

"This is a hard journey for everyone, Marie, but it's especially hard for you." When she kissed the soft hair on Peter's head, he brushed his fingers across her nose. This time it was really good-bye.

With Peter in her left arm, she embraced Marie with her right arm. "You and Peter are going to be fine."

"You be prayin' for us?" Marie asked.

"Every day."

In the candlelight, Anna watched the fear in Marie's eyes melt away. "I ain't scared no more."

Anna kissed Peter's cheek one last time. Then she slowly released her grasp on the child as she gave him back to his mother.

"Go with God," she whispered as her friends turned away.

Their forms faded into the oaks and evergreens like leaves blowing away in the autumn winds. Even the candlelight was engulfed by the darkness.

She reached down and lifted a stack of blankets off the ground, but she dropped them. The Spirit was nudging her to pray. Right now. And so she did, entreating God to protect Peter and whisk him away to safety before the first snow.

For ten minutes she prayed, until the cold settled on her. Something moved in the brush beside her, and she knew she couldn't linger.

She didn't want to meet an animal or another person on this remote trail, especially a person asking questions.

She lifted several blankets off the ground and dumped them back in the wagon.

Her friends would go to the Sutters' home, and she would deliver the blankets to Jacob Sutter's store in Connersville. Then she would go home and wait for the next knock on her door.

Chapter Ten

....

The apple trees along the road to Liberty swelled with bright reds and greens. The crisp air nipped the tip of Anna's nose, and she tugged her shawl closer to her face. When she rounded the edge of the orchard, a marsh robin dipped in front of her carriage and serenaded her with such a sweet tune that she couldn't imagine hearing a prettier song.

She loved the sounds and beauty of Indiana's hills and wilderness, though some days she missed the bustle of college life. It had been four months since she'd completed her degree in English—one of the few women to receive a gentleman's education from Oberlin College— and returned home to help her father with their Underground station. When she was in Richmond, her boardinghouse had been in a constant state of activity, but she'd thrived in the busyness of her studies and long conversations with friends. She didn't know what she would do if Charlotte weren't at the house to keep her company each day, working alongside her to manage the housekeeping and cooking for her father and their guests.

Anna's favorite day of the week was First Day, when she and sixty-one other Friends gathered together at the meetinghouse in Liberty. After the quiet service of reflection, she and Charlotte and her father often stayed in town and spent the afternoon visiting.

Today wasn't First Day, but Esther Cooley had sent a messenger with her promised invitation for a tea, and Anna had responded that she would come. She told herself that it was a business call to discuss a baby blanket woven at the mill, but she was rather excited about the opportunity to visit, even if her host was a worldly woman instead of a Quaker.

Ever since she had taken Marie and Peter and the others to the Sutter home last week, she had flitted around the house, trying to stay busy with her writing and cooking and mending, but she couldn't stop wondering if they had made it safely to the next station...and the next. When the *Liberty Era* arrived on Seventh Day, she skimmed its contents in minutes but found no mention of runaways who had been caught north of Connersville. She comforted herself with the lack of news about their flight.

She checked the address on the invitation and turned onto High Street. Most of the houses on this road were brick, but the Cooleys' large white home shone like a centerpiece made of flowers and ribbon.

She exited the carriage and handed the reins to the Cooleys' hired man, who assured her that he would feed her horses before she journeyed back to the mill. To people like the Cooleys, Silver Creek probably seemed as far away as Cincinnati.

She lifted the hem of her silk skirt, the light copper color the same as a mother robin's breast. On days like this Anna almost felt as if she could fly and sing like the birds in the marsh, but she smoothed her skirt and walked toward the staircase that led to the veranda. She wore this silk dress only for special occasions, and as often as she was invited to someone's house for tea, today was a very special occasion.

The front bell rang at the twist of her fingers, and a housekeeper opened the door. The woman was tall and pretty with thick hair braided on top of her head. She motioned for Anna to come inside, and something about the way she smiled reminded her of Marie. Perhaps Marie would grow up to be an elegant housekeeper in a stately Canadian home. Or she might be the mistress of the house.

The woman introduced herself as Greta and said, "Mrs. Cooley will be down in a few minutes."

"Thank you."

Greta opened the French doors beside her. "You can wait in the parlor, if you'd like."

Anna stepped through the doors and inhaled the aroma of nutmeg. She eyed the couch but was too mesmerized by the beauty of the room to sit down.

The walls were painted mauve. Instead of plain wainscoting, the paneling was decorated with white plaster ribbons. The golden frames on the wall glistened in the sunlight, and to her right was a large hutch filled with porcelain figurines and pieces of china.

Her gaze passed over the figurines and froze when she saw the shiny black piano in the corner of the room. She stepped across the carpet, and, without thinking, she opened the top and slid her fingers over the cold keys. For a moment, she longed to hear the music.

The bright paint and paintings and piano might be worldly, but standing in this room alone, all she saw was beauty.

Closing her eyes, Anna fought against the jealousy that seemed to spring up from within her. Elaborate decor and fancy dress only masked the true state of a person's heart and soul. Simplicity and equality were cornerstones of her faith. Her life. If she put on airs, her Southern guests would never feel comfortable in her home.

True beauty was on the faces of the people who had visited her. And it was everywhere around her, the Spirit revealing Himself in nature.

She enjoyed looking at pretty things, but she was content with the plainness—and the simplicity—of her life.

Anna heard the whoosh of skirts, and she opened her eyes to watch her hostess glide into the room. Esther was dressed in a pale pink dress with a large satin bow on the front and a silver heart-shaped locket around her neck. The woman's cheeks seemed to be glowing in the sunlight, her eyes were soft and clear. Pregnancy was obviously agreeing with her.

Esther smiled at her with joy. "Do you play?"

Her hand recoiled from the piano keys. "No."

"I wish you did." Esther sighed softly. "My baby girl loves music, but I can barely play these days."

Anna hid both her hands behind her back and turned from the piano. "How do you know she likes music?"

"She starts dancing whenever she hears the slightest tune." Esther sat on a padded chair and brushed her fingers over her skirt. "I can almost hear her singing, too, a beautiful song about life and love and happiness."

Anna couldn't help but smile back. "It seems that her mother is quite happy."

"I'm horrible, aren't I?" Esther's smile diminished with another sigh. "I gush and gush like there's never been a baby born in Liberty. It's completely improper, I know, but I can't seem to help myself."

Esther motioned to the chair beside her, and Anna tucked her dress under her as she sat down. "You should be happy about your child."

"I'm ecstatic," Esther's lower lip twitched, "though few people can understand why I'm so excited."

Esther's shoulders shook lightly when she turned her head. Her voice was hushed, but Anna still heard her next words. "I've waited so long...."

Anna's hands twitched in her lap as silence filled the room. She wanted to reach out and comfort this woman, yet she didn't want to make her feel uncomfortable. So she waited.

Esther didn't speak again until the door beside the piano opened. Greta entered with a silver tray that glistened as she crossed through the rays of sunlight.

"Thank you," Esther said simply, her lips pinched into a tight smile. She lifted the bright blue porcelain teapot garnished with gold and poured black tea into Anna's cup. Steam wafted out of it, and

Anna smelled a hint of jasmine. She dropped a sugar cube into the hot drink and stirred.

Esther tapped on the side of her cup as she sipped it. Anna felt the woman eyeing her, like she was trying to decide if she would be a close friend or a mere acquaintance.

"Come here." Esther set her cup down and reached for Anna's hand. "You can feel her dancing."

Anna warily placed her fingers across Esther's swollen belly. "I don't feel anything."

The baby gave a swift kick, and Anna jumped. A giggle escaped her mouth, and Esther laughed beside her. The baby's toes and hands danced across Esther's skin, and Anna marveled at the beautiful signs of creation.

She lifted her hand and put it back into her lap. Bitterness swelled inside her again, and she finally recognized it for the sin that it was.

She, with her heritage of Quaker plainness and propriety, was jealous of Esther Cooley's fine china and lacy curtains and piano. And most of all, she was jealous because Esther Cooley had a baby dancing and singing inside her, and Anna could never even dream about having a child of her own.

Her work on the Underground was worth the cost, yet the thought of holding a baby like Peter or Esther's little girl was like dumping salt into an open wound. Her desires might always sting, even if just a bit.

Esther wrapped her slender fingers around her teacup and lifted it to her lips. Her belly still moved, but she wasn't watching it anymore. "It's marvelous, isn't it?"

Anna nodded, her eyes wandering toward the window, to the natural beauty and warmth of God's light. "A miracle."

"A miracle," Esther repeated, gazing out the window like Anna. She seemed to catch herself and looked back at Anna. "How about you, Anna Brent? Will you ever marry and have babies?"

Anna balanced her tea with both hands. She didn't want to talk about her future with anyone, especially someone like Esther Cooley. She was glad to come here and have tea with this woman and even admire her pretty things, but she would never confide in her. "I don't think I will ever marry."

Esther leaned closer. "Surely there is a young man in Liberty that has caught your eye."

The only man who had caught her eye hadn't caught her heart. And he would never catch it. Matthew may be winsome, but he wasn't for her. In the stolen moments that she allowed herself to imagine the type of man she'd like to marry, Matthew wasn't even a consideration. She wanted a man of passion. A man of dedication to God and to the abolition of slavery. That was part of the reason she would never marry. She wanted a hero as well as a husband.

Esther's nose was inches away from hers. "There is someone, isn't there?"

Anna moved back and glanced down at the teapot, admiring its gold ribbing, the white flowers painted on the blue sides. Esther had asked her to come to discuss the blanket for her child, not Anna's future. She lifted her teacup again. "Where did you get this tea?"

"From England," Esther responded quickly, and then she grinned. Before she spoke, she fed another lump of sugar into her cup. "Someday I shall introduce you to my brother. He swears that he will never marry either."

Anna didn't want to talk about marriage or babies or Esther's brother. "Some people are not meant to marry."

"I don't believe that."

"Sometimes circumstances are such that marriage is not appropriate." Her protest was weak, but she wasn't going to discuss specifics. It shouldn't matter to Esther in the least if she did or did not plan to marry one day.

"Two people can be smitten by love even in the direst of situations."

"Did you meet your husband under dire circumstances?"

"Oh, no." Esther's laugh sounded light again. "We met in Ohio. He was a colleague of my father's at the Cincinnati hospital, and my father decided to bring him home."

"And you were smitten?"

"Immediately."

Anna didn't want to think about falling in love, but her mind wandered. Like Esther and Joseph, her parents had loved each other from the first time they'd met on a plantation in North Carolina, more than thirty years ago. Her mother once told her that it was as if God Himself had brought them together. They moved north to Indiana weeks after they married.

Esther glanced back at the piano. "Do you want me to teach you a song or two?"

Anna shook her head. "We're not allowed to play the piano."

"Oh, I know all about your rules," Esther said. "My mother's parents were Quakers."

"And your mother?"

"Decided to marry a Presbyterian."

"She couldn't convince him to join?"

Esther shook her head. "My grandparents were devastated."

"I can imagine."

Esther unclasped the silver locket from around her neck and held it out for Anna to see. A vine had been engraved into the silver. "When we left home, my grandmother gave both my brother and me a locket."

"It's beautiful."

Esther traced the vine with her fingers. "It's supposed to remind us of our Quaker heritage and of all the people we love today."

"Why don't you and Joseph join our Meeting?"

"I'd never make a good Quaker. I love to sing and dance and read...."

"We're allowed to read," Anna interjected. Not only was this woman questioning her future, now she was questioning her faith.

"Not *Godey's Lady's Book*."

"We don't seek out worldly pleasures," Anna tried to explain. "Not because we don't enjoy God's blessings, but because we're devoted to protecting our hearts and minds—like Jesus when He rejected Satan's temptations in the wilderness."

A long pause settled in the room before Esther spoke again. "Surely you have something to entertain you during the long winter evenings."

"I like to write," she replied, and then wished she hadn't. She didn't have to defend her faith to this woman or tell her that more than anything she liked to lose herself in words. Her desk, with its pen and fine paper, was her favorite place to be.

But it was too late. Esther's eyes had a fresh spark in them. "What do you write?"

Anna hesitated this time. "All sorts of things."

"Poetry?"

"A little."

"Oh, good." Esther clapped. "Next time you come visit, you will have to bring your poems for me to read."

"I don't think..."

"Nonsense," Esther said. "I love poetry almost as much as I love music."

Anna lifted her cup to her lips, embarrassed at the thought of Esther reading her private stash of poetry. Yet another part of her wasn't embarrassed at all. Someplace deep inside her, she was pleased that someone wanted to read her work.

The pride in her heart was as stalwart as the rock walls of Liberty's jail. Perhaps the only way to humble herself was to let Esther pore over her poetry and critique it. She was certain Esther would help keep her pride at bay.

"You will bring your writings to me, won't you?" Esther insisted.

Anna studied the way the sun reflected off the gold rim of the cup in her hands. "Next time I come," she promised.

A Quakeress never broke her word.

Chapter Eleven

....

With his ink-stained fingers, Daniel dropped the last three letters for the page into the composing stick and positioned the stick on the galley tray. The rapidly fading light cast shadows across the counter and tray, but he didn't stop to light a lantern. The lamp's reservoir needed to be refilled, and he didn't want to bother with the funnel and oil until the entire tray had been compiled and was waiting for him on the press.

The paper was due to local subscribers by daylight. Printing it would take most of the night, but he had assured Isaac that it would be done by morning. In nine hours, he would hand off the finished stacks of the paper to a team of schoolboys who would then deliver it across the county and to the residents of Liberty.

He may be late in setting the type, but he wouldn't miss the deadline. When the first rays of morning shone through the window, he would be surrounded by stacks of newspapers.

The brayer in hand, he rolled ink across the tray and then placed a long piece of paper over the ink. With a wooden hammer and a block of wood, he pounded the paper over the type and created the proof so he could check for errors before he made a thousand copies on the press.

He wiped his smudged glasses on his coat and began to review the draft of his newspaper. In the last week, apples had begun ripening in the orchards around Liberty, the furniture store had received a load of coffins, and Union County farmers were preparing for the annual Battle of the Bang Boards. Hardly the pressing news he'd envisioned when Isaac had asked him to take the position of editor.

Yesterday he finished his editorial about slavery, a full column on the destruction that would ensue if the president signed the Fugitive Slave Act. Congress had somehow approved the blood-soaked piece of legislature and was now waiting for Millard Fillmore to either sign it or veto the bill that would punish anyone who helped slaves go North.

Daniel was convinced that the president would never sign a bill like this into law. It was only a patch, slapped on to piece together the chasm across Mason and Dixon's Line. If the president passed it, the government would keep together the Union of the North and South, but it would punish Negroes for simply desiring freedom. And it would punish the good people who abetted them.

Instead of using their power to indict people who'd committed a real crime—like slave owners who beat and sometimes killed their slaves—Congress wanted to force people to look away when they saw someone in need. No person who had dedicated his or her life to following God could look away. No legislation would keep the Union together as long as certain people in their country didn't value the freedom of those whose heritage happened to be from Africa instead of Europe.

People like Enoch Gardner craved freedom, and they deserved it. Daniel didn't have any idea where Enoch went after he ran away from his owner in Richmond, but as far as he knew, no one had found the man. He prayed they never would. Enoch might be safe in Canada at this very moment, ready to start a new life, have a family, and work to earn a living.

Daniel placed the galley tray into the metal chase and began putting the little pieces of wood called furniture around the tray to hold it into the chase.

Instead of growing in their support for runaway slaves like Enoch, their country and state and even their county was becoming polarized by it. People were either for abolition, or they were for slavery. In his opinion, no one could be against slavery and not fight for abolition. The Bible refused to condone people who were lukewarm in their faith. In fact, the book of Revelation clearly stated that God would spew those out of His mouth.

How could someone see what was happening and not take a stand?

He didn't understand it. If someone had a strong faith in God, how could they not believe these people should be free? In the book of Jeremiah, God clearly commanded the house of David to deliver those who were spoiled out of the hands of the oppressor.

"Deliver him that is spoiled."

The words called out to him morning and night. He would do whatever it took to deliver slaves from those who oppressed them.

There was a quick knock on the door beside the printing press, and his employer and friend, Isaac Barnes, rushed into the room, waving a piece of paper as if he were mad. "They've done it!"

Daniel slumped forward against the counter. Part of him didn't want to know the truth, wanted to stay in denial that their president would side against freedom, but he had no choice. He would learn about it, and he would fight. "The Fugitive Act?"

Isaac slapped the paper in front of him. "Fillmore signed it yesterday."

Daniel shoved the tray of type, and it spilled over the counter. Metal clanked when it hit the ground, and type sprayed across the floor.

How could Millard Fillmore have done this? He was supposed to be a man of integrity. He was supposed to be fighting for the freedom of the slaves, not punishing the people who were trying to help them. "They made it a federal crime?"

"That includes sheltering runaways or giving them food." Isaac kicked away the type at his feet and spread the telegram over the countertop. "They've called it 'stealing negroes,' and it's punishable by a thousand-dollar fine and six months in prison."

Daniel read an abbreviated version of the new law and pushed the paper back toward Isaac. "Indiana is supposed to be a free state."

Isaac shook his head, shoving the paper into his coat pocket. "It's not free for runaway slaves anymore."

"Or for the people who want to aid them." Daniel smacked the countertop. "What can be more American than helping an injured soul?"

"This law won't stop the abolitionists."

Resolve swept through him. Isaac was right. This type of legislation would never stop him and those who spoke out against slavery. They were called by a higher law that demanded justice and righteousness and compassion. God would never want him to stop fighting for the millions of colored men and women who would be punished if they tried to fight for themselves. "It will only make us stronger."

"That's what I wanted to talk to you about—" Isaac paused, but the weight in his voice felt like an anvil about to fall.

"You can't ask me to compromise on this!"

His employer walked to the window. Daniel couldn't imagine that Isaac wanted them to compromise on their stand in the paper, as well. Isaac had started this paper specifically to counter the pro-slavery propaganda coming off Milton Kent's press.

No matter how much it hurt, Daniel wouldn't concede on this issue. Not writing about slavery was the very same thing as writing articles that supported it. He might as well go to work for the *Union County News*.

It was the silence of so many on this issue that was strengthening slavery. Words, not weapons, would give them victory in this battle. He only needed to convince those in Union County that slavery was of the devil. Their pro-slavery sentiments could spread to other counties in Indiana and throughout the state.

But he couldn't influence anyone if he couldn't write.

Isaac turned toward him, but before his employer could speak, Daniel said, "I have to do this."

"I'm not asking you to stop writing about abolition." Isaac wiped the sweat off his forehead with a handkerchief. "We just can't report anymore on specific slaves who have run away."

"You're going to let them win?"

"This isn't a battle against flesh and blood, Daniel. It's against darkness and principalities." Isaac ran his hands over the press. "And no, I don't want them to win. I just don't think we can help anyone if we're sent to jail."

"I'll go to jail if I have to."

Isaac smiled the same way his father used to smile when Daniel pestered him. "What good are you going to do in jail?"

"At least I'd be taking a stand."

Isaac clapped him on the back. "I don't want you to falter on your stance against slavery, but I also don't want you to incriminate yourself or me. Unless the good Lord wants us in chains, I think we could be more effective on this side of jail."

Daniel leaned down and began picking the type off the floor. He didn't care about himself; he would go to jail if he had to, but he did care about Isaac. There were few people who had put so much of a personal stake against slavery as Isaac. He didn't just speak against slavery; he had spent much of his income and sacrificed his reputation to fight it.

Daniel dumped the letters onto the counter. "I'm still going to write editorials."

Isaac nodded. "I wouldn't want it any other way."

"And a cover story condemning this new act."

"I certainly hope so!"

Daniel scooped another handful of type from the floor and began sorting the letters on the countertop. "I don't want to stop telling the stories of individual slaves."

Isaac stepped toward the door. "I respect you, Daniel, and your decisions. If you want to use your talents at another place, there will be no ill will from me."

"Thank you."

"In the meantime, if you can get the article on the Slave Act done tonight—"

Daniel finished his sentence. "We'll beat Milton Kent's edition."

"Exactly."

Daniel glanced over at the clock. He had eight hours to compile and print it, but the absurdity of the deadline didn't deter him. Who needed sleep on a night like this?

"I'll have it ready in the morning."

Isaac reached for the door handle, and chilly air filled the room when he swung it open. "The boys will be here to deliver at five."

Daniel shivered, but he didn't stop to throw more logs on the fire. He'd spent the past two days writing copy and now most of that would be scrapped, but maybe people would actually read this edition. The new act would impact every person in the county, every person living in states that were supposed to be free.

He finished organizing the next line of type in the tray and began popping the next letters into the stick. Usually he wrote the article first, longhand, but there was no time for him to write now. He would have to compile the story in his head, and as he placed the type into the stick, he would pray it made sense.

Expediency was the key, not eloquency. He had to get the facts on the paper, along with his opinions, and out to the subscribers before Milton released a paper applauding the justice of the new act.

His paper was a meager offering in comparison to what so many had to endure down South, but he would do it and do it well. He couldn't do much to fight against the act, but he could speak out.

FILLMORE PASSES FUGITIVE SLAVE ACT

Private Citizens Criminalized for Helping Runaways

The clock chimed that it was ten o'clock, but he didn't panic. He would finish this story and set the rest of the paper. Then they would distribute it in the morning.

He wouldn't let Isaac or their subscribers down.

Chapter Twelve

....

Marie winced as her elderly hostess cleaned the wound on the bottom of her foot with soap and water, but she didn't complain. An injured foot was only a small obstacle to getting her baby to freedom. It might hurt, but nothing would stop her from reaching the Canadian shore.

She had already berated herself for the injury. She should have been more careful, holding her candle in front of her instead of to the side.

It had happened three nights ago when she and their small group of runaways had crossed the dark field to Mrs. Adeline's home from Mrs. Betsy's. She had sliced her heel on something sharp, the pain instantaneous as it shot up her leg. She didn't stop to see what she had stepped on—it didn't matter anyway. What mattered was that she kept moving.

Mrs. Adeline apologized as she rubbed the ointment into her foot and wrapped a cloth around the wound, but Marie told her not to worry. The pain wouldn't last. Their group was supposed to move again on Saturday, and she was going with them.

"Maybe you should stay here a few extra days," Mrs. Adeline said. "I'll make sure you and Peter get to the next station when your foot heals."

Marie's gaze settled on the crib at her side. Sleep had overtaken Peter, and he rested by the fire. It was tempting to stay here longer and let Peter rest and her body recover. Yet Master Owens and his posse were close behind her—she could feel it in her bones. No injury would stop her and Peter from pressing northward. If she left on Saturday night as planned, Mrs. Adeline said she could be crossing the great lake in three weeks' time. She was so close to freedom. Sweet freedom! She couldn't stop now.

"I'm goin' with the others."

Mrs. Adeline leaned forward, imploring her. "I wish you would stay, just until you are well."

"There won't be any well in me, Miz Adeline, until I reach Canada."

Mrs. Adeline paused and then patted Marie's knee. "Wait right here. I've got something for you."

Marie leaned her head against the curved back of the rocking chair. With her good foot, she pushed away from the floor and rocked beside her baby. She never thought she'd see such kindness in white folk, yet so many had been kind to her along her journey. Miss Anna and her father. Mrs. Betsy. And now Mrs. Adeline. They had all cared for her and Peter like they were white, too. Like they were equals.

Maybe in Canada they would be equal, as well. The Promised Land would be a land of opportunity and kindness. Only heaven itself would be more glorious, she was sure of it. She would make a home for her and Peter in the new land, and they would be safe and warm until God Himself called them home.

The door squeaked open, and Mrs. Adeline held out a pair of ankle-length boots to her. Marie didn't think she'd ever seen anything so fine. They were black leather with laces strung to the silk tops. On the toes were cream-colored bows.

She took the boots in hand and ran her fingers across the smooth linen inside. They were beautiful, made for a lady. Why was Mrs. Adeline, who had been so kind to her, showing off her fancy boots? Only a proud fool, her mama once said, flaunted their possessions. Mrs. Adeline didn't seem like no fool.

Marie handed them back to the lady. "They's very pretty."

Mrs. Adeline folded her hands, refusing to take the boots. "They're for you."

Marie stared down at the boots and then looked back up. "They much too fancy for me."

Mrs. Adeline reached for one of the boots and held it up to Marie's good foot. They were about two inches too big. "Not a perfect fit, but they'll protect the bottoms of your feet."

Marie sat frozen for a moment, words and thoughts paralyzed in her mind. Even when she'd worked in Master Owens's house, taking care of his babies, she hadn't been issued a pair of shoes. She'd watched the wife and daughters of Master Owens parade around the house when they purchased a new pair of boots or a dress, but she'd never had anything fancy of her own.

Mrs. Adeline pulled a pair of stockings out of her pocket and set them on the side table. "We'll bandage your foot before you leave, and then I want you to wear these boots and stockings over it."

Marie refused to take back the boot in the woman's hand. "I cain't take these from you, Miz Adeline. They's much too fine."

The woman met her eye. "They're a gift, Marie. You can't give them back."

A gift? Tears wet her cheeks as she reached for the boot and pulled it to her chest.

Miss Anna had given Peter the gift of clothing, and now this woman was giving her the gift of boots. And she hadn't done a single thing to earn them. Mrs. Adeline refused to let her help with the ironing or food preparations, saying it was her job to rest and care for her baby so they would be ready for the next leg of their journey.

"I ain't deservin' these, Miz Adeline. I ain't good like you."

"Only God is good, Marie." The older woman bent down and kissed her head. "That's why He sent His Son to die for me and you both. He loved us even when we were doing things that hurt Him."

Marie had heard plenty of stories at Master Owens's church about how God had sent Jesus to die for His children, but she'd always thought Jesus had died for the white children. The good children. Not for her.

She wiped off her tears with her sleeve. "He didn't die for me."

"Oh yes He did, Marie. He died especially for you and that beautiful baby of yours." She squeezed Marie's hand before she stood up. "He loves you so very much."

Someplace deep in her heart, she had known that God loved her. Before her mama had passed, she'd talked about God's love, but Marie had never really believed her. God had protected her along her journey—she had felt Him there—but she had never understood how a loving God could take away her mama and leave her with Master Owens.

She'd never stopped to think that maybe God wasn't at fault for her being born into slavery. Or that maybe He loved her in spite of where she'd been born and what she had done.

Mrs. Adeline stepped out of the room, and when she was gone, Marie thanked God for all of His gifts to her.

* * * * *

Five boys, ages ten through thirteen, gathered in the small newspaper office and waited by the wall for Daniel to finish the printing. He'd been up all night setting type, proofing, and finally printing and folding the paper one copy at a time.

His arms ached from inking the plate and cranking the press over and over a thousand times. It had felt like ten thousand times. His shirt was soaked with sweat, and the long apron he wore over his clothes was splattered with ink. With every crank, he told himself that people needed to read about the Fugitive Slave Act before Milton Kent published his paper supporting the act. They needed to read about it today.

The truth would prevail; he was sure of it, in spite of the government's opposition. In spite of the millions who thought that slavery was critical for their country's survival. The truth would come out, and no one could ever accuse him of running from the front lines when a very real battle was being fought. Even if, like Isaac said, the battle was against the dark rulers of the world instead of his fellow man, his fellow man was allowing himself to be used by the devil. As long as men and women volunteered to support evil's schemes, he would speak out against them.

The sun was stealing over the horizon when he handed the remaining boy his stack of papers for delivery.

"Run!" he directed, and the boy flew out of the building like a hawk chasing a rabbit.

Daniel collapsed in the chair by the window and rubbed his eyes.

He'd done it! The paper was out. Their readers would learn about the atrocious slave act before anyone else. Then they could pass along the information to their neighbors. All it would take was a slow swelling in their community to overturn this legislation, not just among Quakers but among every denomination of people who called themselves Christian. Even if the law remained, the county of Union could band together to fight this institution. In spite of the law, they could be a safe haven for runaways.

Outside the tempered glass, orange and red rays crept through the sleepy village. Most of the town would wake soon, many of the residents with a copy of the *Liberty Era* on their doorsteps, but he couldn't keep his eyes open.

He forced himself to stand. If he fell asleep in this chair, he would awaken with an aching neck and back that would bother him for days. He needed to walk across the street to his boardinghouse, change his clothes, and crawl under the heavy quilt on his straw bed.

He glanced back out the window. The boys had dispersed with their papers. The street was quiet for now, but in an hour it would be bustling with carriages and carts and horses. Once he fell asleep on his bed, he wouldn't hear any of it.

Greta Lawson crossed the street toward his office, on her way to work for the day at his sister's house. She was one of the hardest working women Daniel knew—and flexible enough to embrace his sister's many whims.

Esther was deceived when it came to the evils of slavery, but deep down she had a kind heart. And she kept everyone's life around her interesting. Her house bustled more than the streets of Liberty at noon.

At this moment, in the still of the morning, Greta was probably wondering what whim Esther was preparing to pursue today.

The sudden sound of horse hooves startled him, and he turned his head to the right to see who was interrupting the quiet morning hour. He recognized the black man who galloped toward them, iron chains clanging on the back of his horse. It was Simon Mathers, the slave hunter who had pursued and captured Bradley over in Bloomington.

When Simon saw Greta, he pulled back on the reins of the horse and hurled his leg over the saddle, dropping down in front of her. Greta jumped backward, clutching her hands to her chest.

Exhaustion vanished as Daniel sprang to his feet. He ran toward the door and flung it open. He couldn't stop slave catchers from riding through their town, but he wasn't going to let someone like Simon harass their citizens, white or colored. Greta was an honorable woman, a hard worker. Just because her skin was a shade darker than most in their town, it didn't mean she had to subject herself to an inquisition. She'd done nothing wrong.

Daniel stepped in front of the man, his head stopping an inch short of Simon's crooked nose. Daniel was taller than most men in Liberty, but the man in front of him was part Hercules with eyes darker than an impending storm. No wonder slaves were afraid of running away. The men they sent after them were huge...and brutal.

Daniel stared at the man. "What's the problem?"

Simon sized him up like he was trying to determine the best way to defeat his opponent. It wouldn't be hard for the man to crush him—a couple belts with those fists and he'd be on the ground—but Daniel held strong. If young David could face the giant Goliath without wavering, Daniel could stand up to a bounty hunter.

The man coughed, his rancid breath reeking of tobacco and ale. "It ain't none of your business."

Daniel reached out and took Greta's arm. Her body shook, but she didn't cower from the man or his intimidation. Both of them would stand strong together.

"Greta is a family friend," he explained calmly. "So it is my business if you need to talk with her about something."

Simon snorted at him. "I ain't here to talk."

"Well, good." Daniel released Greta's arm and propelled her forward with a small push on her back. "Then my friend can get along to work."

The slave catcher blocked her steps. "Oh, no she cain't."

"Then we do have a problem, because Greta has an important position in town." Daniel pulled his watch out of his apron pocket and glanced at it. "It's already 6:20, and she is required to be at the home by 6:30 to build the fire and begin breakfast for the family."

Simon clenched his jaw, and he looked like an angry bloodhound about to be denied his catch. In the daylight, the fury in his eyes seemed almost comical, but if Greta or another colored woman met this man at night, they'd be terrified. It was bloodthirsty men like him who often determined their fate.

"I've been lookin' all over the county for a Negro named Marie Owens, and now I'm thinkin' that I'm looking right at her."

Greta shook her head quickly. "I've never been known as Marie."

Simon reached out and looped one of Greta's curls around his fingers. "I bet you've been known as a lot of names in your lifetime."

Daniel slapped the man's fingers away from her hair. "She said she isn't Marie."

Simon faced him, his hand reaching for the lanyard that dangled from his neck like he might need to use the knife inside. "You don't want to mess with me, boy."

Daniel refused to back down. The man could kill him—and probably get away with murder since Daniel had been killed defending a colored woman—but God had appointed him to defend the powerless. If he had to die for it, he would die with honor.

He held his shoulders high. "What do you want from her?"

Simon's eyes wandered back toward Greta. "Marie Owens has a red scar on the back of her neck and a five-hundred-dollar reward on her head."

The man reached for Greta's hair again.

"Don't touch her!"

A dog barked in the distance, and Daniel held his breath as the man contemplated what he was going to do to get rid of him.

"I'm a lawyer by trade." Daniel checked his watch again. "We can take this before a judge in two hours and determine your legal rights."

The man snorted again. "I don't need no judge tellin' me my rights." He slipped his knife out of the sheath and held it to his side. "If you'd read a few of your lawyerly books, then you'd know it's my right to see if this here woman is the one I been searchin' for."

Greta looked at Daniel, her gaze sad but resolute. She turned her back toward the man, lifting her hair with one hand while she pulled down the collar of her dress with the other. There was no scar.

Simon shoved his knife back into the sheath. "It's too bad," he said, licking his lips. "Marie's owner is just south of town, and I'd a sure enjoyed taking you to him."

He didn't apologize to Greta or say anything else. Instead, he jumped back on his horse, the empty chains on his back clanking together as he rode away.

Greta smoothed her fingers over her hair and straightened her dress. She stepped off the curb and, with her head high, began walking toward the Cooleys.

Daniel walked beside her. "You didn't have to show him your neck."

"Yes, I did," she replied, her voice smoother than freshly churned butter. "He wouldn't have left me alone until he found out I wasn't Marie."

He sighed. "I suspect you're right."

She glanced back at the dust cloud that shadowed the hunter. "How sad for Marie..."

"We'll pray God's protection for her."

"Please pray for God's protection over all of us." They passed the owner of the furniture store and nodded at him. "Free blacks aren't even safe around here anymore."

He wanted to disagree with her, but he couldn't. The passage of this new law would make the North an even more hostile place toward colored people—whether or not they had their free papers. What was stopping a hunter from kidnapping a free Negro and claiming that he or she was an escaped slave? They could steal away even the legally free and sell them down South for a substantial profit.

It was despicable to God, and it should be despicable to His people as well.

When they got to the house, Greta turned to him and shook his hand. "Thank you for helping me, Mr. Stanton."

"Daniel," he replied, and then he admitted the truth to her. "I was scared."

Her eyes fell, studying the white planks of the porch steps. "Me, too."

"He won't bother you anymore."

She took two steps up to the porch and turned back to him. "Mr. Stanton?"

"Yes, Greta."

She hesitated. "You helped me so much that I hate to even say it."

"What is it?"

"Well—"

He cocked his head. "When did you ever have trouble speaking your mind?"

She lowered her voice and leaned toward him. "It's just that, if I were you—"

"Yes?"

"If I were you, I'd think about takin' a bath before you help anyone else this morning."

He glanced down at his ink-stained hands and then grinned at her, pleased that her spirit was returning. "Does that mean you don't want me to stay for breakfast?"

"Not until you look presentable."

He took a step back. "I'll think about a bath."

Her hands flew to her hips. "You better do more than think."

On the way back to his room, he whistled. In spite of his fears, and in spite of the odds that he'd be whooped, he had stood up against the slave hunter. When confronted with the truth, the man had eventually backed down.

The truth is what would continue to drive him. The truth is what he would print in the paper. He didn't need to name runaway slaves by name. He would protect their anonymity as closely as he would protect their stories.

He would sleep for a few hours and take a bath. Then he'd start on a new edition of the paper, a special edition to highlight the heroic efforts of those committed to helping runaways in spite of the new law. He wouldn't name names—he didn't even know anyone in their town who was part of the elusive Underground Railroad. But he would talk to a few people at Meeting. Without using their names, he could tell some of their stories...and perhaps inspire others to sacrifice, as well.

Greta and other colored friends, slave or free, wouldn't be harassed on his watch. He'd faced the enemy square in the face, and he would do it again and again until God ordained that it was time for him to go home.

Chapter Thirteen

Anna's pen wasn't fast enough to capture all that tumbled out of her head and her heart. She was certain of few things anymore, but she was absolutely convinced that she was doing the right thing during this season of her life.

Nothing would stop her from harboring those who sought freedom, though neither she nor her father would talk about it in public. For that matter, they rarely talked about it in private, as if the very acknowledgment of their actions might travel out the window and over the doorstep of one of their neighbors who felt it their moral obligation to report anyone helping slaves.

Yet the words begged release, so she poured them out on paper. No one needed to know that the words came from her. She didn't seek fame or recognition. All she wanted to do was communicate that which erupted inside her. It was a plea for others to value the gift of freedom and desire to bestow that priceless gift onto others. It was a petition for her friends in the county and across the state to recognize the horrors of slavery and be incited to do something to stop it.

The stories she painted weren't pretty, but they were true. Every story of love and loss and brutality was one she'd heard from the fugitives who had stayed in her house. The latest one was about the fearless girl who was running to protect the life of her baby. Who could condemn a mother for escaping slavery to protect her child?

Those who thought that colored people didn't have the same feelings as those who were white had never met a Negro mother. Marie's devotion to her child was equal to any other mother—and maybe even more protective because she knew that at any moment her child could be whisked away from her and sold down South. The prayers of enslaved mothers must flood the very throne room of God.

Even when evil still prevailed, Anna knew He heard every one of those prayers, but it frustrated her, knowing that God was all-powerful, yet darkness ruled the world. Her father often reminded her that it was a human choice, back in the garden, to disobey God. With disobedience came disorder. When evil ruled in the hearts and minds of creation, it was the smallest, most innocent of them all who seemed to hurt the most.

Someday it would all be reconciled. Evil would be punished and good restored. In the meantime, she would use her pen to promote the good.

Charlotte slipped into the room and slid a newspaper in front of her. "This came out yesterday."

Anna read the *Liberty Era*'s headline and sighed, the sadness in her heart almost unbearable. "They passed it?"

Charlotte nodded slowly. "Everyone is talking about it in town."

She pushed the paper away from her and picked up her pen again. "Then we'll have to be even more careful, won't we?"

"You don't understand." Charlotte swung Anna's chair around so she would have to face her. "They are going to jail people for aiding slaves, and those in Liberty who've looked the other way at what you and your father are doing will be forced to testify against you in a court of law."

Anna rested her pen on the armchair. "God is on our side, Charlotte. We can't be afraid."

"God may be on the side of freedom, but if you get caught, Sheriff Zabel will lock you up in jail."

Anna's smile was confident, but she trembled inside. One of the reasons she fought for other people's freedom was because she valued hers so much. She liked to pretend that she was strong, but she knew she would crumble in a second if they put her in jail.

She blinked, and in her mind's eye, she saw the coffles she'd walked past around Liberty—fugitive slaves caught and strung together like trout on a line. How could she complain about a few nights in chains when so many spent their lives in shackles?

God knew that she didn't want to go to prison, but she couldn't live with herself if she didn't answer her door when a runaway knocked. She couldn't turn her back to those on her doorstep.

She would be more careful, but she wouldn't stop hiding those who had escaped slavery. No matter what this law said, her father wouldn't hesitate to welcome them into their house, and neither would she.

Anna clapped her hands together and folded them in her lap. "We aren't going to change a thing."

"There are plenty of other people who run stations on the Underground." Charlotte glanced out the window and looked back at her. "I can tell Ben to wait a few weeks before he brings anyone else here, just in case Will Denton talks to Sheriff Zabel about what he heard on the road the other night. Then you can start up again."

Anna shook her head. "There have always been risks with having a station. Now the stakes are just a little higher."

"But your father—"

"I'll talk to him tonight, but I don't think he will change his mind, either."

Charlotte's voice turned into a plea. "What if they fine you a thousand dollars for every person you've helped? What if they put you in jail?"

Anna scooted toward her friend and took her hand. "You don't want me to stop helping runaways, do you?"

Charlotte stepped back, seeming to contemplate her words. Her friend had experienced the horrors of slavery. Her master in North Carolina had tried to seduce her, and when she refused him, he'd cut her with his knife. Still she'd refused him, so he put her on the auction block and sold her.

Anna's parents, on a trip to their hometown in North Carolina, purchased Charlotte, and when they reached Indiana, they set her free. Instead of trekking out on her own, she had insisted on working for them.

Anna knew that her friend must be torn up on the inside about this new law. She wanted to help those slaves who had escaped from abusive masters because she'd experienced the abuse herself. But she also wanted to protect the Brents. The only winners of this new law were the slave owners, and Charlotte had no interest in protecting them.

Charlotte rubbed the scar on her cheek. "If you get discovered, they will want to hurt you."

She squeezed her friend's hand. "But they can't hurt my soul, and that's what really matters."

The doorbell rang, and the women looked at each other in surprise. Rarely did they have unannounced visitors out here on Silver Creek. A fugitive would never arrive in daylight, nor would they ring the front bell.

Anna hoped it was a neighbor until she heard dogs braying. When she pulled back the curtain, she saw that trouble had arrived.

Three men stood outside her door. The one ringing the bell was a middle-aged gentleman with a silk top hat and buttoned suit jacket. He held his head high and a black walking cane in his gloved hands.

The two men behind him, though, would never be confused with gentlemen. They were burly with scruffy beards, long hair, and skin as black as coal. They both wore dark brown buckskin jackets and long leather chaps. One of them held a whip and a set of chains in his hands. The other was struggling to hold the ropes that kept two bloodhounds at bay.

She stepped back from the curtains and looked into the strong brown eyes of her housekeeper. "You'd better go upstairs."

Charlotte stood tall, her shoulders back. "I'm not hiding from them."

"You don't have to hide," Anna insisted. "I just don't want them to see you when I open the door."

Charlotte's skirts swished with her sharp turn.

The doorbell rang again, and Anna moved slowly toward the door, waiting until Charlotte was upstairs. Her father would be upset at her for opening the door, but there were no runaways in their house this afternoon. If she didn't answer their ring today, these men would come back, and when they returned, she might have guests. Better to get rid of them now, before the hounds caught the scent of one of their friends.

These men may not hesitate to harm a slave, but she felt confident that they wouldn't harm a white woman in broad daylight. Or somewhat confident, at least. If they were caught harming a white woman, they would be hanged in the public square.

She wiped the sweat off her palms before she opened the door.

The gentleman flashed her a broad smile, his white teeth almost glistening in the sunlight, and he extended his hand. His features weren't exactly handsome, but his blue eyes were as intense as the shake of his hand. Whether or not they knew his name, most people probably didn't forget meeting him.

"I'm sorry to bother you, ma'am," he drawled when he released her hand. "I've been searching for a lost girl, and I wondered if I could trouble you with a few questions."

Anna nodded her head but didn't invite him inside. It was almost as if his very presence would taint her home.

"My name is Noah Owens, and I'm concerned about one of my servants who went missing from my plantation in Tennessee."

She wiped her palms on her skirt again. "Why are you concerned about her, Noah?"

The man looked shocked that she would use his first name. Or maybe he was shocked that she might question his motives. Apparently he'd never met a Quaker before.

"I'm always concerned about the people in my care, Miss, but I'm especially concerned about our little Marie. My wife and I raised her since birth, you see, and now she is expecting a child herself. My wife misses her terribly, and we're both worried sick."

"You must care for her deeply to travel such a distance."

He bowed his head. "I would be a real scoundrel to ignore her fate and let her and her child succumb to certain death up here."

Slime pasted the lips and whiskers of his bloodhounds, and Anna wondered why the master of an estate needed dogs to rescue someone he cared about so deeply.

"She looks like this." The man held out a flyer to her with an ink portrait, the remarkable likeness of the girl she'd befriended. "She's probably carrying a baby with her."

Anna wanted to tell him that Marie did have a child with her, a beautiful baby boy with the same blue eyes and head full of blond hair as the man who stood before her.

The man covered his chest with the flyer and blinked back a tear. "She's like a daughter to us."

It took everything Anna could do to control her tongue. Words wanted to tumble out of her like they had done moments ago from her pen, but this time she stopped them. She would write later...and burn her words.

How could this man, who had done so much to hurt Marie, say that she was like a daughter to him? If that's how he treated his children, she felt sorry for them as well.

The story came back to her quickly, the one Marie had told her of the baby born to her friend and fellow slave. The one who had been taken away and either sold or left someplace to perish.

Noah Owens was not kind to his children, either.

He didn't seem to notice the anger sparking inside her. He continued. "She was last seen at the mouth of the creek, a mile or so from here."

She forced a smile. "I know where the mouth of our creek is located."

"Of course you do." He winked at her. "You have a beautiful home, Miss—"

"My name is Anna."

He laughed. "You don't stand for much pomp and circumstance around here, do you?"

She didn't explain to him the Quaker disdain for any title that esteemed one man or woman over another. "Is there anything I can do for you?"

"I'd like to know if you've seen Marie."

She shrugged her shoulders. "Hundreds of colored people travel through our town, Noah, and they all look the same to me."

"I understand." He turned back to the men behind him. "She hasn't seen her."

He took a step down like he was leaving but then pivoted toward her again. "There is one more small thing you could do for me."

She didn't want to ask, but there was no other way around it. "How can I help you?"

"If it's not too much trouble"—he hesitated only for a moment—"I'd like to take a quick look inside your home."

Chapter Fourteen

....

Both hands firmly on her hips, the fury inside Anna blazed. How dare this man ride all the way from Tennessee, in pursuit of a girl he had probably raped, and then demand that Anna allow him and his rogue hunters to search the house for her?

The audacity astounded her. It was as if he had no idea that what he had done was wrong or that Marie was willing to risk everything to get away from his "kindness."

"You think I'm hiding your slave?"

"Of course not." Noah waved his hands at her. "I'm not accusing anyone around here of doing anything wrong. I just wouldn't be doing my job as a Christian man, you see, if I didn't search every house along this creek to try to find Marie and beg for her to come back home to her family."

She held out one of her hands. "Do you have a search warrant?"

"Aw, Miss Anna, all your neighbors let me glance in their houses without a warrant, so I didn't even think to get one." He stepped down the stairs again. "But I'm a gentleman, not one to force my way into someone's home. I'd be glad to get one from the sheriff if that would help you open your door for me."

Anna sighed. He wouldn't have any problem in getting the warrant— if not this afternoon, then when the court opened again on Second Day—and he'd return, perhaps with Randolph Zabel and Will Denton in tow. Better to let him go through her home now and be on his way.

She nodded toward the two slave hunters behind him. "I don't want them in my house."

Noah smiled at her again. "That won't be a problem, will it, fellas?"

He didn't turn around, but like obedient dogs, the men stepped back. Then with the quick removal of his hat, Noah Owens stepped over her threshold and into her house.

"My housekeeper is working upstairs." Anna shut the door behind him and turned. "I hope you won't disturb her."

Noah gave her another broad smile. "Of course not."

"You can look wherever you'd like."

He took off his coat and strung it over his arm. "Thank you for letting me intrude on your day."

She nodded, like he had given her a choice.

Noah brushed past her, and she moved into the parlor to wait for him to finish looking for Marie on the first floor. She folded her papers and the *Liberty Era* and slid them both behind a stack of books. He may never leave if he found abolitionist papers on her desk.

She shoved the edge of the newspaper down behind the books. What the world needed was more men like Daniel Stanton, men who were willing to stand up for slaves instead of hunting them down. He was sure to get a lot of local flack for condemning this new bill, both from people who were pro-slavery and from Quakers who believed that the Society of Friends should support the government and its laws protecting slave owners.

She closed the top of the secretary and wiped off her fingerprints with her sleeve. She could hear Noah's boots stomping through the dining room.

Never before had she been so thankful that they didn't have any runaways staying at their home. All it took was one cough. One sneeze. One cry from a baby, and the waiting bloodhounds would barge through her front door.

Having a man like Noah find even one fugitive in her home

would be catastrophic. Not only would the runaway be returned to slavery, but she and her father would have to shut down their station for good.

She was called to help fugitives, "aid and abet them" as the new bill said, though the government meant these words to be an act of evil instead of good. Nothing would devastate her more than being forced to stop helping slaves find freedom from people like the man currently tramping through her house.

The door squeaked open to the basement, but she didn't follow Noah downstairs. He could spend all day down there if he wanted. Drink from their spring. Eat some bread or meat. There was nothing incriminating in the kitchen.

Out the window, she saw the two colored men and their dogs still standing, waiting for Noah. At least they weren't trying to sneak around her property while their master was inside.

She eyed the men. Beyond the harshness of their faces, she saw a hint of raw sadness in one of the man's eyes. Why didn't he try to run while he was in Indiana, like the man Daniel had reported about in Richmond?

Running on his own, he could easily make it to Canada before the first snow. Most Northerners wouldn't dare stop a hardened escapee like him. It was the most vulnerable, people like Marie or elderly Auntie Rae, who were apprehended if friends didn't help them along the way.

The man didn't even look around him like he was contemplating the idea of running. Noah probably made it worth his while to stay in Tennessee.

How sad to have dark-skinned men hunt down a colored girl for money. Or perhaps Noah had beaten them both into submission and they truly feared him. It was hard to say. Maybe they were free blacks he'd hired in Indiana. These hunters preyed on runaways across their state and used their muscle and weapons to capture them for handsome rewards.

Did either of these men wake up in the middle of the night ashamed of what they had done? Or had their consciences been so seared that they no longer cared about the pain they inflicted on others? Either way, it was tragic.

"Nothing down here," Noah reported with gaiety, like the search was a game.

Anna followed him to the staircase in the hallway. "Of course not."

He placed his hand on the banister. "But your turkey smells wonderful."

"We're expecting guests tonight."

"It's too bad I'm not invited."

Too bad.

As he climbed the staircase, she thought it awful that he could joke about dinner when a woman's life was at stake. He acted like a casual hunter, tracking a fox or goose for pleasure.

What would happen if Noah's facade crumbled and his heart was exposed? She imagined that under his cool exterior was a swell of anger that could surge at any time. Even if she had to face his wrath, she wouldn't let him walk around upstairs unattended. Not while Charlotte was working up there alone. She trailed Noah up the staircase, and when he entered the first bedchamber, she waited for him in the hallway.

Minutes passed, and she finally peaked into the room. The man was under the bed, pounding on the floor planks. So much for a casual tour through her home.

"Anything loose?" she asked.

His voice was muffled. "Not yet."

He pushed himself out from under the bed, his black jacket speckled with gray. Bits of hair stuck up across his head. He brushed off the jacket, but already he was looking less like a gentleman.

He walked toward the door. "Are you planning to follow me around?"

"Of course," Anna replied. "If you find your servant hiding under my floor, I want to know about it."

His smile wasn't as big this time. "I wouldn't be doing—"

"I know," she interrupted. "You're doing your Christian duty to help this girl."

"Right."

So she followed the man into the next room and the next, watching him pound on the walls, open wardrobes, and check under each bed.

In the hallway, he opened the door to the dumbwaiter, and she held her breath when he looked up, hoping that someone had remembered to cover the opening to the attic so he wouldn't ask questions about the dumbwaiter traveling past the second floor.

He didn't ask.

When he came to the last bedchamber, Anna forced her expression to maintain the annoyance she'd displayed while he searched the other rooms. This was the only room that really concerned her. It wouldn't take much tapping inside the cabinet to discover the false wall.

Charlotte was making the bed in this room, the look on her face as cold as stone. She didn't nod at the man when he entered even though he stared at her like so many men did. His mouth was agape, his focus solely on her friend. "You've made a fine choice for house help, Miss Anna."

Her blood curdled at the lust that thickened his tone. He looked directly at Charlotte yet spoke to Anna like Charlotte wasn't worthy of his address. "Charlotte chose us, Noah. We didn't choose her."

"Even so..."

Anna shivered to think what would happen if Noah met Charlotte under the cover of night, without someone nearby to help or protect her.

Anna tapped him on his shoulder. "Is there anything else you'd like to look at in this room besides my dear friend?"

His eyes broke away from Charlotte, but he didn't look the least bit embarrassed at being caught.

At that moment, she knew with certainty that Marie had told the truth. If she ever returned to Tennessee, Noah Owens's wife would sell her off the plantation. No woman would want her husband steaming with such a blatant desire for another woman, especially right in her own home. Not that Anna could justify the woman's actions, but she could understand her resentment. Noah's wife probably felt trapped as well.

Noah didn't crawl under the bed in this room, but he stuck his foot under it and stomped on the planks. He pounded on the walls around the bed, and when he opened the cabinet doors, Anna clutched her hands together so he wouldn't see them shaking.

Charlotte stepped forward and forced a tepid smile. "Would you like a cup of coffee, Noah?"

He turned back around, obviously pleased when she spoke his name. "That would be mighty nice."

"It will be ready in ten minutes."

Anna nodded at Charlotte, and the woman fled the room. Perhaps the awaiting cup of coffee, along with the thought of seeing Charlotte again, might distract the man.

Noah pushed through the towels and pillows that Charlotte had stacked inside the cabinet to cover their hiding place. All it would take was one strong thump on the board that hid the entrance for him to know that it was hollow on the other side. Then it wouldn't take him but a second to figure out how to slide the board into the wall.

The man must have been distracted, because she didn't hear a single knock against the wall before he backed out of the cabinet and brushed off his pants. At that moment, she was thankful that the Lord did indeed work in mysterious ways. Blinded with lust, Noah Owens couldn't see what he'd come looking for.

"Where's the entrance to the attic?" he asked.

She turned her face abruptly, the absurdity of it almost too much. Here was this man, standing beside the most important entrance to the attic, yet she couldn't say a thing.

Chapter Fifteen
....

Anna clasped the banister as she followed Noah Owens up the steep attic steps. In minutes, she would send him and his men on their way, and maybe all he would remember of his time here was receiving a hot cup of coffee. And seeing Charlotte.

Even before they entered the attic, she could smell basil and onions and mildew. Light seeped into the room from the two windows on each end, and herbs and garden vegetables dangled across the room like vines in a jungle. The floor was covered with trunks, blankets, and milk crates.

Noah ducked under a garlic braid hanging from the ceiling as he crossed the room, and then he stooped over to investigate the eaves of the slanted ceiling. When he came to the wall on the north side, he stopped and pounded on the brick.

Anna watched him quietly. If he could see through the brick, he would find a small room filled with cots, water, and wool blankets. His hands traveled across the rough brick, searching for an opening. "How do you access this part of the attic?"

She shrugged even though he wasn't looking at her. "We've searched for an entrance up here but have never been able to find one."

"That's a strange way to build an attic."

She walked beyond him, and her hands slid across the brick on the other end of the wall. "I haven't thought much about it."

He mumbled as he backed away, swearing about Yankees and inept construction. She didn't mention to him that her parents had built the house and that the design was quite ingenious with its dumbwaiter and secret door and hiding space. Nor did she mention that she thought certain people were inept for not discovering the entrance on the second floor.

The attic floor was filthy, dust having no place to settle except on the ground. She and Charlotte had no real urge to clean it either, hoping the dirt would discourage men like Noah from hunting around.

But it didn't discourage him in the least. When he realized the brick wall was intact, Noah sank to his knees, testing dirty floorboards with his hands. He opened trunks and moved pieces of furniture, like Marie and her child might be hiding behind a rocking chair.

After he'd scoured every inch of the room, prodded every box and floorboard, the man finally gave up his search. Anna followed him down into the hallway and closed the door behind them. Her emotions teetered between fear and madness. It was all funny, in a delusional sort of a way. This man who was so sure of himself really didn't know a thing.

When she faced the man, she had to gulp back a laugh.

Noah no longer looked like the suave Southern gentleman who had appeared at her door an hour ago. His black coat and light hair and even his eyebrows were so heavily coated with dust that it looked as if he'd worked for days on the mill floor. His face was smeared and splotched red from exertion. His pants were crushed with wrinkles.

No one could accuse him of not scouring her home. Not only had he searched, but he was taking most of the attic dirt with him.

"Anyplace else you'd like to look?" she asked.

"I think I've covered everything."

"You haven't searched the barn or the outbuildings."

He gave her an odd look, like he was trying to determine why she was suddenly being helpful to him. She wasn't being kind. She wanted him out of her house.

He brushed his hands over the dust in his hair, but it did nothing to improve his appearance. Instead of removing the grime, he only smeared it.

A proper hostess would ask if he wanted to wash his hands and face, but she hadn't invited this man into her house nor did she want him staying a moment longer than was necessary.

Though it rarely happened, runaways had arrived at their house in broad daylight before. With the sight of the bloodhounds in the front yard, any newcomers should stay hidden behind the trees until Noah Owens and his men left, but the dogs still might catch their scent. And even though Marie was no longer at their home, Noah Owens would know she had been hiding runaways.

She was ready to send this man on his way and pray that Marie and Peter would cross Lake Erie soon. Once they reached Canada, no one could force them back to Tennessee.

The man walked briskly down both flights of stairs to the kitchen. The coffee was boiling over the fire, but Charlotte wasn't in the room.

He glanced back at her like he'd just realized that she had been following him again. "What happened to your help, Miss Anna?"

Anna swung the crane out of the fire and removed the pot with a cotton holder. "Probably went into town for something."

She poured the coffee into a cup.

"You don't know where she is?"

Her amusement over his disheveled appearance disappeared. "Charlotte doesn't have to report to me every time she leaves the house."

Disapproval weighed down his voice. "But how do you know where she went?"

"She often goes to town for supplies."

"But what if she—"

She handed him the mug of coffee. "I'm not worried about her running away."

Noah didn't ask for cream or sugar, and she didn't offer. Without Charlotte to entertain him, he was ready to move on with his search.

He gulped down the black coffee, and the cup clinked when he set it on the table.

"You've been a gracious hostess, Miss Anna."

She bowed her head like a shy schoolgirl, and then he hustled up the kitchen steps and out of the house.

Seconds later, she walked upstairs to the parlor and watched him from the window seat. He shouted something to the other men, and they all mounted their horses. Dust clouded her front yard as they rode away, the bloodhounds barking behind them.

Anna collapsed on the seat and clutched her hands to her chest. She hadn't even realized that her heart was hammering against her ribs. The strength that had energized her when Noah stepped into her house vanished when he shut the door. Power drained out of her, and she couldn't move.

Maybe she should have kept him here longer, all day even, to give Marie and the others extra time to travel north. If only she knew where Marie was, she could send a message and tell her that Noah was coming.

She tried to stand up, but her legs wobbled under her and she fell back onto the window seat. She would sit here all afternoon if she needed to. Sit and pray for Marie and the others.

"Charlotte!" she called out. Her friend wouldn't have left the house. It was too risky, having a man like Noah find her alone, outside these walls. "He's gone."

The door to the front closet opened, and Charlotte stepped out. She ran her fingers over the loose knot on the back of her head and straightened her skirt. Anna didn't say anything about her choice to hide. Noah Owens probably reminded Charlotte of her own master from North Carolina. Anna would have hid as well.

"Poor Marie," Charlotte whispered. "He'll kill her if he finds her."

"Noah's wife might kill her, but he wants her for himself."

"Lust and anger stem from the same place." Charlotte glanced at the door as if fearing Noah might march back inside and steal her away. "Marie has humiliated him, and a man like him would rather kill than forgive."

"But he's offered money for her—"

"He doesn't need the money." She twisted her hands in her lap, and Anna listened in sadness, wondering how many of Charlotte's words were from personal experience. "He's paying money so he can punish her and make an example of her for the others in his house."

It was stunning, really. Ironic. A powerful plantation owner, a master of many slaves, being ruled by his own anger. Noah Owens had left his family and his profitable work to hunt down one young runaway girl even though it could take weeks or even months to find her. Without knowing it, Noah had lost control of himself. And he'd given it to his slave.

"How did he find out she was here?" Charlotte asked quietly.

"That first night she came, Marie knocked on another door first. A family down the creek."

Charlotte sat on the cane seat across from her, her eyes focused above Anna's head. "But someone had to have tipped him off about our house," she said. "He wouldn't have wasted time in searching so thoroughly unless he believed she might be here."

"But who would have told him?"

They both sat in silence, listening to the clock chime. She thought about the man's face, polite but intense. He would use honey to catch his prey until he met resistance. Then, she was certain, the men who accompanied him would force cooperation.

Perhaps Roger or another one of the fugitives in that party had gotten caught and tried to bargain their freedom by talking. Yet in the five years that the Brents had had a house on the railroad, she didn't know of a single fugitive who had exposed their location. Ben was a meticulous agent. He directed only runaway slaves to their home, not colored men or women who purported to be slaves but were paid to expose stations on the route.

Her father and Charlotte both trusted Ben. Even though she had never met him, she trusted him as well.

Someone besides Will Denton could have suspected her wagon delivery, but even so, how could they have known she carried the girl and her child?

Then she remembered the cries. Peter had been crying when Matthew was here, but she had shrugged it off, saying it was a wolf. Could he have suspected the child was Marie's? And even if he did suspect it, why would he report the incident to someone like Noah?

The Nelsons might not condemn the legality of slavery, but surely they wouldn't report an escaped slave. Perhaps one of the men had talked about it at the pub or in a shop and someone else had guessed at the origin of the cries.

No matter who talked, or if anyone actually did send Noah their way, his search had come up dry. He hadn't found the room or any evidence of fugitives hiding in their home. Any rumor had been stopped.

At that moment, a new energy seemed to balloon within her. They had triumphed over their opposition. They had won! They'd beaten Noah and his little posse.

As she reveled in their victory, she realized suddenly that this new energy wasn't strength at all. It was pride. Pride led to carelessness, and ultimately it could lead to a fall.

Noah Owens was a proud man, and pride had overtaken his life until he had become obsessed with finding the one person who threatened it. He'd become blinded to the goodness in his life, seeking instead to pursue the darkness in his heart.

By God's grace, she would battle against a proud heart. It was only by His grace that Noah hadn't exposed their station. Only by His grace that Anna and her father hadn't yet been carted off to jail.

There was too much at risk, too many people whose secrets she needed to guard, for her to let the pride of a victory overtake her life.

Charlotte interrupted her thoughts, her voice urgent. "We need to pray for Marie."

"Yes, we do." Anna's thoughts moved from the condition of her heart to the fear she had seen in Marie's eyes when she sat in the rocking chair, clutching her baby to her bosom like someone might pry him away from her.

"And we need to pray for her baby."

Charlotte's head was in her hands. "Of course."

She didn't just want to pray for Peter's protection. They needed to pray that God would fill his heart with love instead of lust. Compassion instead of anger.

They needed to pray that Peter didn't turn out like his father.

Chapter Sixteen
....

The wild duck tasted even better than the duck their mother had made for Christmas dinner. It was perfectly crisp on the outside, and when Daniel slid his knife into the meat, it cut like butter.

It wasn't a holiday, though. Wasn't even December. It was Seventh Day morning, mid-September, and once again Esther and Greta had outdone themselves with this meal.

Daniel ate a bite of stuffing seasoned with pepper, sage, and onions. He often found himself complaining about his sister's obsession with being the perfect housewife, but he wouldn't complain about her skills today. Toast and coffee were usually all he had for breakfast. Never duck and stuffing, though he'd heard that some of the farmer's wives in the county created entire meals for breakfast. He didn't need wild game and potatoes every morning to operate a printing press, but he could sure enjoy it when he had it.

Joseph had left for a house call long before Daniel arrived. Esther and Greta were already preparing for a dinner party in the next room. He would appreciate the duck and stuffing and the biscuits smothered with currant jelly in solitude.

He unfolded a copy of the national anti-slavery paper called the *Independent Weekly*, marveling at the perfectness of the morning. He was alone with this wonderful meal and his favorite newspaper.

Sunshine streamed through the window, and there wasn't one person in sight who was trying to contradict him. Not that he didn't thrive on a good debate—he liked to argue a point if it meant that someone might be swayed toward the truth—but sometimes he needed to escape to a quiet place. Just to think for a bit. Even if Esther and Joseph didn't support his work or his views, their home was the perfect place for him to rest.

He glanced at the corner of the room and saw the waiting cradle. Once the baby girl, or boy, was born he imagined the house would become louder. More chaotic. Though with his sister at the helm, she would require order from even the smallest parties.

The house would still be a haven for him, though he planned to spend more time playing with his niece or nephew than reading his paper. And though he would never admit it, he was actually looking forward to becoming an uncle. With his parents living down in Cincinnati, he was thankful to be close to Esther even when they disagreed.

He never planned to marry, himself. It was a rare woman who would sacrifice everything to stand up and support an outspoken abolitionist. He'd yet to meet one who wasn't already married, and even if he did, he didn't want to spend his time entertaining the whims of a wife.

No, it was much better for him to be single, like Paul had said to the Corinthians. Children weren't in his future, but he would enjoy his time with the many nieces and nephews that his sister would surely produce.

He took another bite of the moist meat. At the top left of the newspaper was "Liberty Line," a monthly column from his favorite writer. Adam Frye was a poetic writer, weaving together stories about fugitives who traveled the Underground Railroad. They were personal experiences, heartfelt yet not so coated with drivel that they lost the meaning. The men and women he featured were real people trying to escape the cruelty of their master's hand and the loss of their family.

Although he'd interviewed many people at the Anti-Slavery Meeting, Daniel still didn't know anyone who ran a station. He'd heard rumors about secret meetings, but he'd never been invited to one. He'd also heard rumors about the secret railway passing through their town.

As outspoken as he was, he figured that no one would ever give him the specifics about these stations, and that was fine with him. They could do their job of subversion. His job was to be as bold as possible, directing people toward the truth through the written and spoken word.

And he would live vicariously through people like Adam Frye.

He put down his fork and savored the "Liberty Line."

In the book of Philippians, Paul said he had learned to be content in every circumstance, but many slave owners use this passage to justify the enslavement of people and then demand that their property be content in chains.

Does Paul's teaching apply to slavery? I believe each of us, myself included, are called upon to listen and decipher God's scripture with the guidance of the Spirit.

As I wrestle in my own heart with this area of contentment, I am convinced that, yes, God wants even those who are living in slavery to be content, but this does not mean that the runaway slaves who pass through my home are not supposed to seek freedom. Just because we are content with a broken arm or leg, does this mean we shouldn't seek a physician to mend this limb? Or if we are content with a leaking roof or a smoking stove, does this mean we should not have these repaired? Of course not.

Should the young mother whose child is about to be sold away from her not seek freedom for her son? Should the son, years later in life, not protect his elderly mother from the beatings of her master?

I believe that God does want us to be content in every area of our lives, but we are responsible for fixing those things that are broken. Some people refer to slavery as a "peculiar institution," but I believe it is a "broken institution" that must be fixed.

How can we listen to the cries of these slaves without acting?

How can we ignore their pleas? The only way for each of us to find contentment is to set those prisoners free.

The last lines resonated with him. Men like Adam Frye didn't just report the stories. They were part poet and part preacher, taking their stories beyond the hard facts and inspiring their readers. Adam painted faces on the people who were running toward freedom and made you laugh and cry with them. Then he made you want to stand up and cheer when the runaway slaves finally stepped onto Canada's fine soil, fugitives no more.

That's why people like Adam Frye wrote for a national anti-slavery newspaper while Daniel wrote, edited, and printed a county one.

He wasn't a good writer, he knew that, but he was trying to master the basics of reporting so he could at least communicate clearly and accurately even if his words didn't tug on his readers' emotions. He would never have as much talent as the writers at the *Independent*, but he was passionate. As long as Isaac wanted to print the paper—and as long as Isaac wanted to employ him—Daniel would keep writing.

Esther hobbled into the dining room, one hand on her belly and the other carrying a basket that billowed with steam. He jumped up from his chair and took the biscuits from her mere seconds before she seemed to melt into the seat across from him.

Her hair and skin looked greasy. Her face was red, plastered in sweat from the hot fire. Here he was sitting leisurely at the table, reading a newspaper, while Esther had already baked biscuits and stuffing this morning. And roasted a duck.

"You need to get out of that kitchen." He fanned her face with the newspaper, and she closed her eyes. "Go rest upstairs."

"I'll go crazy upstairs."

"Don't you have one of those women's magazines to read?"

"I've read every one of them at least three times each."

He handed her the *Independent Weekly*. "You can borrow this if you'd like."

She saw the masthead and waved it away. "I don't need to read anything depressing. It's not good for the baby."

"It's not depressing."

Greta stepped around the corner. "You okay, Mrs. Cooley?"

"I'm fine, fine." She waved her hand again. "I'll be back in a few minutes."

Daniel looked at Greta's face, and she seemed concerned about Esther, as well.

"I'll wash the pans," Greta said. "You just sit here with your brother and rest awhile."

Esther pushed herself up in the seat. "But I want to start the ice custard."

"Now, we don't need to start that for two more hours, and I've got kind of an affinity for ice custard anyway. I'd like to make it all by myself."

Daniel handed Esther his handkerchief, and she wiped her forehead. "I suppose you can start it if you'd really like."

Daniel stood up. "Can I fetch the ice blocks for you?"

"They delivered them an hour ago." Greta shooed him back into his seat as she stepped toward the kitchen. "You just set and talk with your sister."

Daniel reached for a biscuit and smothered the hot bread with jelly. When he handed it to Esther, he prepared himself for a fight, but she didn't refuse the food or the glass of water he poured for her. "You're working yourself too hard."

"I try to rest."

He lifted an eyebrow, but she persisted. "Really, I do try, Daniel. It's just that I keep thinking of all these things I need to do before Lilith is born."

"Lilith?"

"After our great-grandmother."

He wanted to tell her that she didn't know it was a girl, but he also didn't want to argue with her this morning, especially about her child. If Esther had decided it was a girl then he'd say it was a girl as well. Lilith was as fine a name as any unless the baby surprised them by being a boy.

"You do what you need to for your child, but don't make breakfast for me anymore."

His sister grinned. "But I like to take care of you."

Esther was four years younger than him, but she had doted on him almost from the time she could walk, making him and her friends teacakes and lemonade and cookies. Once, when she was five, she threw a grand party with sugar water and stale bread because she wanted so badly to entertain.

"I can eat breakfast at the boardinghouse and then come visit on Seventh Day."

She grimaced like he'd said he was eating at the poorhouse. "The food there isn't fit for consumption."

"No one can compete with your duck and stuffing, but I can survive on toast in the morning."

"Burnt toast." She leaned forward and tweaked the edge of his paper. "Why can't you come here and relax on Saturdays?"

He didn't even crack a smile. "I'll try to follow your example."

"Very funny." She took a deep breath and sat up straighter. "I saw Mrs. Gunther at the millinery yesterday."

"I hope she acquired the perfect hat."

She ignored his sarcasm. "She said she saw you helping a Negro woman a few days ago."

Daniel lifted the paper from the table and folded it. He didn't want to have this conversation. "It would have been nice for the Gunthers to stop and help, too."

"She said the woman was being apprehended by the law."

"It wasn't the law stopping her. It was a slave hunter."

Esther sighed, and he knew how much she hated talking about anything that tainted the pearly whiteness of her mind and her home. Slavery was a messy issue, blood and grime everywhere. She could tolerate blood, but she didn't like the grime.

"You've got to leave these people alone," she begged. "You're going to get yourself into trouble, Daniel, and no one will be able to bail you out this time."

He was going to get himself into trouble? Women like Greta were in trouble for simply walking down a public street, in daylight, and Esther wanted him to ignore it. If he hadn't helped Greta, the hunter probably would have taken her and sold her even though she wasn't Marie. Her life would have been on his head.

Daniel stood up and pushed his chair under the table. "Do you know who was being accosted on Main Street?"

She waved her hand in front of her face. "It doesn't matter."

"It wasn't just some 'Negro woman,' Esther. The man was trying to hurt your housekeeper."

The name escaped from her lips in a gasp. "Greta?"

"Yes, Greta." He snatched his paper off the table. "And it's people like you who sit back in their pretty, protected homes and let him do it."

Anger burst in his gut when she didn't reply. He was sorry his sister was tired, but he couldn't stay here and listen to her demean "these people," as she called them. Nor could he tolerate her silence when she refused to defend the woman who cared so much for her.

He grabbed his hat and coat before he stomped out of the room.

Chapter Seventeen

....

Dry leaves crunched under Marie's feet as she and five others pressed through the dark, tangled brush. With Peter swaddled in a blanket tied over her chest, she couldn't see her feet, so she tested each step before she took it. In spite of Mrs. Adeline's fine boots and the bandage, pricks of sharp pain shot up her right foot. Her leg throbbed with every step, and her face and arms were icy cold in the night air.

Neither the pain nor the cold would stop her. No matter how many more hours they had to walk. No matter how many more days it would take to reach Canada. There was nothing that could make her turn back.

She had to keep moving, keep fighting. This run wasn't about her or her feet, no matter how much they hurt, or even her personal freedom.

This was about finding a safe home for her son.

Except Auntie Rae, the other runaways in their group walked far in front of her like they'd done ever since Peter had cried out from Miss Anna's wagon. It didn't help that the deputy had been looking for her. They all treated her like she was cursed.

Marie's lips brushed over the top of the wool blanket. Peter was wrapped so close to her that she could feel the steady rhythm of his breath on her breast. It made her happy, knowing he rested even as they ran through the night. His contentment seemed to renew her strength, and she marched forward through the brush, forgetting for a moment the pain in her foot.

"*On my knees when the light pass'd by, I thank God I'm free at last,*" she hummed quietly. "*Tho't my soul would rise and fly, I thank God I'm free at last.*"

When she was a child, her mama used to sing "Free at Last" to comfort her in the shadows of night. Others hummed the spiritual around the plantation and even in the house, but no one ever sang the lyrics except in the privacy of their own rooms or cabins.

They may not have sung the words in public, but even as they hummed it, all the slaves knew what it meant. They were dreaming of freedom. Longing for it.

Marie glanced up at the starlit sky. The tip of the Drinking Gourd pointed them toward Canada—like the flame burning the wick of a candlestick, its brightness always climbing upward and away from the narrowed mold. It was almost as if God was guiding them north with the stars. Calling them to be free.

She started humming again until the man in front of her hushed the music from her lips.

Earl was the conductor to their next station. If you were going to find your way to Canada, you had to listen to the conductor and do exactly as he or she said or you'd be caught for sure. Marie stopped humming, but the lyrics sang on in her mind.

Auntie Rae took her hand and squeezed it as if to say that she understood the music.

In front of them was a small clearing, and Earl signaled for them to stop. Huddling close around his candle, light danced across their dark faces, and she could see both fear and hope in the eyes of her friends. Marie reached out her fingers to feel the heat from the flame.

Earl whispered so low that she had to step even closer to hear him. "This is where I take leave of you."

They all knew it was coming; most conductors didn't take their passengers all the way to the next station. No one told her why, but she guessed it was to lower the risk of them all being caught. None of their group wanted to say good-bye to Earl, but they had no choice.

The man's words sped up as he pointed to the side of the clearing. "Straight ahead you will pass an old homestead before you come to a cornfield. Turn right and walk through the field."

"Right." George repeated the direction so Earl knew they understood.

Earl nodded. "Go north through the cornfield about a quarter mile."

With one hand on Peter's back, she gazed up at the bright mantle of stars and saw the gourd, its tip the brightest of all, pointing them north. She'd never been more grateful for the stars.

"On the other side of the field is a brick house and a family of Quakers. If there's a flag hanging over their porch railing, it's safe for you to knock."

George shook Earl's hand and promised the man that he'd get their small group to safety before daylight. Earl didn't prolong the good-bye. He wished them Godspeed and then disappeared into the trees behind them.

Marie trailed the others up the path, and in the starlight, she could see the outbuildings of the abandoned homestead. Chicken coops. An outhouse. The root cellar. A brick smokehouse.

It was peaceful out here. Serene. Peter stirred against her, and she whispered softly for him to go back to sleep. Soon they would arrive at the next safe house and she could feed him for the night. Soon he would be warm and dry and content again.

A dog barked behind her, and she stiffened. There were wild dogs in the forest, packs of them. She took a long breath. No dog would hurt them if they stuck together.

At least it wasn't the cry of a panther.

Her pace quickened when she heard another dog bark behind her. But then, like a roll of thunder echoing across a plain, she heard a familiar pounding.

Her heart raced so quickly that it almost blocked the thoughts in her mind. The horses weren't moving fast through the overgrowth, but they were moving. Faster than she could run.

She turned in shock and stared into the trees. The dim cast of a lantern forded through the darkness. Then a shout drowned out the bark of the dogs, and in an instant she knew.

Master Owens had found her.

Her mind screamed for her to run, and she obeyed, sprinting forward. She had to get away from her master. Had to protect her son.

The other runaways scattered in front of her. Her eyes focused on the dark path, but she couldn't see her feet.

It wasn't a log that tripped her. It was a shoelace that snagged her foot and sent her sprawling. She rolled to her back when she landed on the leaves, shielding Peter from the fall, but he woke with a jolt and screamed out in the night.

The horses were getting closer now. And the dogs.

Wild with fear, Marie lifted herself up and scanned the buildings beside her. She couldn't take Peter with her. Not right now. They couldn't outrun the horses together.

She'd distract the hunters. Take them away from her baby and the others. Then she'd come back in the morning and get Peter and they'd go together to the house on the other side of the field.

The ground under her shook. The horses were almost here.

She ripped off her new boots and threw them on the ground. Then she kissed Peter on the head and wrapped her cloak around him.

Flinging open the door to the smokehouse, she saw the barrels and equipment that had been left behind. There was a rug, rolled up and standing against the wall. She pulled it down and quickly placed Peter on it. Then she tucked the blanket under him and dropped her pack beside him.

Suddenly she knew with clarity that she wouldn't need the pack anymore. She had come as far as she was supposed to in this journey. God would now have to carry Peter the rest of the way.

She just couldn't let Master Owens find her baby.

She kissed Peter for the last time, no time for tears. When she shut the door, his cries were muffled through the brick wall, but Master Owens would still be able to hear them.

He couldn't come this way.

Marie ran the opposite direction, adrenaline numbing the pain in her bare foot. Nothing else mattered now except to get the hunters away from her child.

When she reached the cornfield, she screamed once. Twice.

The horses turned away from Peter, toward her. The tip of the gourd pointed ahead so she turned and ran south. Corn batted her face and hands as she zigzagged through the tall stalks. The longer it took for the dogs to catch her, the farther away they would be from Peter.

She yelled as she ran, and she knew they heard her. They were galloping now. The dogs almost on her heels.

All she could do was run. Pray.

She pleaded with God to deafen the hunters' ears and open the ears of someone who could help her son. She prayed that George and Auntie Rae and the others wouldn't get caught. She prayed that God would free Peter's body and save his soul.

Not once did she pray for herself, for there was nothing left to pray. Tonight she was going home to her mama and her Maker. She only hoped she could get the horses and dogs as far away as possible from Peter before she left this world.

Peace infiltrated her soul, mercy blanketing her fear. Without Earl or anyone else to stop her, she sang out loud and strong. Songs about heaven and rivers and Jesus dying on the cross for her.

The dogs were panting now, parting the corn behind her. She was so close now. Close to the light.

Teeth tore into her skirts and her skin as they dragged her to the ground. The dogs snarling above her, she balled up like a caterpillar, instinct protecting her head and her face until she heard the voice of Master Owens.

When she looked up, she saw the face of her earthly master sneering down at her. Sometimes his face was kind, almost compassionate to her, but in the shadows that moved across his face, all she saw was fury—and she knew what that meant.

In one swift move, he pulled her hair down, forcing her head back. Then he punched her in the stomach.

"Where's the baby?" he growled.

Behind him stood two men with whips in hand. If they knew where Peter was hidden, they wouldn't hesitate to kill her child.

"Gone," she choked. "I done lost him a month ago."

"What do you mean you lost him?"

"He died." She shook her head. "Died 'fore he was borned."

There was no baby left for them to find.

Master Owens lifted his hand, and the black hunter handed him a whip.

Marie looked up at the North Star above them as a soft breeze fluttered through the corn. Freedom was so close now. Just beyond the night. She was going home.

She barely felt the whip on her back.

"Some of these mornings, bright and fair, I thank God I'm free at last. Goin' meet King Jesus in the air, I thank God I'm free at last."

Chapter Eighteen

....

Woven into the braids of forest below Liberty was a whitewashed meetinghouse built to last a hundred years. It was rare that an outsider visited the Silver Creek Meeting, though the faithful met every Sabbath Day in its walls without fail.

In the winter, they rode their sleighs to Meeting, toasting their feet with soapstone and covering their clothing with woolen blankets. In the summer, many of them walked from Liberty, swinging picnic baskets filled with cold meat and jars of lemonade.

Today Anna, Edwin, and Charlotte were riding down the well-traveled road toward the meetinghouse where the Salem Meeting and the Salem Anti-Slavery Meeting would converge with the Silver Creek Meeting, setting aside their differences for one morning, to witness the marriage ceremony of Rachel Logue and Luke Barnes. Luke and his family attended the Salem Anti-Slavery Meeting, but their marriage had been approved by the Silver Creek elders and members of which Rachel was a part.

There would be no fanfare at this wedding like the ceremonies held at the churches in town. Luke and Rachel would simply stand up at the end of the service, say their vows, and sign a marriage certificate to become husband and wife.

Rachel didn't need a flowing dress or flowers or music to make this day special. Anna had never known anyone as deeply and completely in love as Rachel and Luke. Her friend was so blinded by her adoration for this man that even if the meetinghouse were filled with hundreds of roses, she probably wouldn't see the blooms. Her eyes would be solely on

Luke and his eyes on her. A few hours from now, Rachel would leave the Meeting with Luke instead of her parents, and together they would enter the world of the happily married.

Anna was glad for her friend, truly glad, but the day was a clear reminder of something Anna would never have.

She reached her fingers into her pocket and felt the envelope waiting for delivery to Isaac. At least she would always have her writing and her work on the line.

Charlotte tapped on her shoulder, and Anna forced herself to stop thinking about writing and weddings. When she turned her head to the back seat of the buggy, Charlotte pointed at Edwin in the driver's seat and nodded her head toward him.

Anna knew exactly what Charlotte wanted her to do, but she still didn't want to tell her father about the visit from Noah Owens. Charlotte was right, of course. Keeping this information was almost the same as lying, or maybe it was lying.

She didn't want her father to be afraid for her, especially for her safety. Harboring slaves was dangerous work, and she knew the risks. Nothing would change her mind—not the new act or threats or visits from Tennessee men. But still, he needed to know what happened.

As calmly as possible, she began to tell him about the visit from Noah Owens.

Edwin's voice sharpened in response. "Did he threaten you?"

Anna thought about the two men and the bloodhounds that stood behind him like *she* might threaten Noah. "He only wanted to search the house."

"Did you let him inside?"

"The slave hunters and dogs stayed in the yard," she explained. "I let him look through the house since we didn't have anyone staying with us."

"You should have made him wait until I came home."

"He wouldn't have waited." Anna tightened her shawl around her shoulders. "He would have gotten a warrant and come back to search whether or not you were home."

Their next group of runaways hadn't arrived yet, but they expected them soon. If Noah had waited to obtain a warrant when the courts opened on Second Day, he may have found them on his return.

It wouldn't take much for him to discover the Brents' secret. Someone could lose a shoe in the bedroom as they ran toward the secret stairs. Or leave the door cracked. Or forget to put the pillows back into the cabinet. Even the simplest sneeze could reveal their hiding place.

"We have to be more careful, Anna." Edwin clipped the rein and glanced over at her. "More people are getting injured by men like him."

She wanted to protest and say she was being extremely careful, but she didn't. Noah didn't seem like the kind of person who would hurt her, but the men outside probably wouldn't have hesitated if he'd found Marie or another runaway in her home. Her father had already lost the person he'd loved most in the world to cholera last fall. In spite of his strong front, she knew he was afraid he might lose her, too. After her mother died, she thought he would shut the doors to runaways, yet he hadn't stopped helping them. His calling was even stronger than hers since her mother had been passionate about helping runaways as well.

Would her mother have been frightened by someone like Noah Owens? Even though she wouldn't admit it to her father or anyone else, some days Anna was scared to continue. Like her father said, an irate owner like Noah could show up at her front door and take the law into his own hands.

Yet even with her personal safety at stake, she wasn't going to stop. God had clearly called her to help these escaped slaves, and she wouldn't ignore this call.

Ahead of their buggy was a small pond blackened with the feathers of coots. The birds splashed and gabbled with each other like they were socializing after Meeting, the sound so loud that Anna had to lean toward her father to speak. "They aren't going to catch us."

He didn't look at her. "I've been seeking the Spirit, Anna. Asking if He wants us to continue with our work right now or enter a season of rest."

His statement jolted her, and she collapsed back against the cushioned seat. She had no idea that her father, like Charlotte, was having doubts about their work. If they were going to continue, they had to stay strong. They were a team.

"We can't quit, Father. Not now."

A bird flew in front of the buggy to join his flock in the pond.

"I still have to ask, Anna. Still have to seek."

She couldn't deny him that. They should always be asking, seeking, but she knew what the Light would reveal.

* * * * *

"The room is packed," Rachel whispered after Anna climbed down from the buggy and stepped onto the pebbled ground that surrounded the meetinghouse.

Anna took both of her friend's trembling hands and squeezed them. Rachel was dressed in a pale pink silk instead of the traditional gray or brown, and even though her hair was covered with her bonnet, Anna knew that Rachel had styled it for herself and her husband-to-be. Around her neck she wore the gold watch and chain that Luke had given her as an engagement present.

People streamed into the meetinghouse on both sides of them, and Anna could understand why Rachel was nervous. Visitors were rare at Silver Creek, but the wedding of Isaac Barnes's grandson was something to be attended and talked about, especially since the marriage was taking place among Quakers. The curious would pack their small house since it wasn't often that one got invited to attend such a peculiar ceremony.

Luke and Rachel had already gone through the passing meeting and been approved for marriage. Today was only a formality to becoming husband and wife in the eyes of God and His people.

"Are you nervous?" Anna asked.

Rachel weaved her fingers through the ribbons that dangled under her chin. "A little."

"You look beautiful."

Rachel glanced around her. "Shh..."

But Anna caught the smile in her friend's eyes. A woman should look beautiful on her wedding day.

"In an hour you will be Rachel Barnes."

The smile in Rachel's eyes flooded onto her face, and she was grinning when they walked into the meetinghouse.

Inside the building, the air was solemn. Most of the benches were already filled, but unlike typical First Day services, the dull gray room was splattered with bright swatches of color from dresses worn by Liberty women. The shutters were open on both sides of the room, and the breeze whisked into the gallery and settled on the crowd, refreshing the staleness of the room.

The men were seated in the benches on the left side of the room. The women sat erect on the right. Motion ceased as each person took their place in the room, and even the children were uncannily still during the first part of the service.

Two tiers of facing benches rose in front of the assembly, lined with elders and recorded ministers. Her father was among this group, as were visiting ministers Isaac Barnes and his wife, Hannah. As was the custom, neither Isaac nor Hannah acknowledged her or their future granddaughter as they sat down. Their eyes stared forward, their spirits focused on His Light.

Anna sat between Rachel and Charlotte. Rachel turned her head toward the other side of the room. Anna knew the moment Rachel saw Luke, because her arms relaxed at her sides. In an hour, the ceremony would be done, and Rachel would join her husband.

The pages of someone's Bible rustled nearby, but Anna kept her gaze on the back of the bench in front of her. Rachel wouldn't be able to focus on anything except the wedding, but Anna wanted to set her heart and her mind on things above. If she looked upon the other side of the room, she was certain she would see Matthew Nelson in attendance, and once she saw him, the doubts would begin anew.

She closed her eyes, and in the quietness of the room she tried to listen. Coots squawked in the nearby swampland, and for a moment, she relished the wild noises in God's creation.

Sometimes she wanted to stand up and rejoice like the coots, but she never spoke in Meeting. Instead she listened and waited for others to be moved by the Spirit. Every once in a while, someone would stand and speak out. When they did, everyone listened intently and determined in their hearts if their word was from God.

What am I to do? she asked softly, inward.

If her father did close their doors to fugitives, how could she continue to help them? Maybe she would talk to Lyle Trumble. Surely he could connect her with the right people.

"The Lord is good unto them that wait for him, to the soul that seeketh him."

She'd read the verse before, but she didn't remember exactly where. More than anything, that was what she wanted to do. Seek after Him and, yes, even wait for Him. He had been good to her. Even in the midst of her mother's death. Even when she was angry and jealous. Even when she had neglected to seek Him.

He had been there.

Often her mind wandered during the quietness, but this was her time to seek Him. She needed to focus her mind and heart on receiving a word from God.

"If we seek the Lord, we will find Him."

The voice startled Anna, and she opened her eyes. Women around her—those who had never attended a Meeting before—breathed a low but audible gasp at the interruption of their thoughts and perhaps prayers. Many of them turned toward the men's side, straining their necks to see who had been led of the Spirit to speak out.

Anna didn't turn. She knew the voice immediately. It was the man who had confronted Milton Kent in front of the courthouse. The man who had written horribly yet passionately about the escape of Enoch and the passing of the Fugitive Slave Act.

Daniel Stanton was speaking out, and her chest constricted so tightly that she had to force herself to breathe.

"God is ready to answer us, if only we seek," Daniel was saying, "and as Friends, we must seek Him deep within our hearts and souls. Would our loving and righteous God approve of how we are treating our brothers and sisters in Christ? Those who were created by Him in a darker shell of skin?"

Daniel Stanton probably had come to witness the marriage of Isaac's grandson along with most of Salem's Anti-Slavery Meeting. She wanted to turn and watch him as he spoke, like she had at the courthouse, but she clenched her eyes shut before anyone could read what was in them. Curiosity was all it was, she insisted to herself. She was only curious about Daniel Stanton, like the worldly people who had gathered here today under the guise of attending a wedding so they could see how Quakers worshipped.

Several of the older women in their meeting could chatter more than the coots at the pond. She didn't want any of them to see even a spark of interest from her at either Daniel Stanton or his words.

"It is for those of us who love our fellow man, those of us Friends who esteem equality among the races and sexes, to offer hope and refuge despite the failure of those who govern us to promote this kindness to our neighbors."

A shiver rose within Anna, and her heart raced. She wanted to stand up and shout that Daniel Stanton was right. They had to protect these runaways no matter what they risked. God had placed the burden on their shoulders to watch over the slaves who ran through their state, their town.

Instead of shouting out, Anna squeezed her eyes even tighter to ward off the temptation of glancing his way. She already knew he was handsome, and there were probably many around her who were distracted at this moment, appreciating his fine features instead of listening to the truth in his words.

"We must seek Him together and find Him." His voice began to escalate, and she imagined the birds and animals gathering outside to listen to his plea. "We can't all fight against slavery or take care of those who have run away from this horrific institution, but in the quietness of this hour, I implore you to ask what it is that God would have you to do."

After he sat down, Anna expected one of the Silver Creek men to rebut the finer points of what the Spirit had so clearly spoken to Daniel, but no one else stood. Perhaps they would save it and share later, next week, when Daniel was attending Meeting on the other side of town.

The minutes seemed to pass by slowly again as she mulled over Daniel's words. Had she ever truly asked God what He would want her to do to help slaves? She had always assumed that He wanted her to work with her father to hide them in their home, but she had never asked for herself.

Maybe it was time for her to ask.

In front of her, a child fidgeted with something in his pocket, and Anna saw the flash of a tiny blue ball fall from his hands and bounce along the floor. The overseer was upon them, plucking up the ball from the floor and pointing his stick at the child. Then, for good measure, Anna watched him turn toward Maisy Templeton, who had fallen asleep at the end of the bench, her lower lip dangling like a shoot of ivy. He poked the stick into Maisy's thick leg, and the woman jumped in her seat.

Anna's gaze swung away from Maisy, and before she caught herself, she was looking at the other side of the room.

Daniel Stanton was sitting on the second bench with his head bowed. She didn't want to stare, didn't mean to, but her gaze rested on his face and didn't waver. What she felt for him was admiration, nothing else, but she did appreciate his strength and determination. She wished she had the same strength within her and the ability to communicate what she felt in public, instead of in secret.

Charlotte elbowed her, and Anna jerked her head back toward the front. She could feel the stare of the overseer upon her, but she avoided his glance. Her father was right. She would have to be more careful. She couldn't align herself with an outspoken abolitionist like Daniel Stanton, either in public or in private. Even her thoughts must refuse to entertain him.

Fifteen minutes later, the head of the Meeting broke the silence when he asked if all hearts were clear. No one responded, so he shook the hand of the man at his right, and the assembly followed his lead. Then he announced with great formality, "It is time for the marriage of Rachel Logue and Luke Barnes to be duly and properly performed."

Anna squeezed Rachel's hand and felt it tremble again, knowing that it wouldn't stop until Luke firmly enclosed it within his fingers. As Rachel stood up and walked to the front of the room, Luke joined her side. No amount of willpower could squelch the smile that overcame his lips. Rachel's face was hidden behind her bonnet, but Anna imagined her smile to be even bigger than Luke's.

The clerk bustled to the front of the room and unrolled a large parchment in his hands. Anna found herself leaning forward with the crowd, listening for Luke's and Rachel's words.

Luke spoke first, slow and strong. "In the presence of God and these our Friends, I take thee, my Friend Rachel Logue, to be my wife, promising with divine assurance to be unto thee a loving and faithful husband as long as we both shall live."

She wasn't supposed to cry on this glorious day, but Anna blinked back tears as Rachel repeated the vows. She was happy that her friend was marrying a fine man like Luke, yet sad because her friend was traveling down a road that Anna would never go.

When the vows were complete, Luke and Rachel sat on the facing bench and clasped hands. They were oblivious to the clerk as he dipped his goose-quill pen into a well of ink and held it up. In a slow line, the assembly shuffled out of their benches to sign their names to the certificate that would be framed and hung in Luke and Rachel's parlor, treasured by them and the generations that followed.

Anna kept her head down as she moved to the front, refusing to look out over the crowd of men and women. She didn't want to see Daniel Stanton or Matthew or anyone else who might distract her from her joy at communing with God today and the happiness of watching her friend marry.

Lyle Trumble signed the certificate in front of her and then handed her the pen. She slowly dipped it into ink and signed her name with a flourish, knowing that Rachel's grandchildren and great-grandchildren would one day read each name with reverence.

When she finished, she lifted her head to pass on the pen and looked up at Daniel Stanton beside her.

He wasn't looking at the document or the newly married couple in front of them. He was watching her closely, a curious expression in his eyes. Did he recognize her from the debate?

She never should have lingered that day. Nor should she have watched him so intently on the podium, thinking he couldn't see her in the crowd. Now he would wonder at her boldness and her interest in his words.

He reached for the pen in her hands, and she shook her shoulders slightly to force herself to move her fingers toward his.

His hand brushed hers when he took the pen, and she hopped back like she'd been burned. Heat seemed to fill the room, stifling her.

With a quick nod toward Rachel, Anna turned away from Daniel and fled.

Chapter Nineteen

....

It was only a brush of the fingers, the briefest of touches, but Daniel couldn't stop thinking about the woman at Meeting. He didn't know her name, but her gracious smile had carried him through his exhausting debate with Milton Kent. Today she hadn't smiled at him. She had confused him.

When she saw him this morning, there was fear in her eyes, almost as if she were scared of him. Instead of even a simple nod of acknowledgment, she had turned and run away.

Not that he could blame her; many people ran when they saw him coming. He didn't want to scare people, but he said exactly what he thought God intended him to say, no matter how unpleasant. It didn't attract many people, men or women, to him, and he usually didn't care. But if he had said or done something to offend this girl, he'd like to know why. Just so he could ask her forgiveness.

During the debate, it had seemed like she agreed with him. It was her smile and the encouragement in her eyes that helped him push through to the end. He may have had more than one supporter on that lawn, but the only one he had seen was this nameless girl who either didn't remember him or had been upset by something he'd said.

"Such a morbid affair," Esther ruminated to Joseph from the front seat of the buggy. "All dark and gloomy."

Joseph slowed the pace of the horse so the carriage wouldn't bounce his wife and unborn child over the ruts in the backwoods road. "That's how all Quakers marry."

"I know that." She crossed her white-gloved hands across her chest. "But it's more like a funeral than a wedding."

Daniel couldn't help but smile. There had been nothing plain or simple about Esther's wedding. Even though Joseph had shown up at the ceremony, it was definitely Esther's wedding. Joseph would have been satisfied with a clerk, a pen, and a marriage certificate, but he endured almost a year of selecting colors, silver, and flowers for their grand church extravaganza. In the end, the ceremony itself was as elegant as Queen Victoria's wedding.

In spite of the prewedding stress, Joseph and Esther's marriage had lasted for six years. With the birth of their child, they would finally become parents. He had never seen his sister happier. She had been a loving wife to Joseph, and he had no doubt that she would be a wonderful mother, as well.

At the time they were married, Daniel didn't know if Joseph could endure the notions of his sister, especially since he was almost a decade older than her, but Joseph had treated her with the respect she deserved.

He and Joseph may not see eye-to-eye on the issue of slavery, but his brother-in-law was a moral and upright man, and he loved Esther. One day, Daniel prayed, his brother-in-law would befriend runaway slaves the same way he befriended the many patients he cared for across their county.

Daniel balled up his hand as the Quaker girl's pretty face wandered through his mind again. He couldn't rid himself of the intense blue in her eyes or the softness of her fingers. She would be the type of person who would be kind to a runaway.

The buggy bumped over a hole, and Esther choked back her gasp. Joseph apologized, slowing the horse to a crawl.

Daniel knew he had to stop thinking about the woman at Silver Creek. He wouldn't court a woman without the prospect of marriage, and since he would never marry, he had determined not to let his heart or mind get involved with another woman, no matter how earnestly her heart sought after God.

When he had lived in Cincinnati, he'd courted a Quaker girl named Jane for almost eight months. At the same time they were talking about their future, he had been seeking God on the divisive issue of slavery. He'd known in his heart that the institution was abhorrent, but as a young lawyer in a big city, he hadn't known what to do about it.

Then he met Isaac Barnes when the minister visited the Cincinnati Meeting. The man had inspired him to speak out in public about slavery so others could learn the truth instead of what they were reading in local propaganda papers and hearing from the slave owners who perpetuated Cincinnati's thriving import business.

His decision to speak out against slavery clinched the end of his and Jane's plans to marry. She had dreams of marrying a successful Cincinnati lawyer, and those dreams dissipated the day he announced he'd taken an editorial position at an abolitionist newspaper—in Indiana.

He couldn't blame her for ending their relationship. He had changed significantly from the day he had met her, and she was still the same woman he had met at Meeting. If they had married, he never could have given her a secure home life like Joseph had given Esther.

It was unfair to Jane, or any woman, to marry someone who had been called into a lifetime of insecurity. Abolition was a dangerous and often disdained line of work. He tried to listen to the quiet voice of God's Spirit, and sometimes that voice prompted him to leap right into a battle.

He rubbed his hands together like he could scrub away the woman's touch.

He couldn't ask anyone, especially a devoted Quaker woman, to join the battle beside him.

*　*　*　*　*

Billows of smoke puffed out of the hotel and lingered on Liberty's Main Street. Instead of inviting friends and family to their house in town, the Logues had reserved the first floor of the Downing Hotel to celebrate the marriage of their daughter. All the people who had attended the wedding now poured into the town's center on horses and in buggies.

As they rode into town, Anna twisted her hands in her lap and then clutched the side of the buggy to let the cool air wash over her fingers. She had to stop thinking about the most innocent of touches, but the man who had spoken out at Meeting—and watched her so intently—had invaded her thoughts.

The next time she saw Daniel Stanton, she would walk the other way. If someone tried to introduce them, the strange feelings that haunted her would be exposed for all to see. Later she would ask God to remove her desires, but in the meantime, she would have to avoid the man, especially if he decided to join the wedding party at Downing's.

As her father tied the horses, she climbed down from the seat and rushed toward the hotel. She wanted to get inside and find a safe place to sit before he arrived.

Charlotte retied the ribbon on her bonnet while they walked. "I'm half starving."

Anna smiled. "You're always hungry."

"Well, today I could eat a whole goose by myself."

The aroma of roasted goose and lemon pastries wafted from the hotel, but Anna wasn't the least bit hungry. She reached for the door handle in front of them, but before she opened it, a groan escaped her friend's lips.

"What is it?" Anna whispered though she refused to turn her head. She didn't want to see if Daniel Stanton was behind them.

Charlotte nodded toward the street, and Anna finally turned.

"Oh no," she murmured.

Trotting down the street on his horse was one of the black slave hunters who had stood outside her door behind Noah Owens. The one who had held the chains in his hands. Dust plastered his leather coat and hat, and he was searching the buggies like Marie might be hiding away in one.

Hands on her hips, Anna stepped off the slats and onto the street. She would tell the man to go home, wherever home was for him. He wasn't welcome here. No one, especially a greedy slave hunter, would spoil Rachel and Luke's special day.

Before she could take another step, Charlotte caught her arm and pulled her back up on the platform.

"He can't be here," Anna persisted, shaking her arm away from Charlotte's grasp. "He'll ruin everything."

"Someone else has to stop him."

Anna glared at the man across the street and the slow gait of his horse. It was apparent that he was in no rush to leave Liberty. Everything within her wanted to confront him and demand that he leave, but Charlotte was right yet again. She must stay quiet. If she challenged the slave hunter, people around her would ask questions. Why had he been at her house, and why was she so angry that he reappeared?

She was relieved, if only a bit, that the man was still searching for Marie and Peter. It meant that they were still plodding toward freedom. She could only pray that her friends were miles and miles north of here.

"Anna!" Matthew called her name from across the street. The smile she forced on her lips never reached her eyes. After the disaster of their last visit, she supposed she should be glad he was speaking to her again.

He sprinted up the steps toward her, oblivious to the hunter at his back. "Could I escort you ladies inside?"

"Of course." Anna nodded, glancing over his shoulder one last time. Daniel Stanton was behind her, but he wasn't watching her this time. He had jumped from a buggy and was approaching the fierce-looking hunter.

Her anger melted quickly into respect. She wanted to hide herself away on the patio so she could watch him. Surely he wouldn't let this man search through the buggies while their friends were enjoying Rachel and Luke's celebration. Even if Daniel could never hear her, she wanted to cheer for his courage from her place on the sidelines.

"C'mon," Charlotte prompted her again.

Anna looked back at Daniel one last time and then reluctantly stepped toward the door, trying not to worry about Marie and her child.

And trying not to think about the man willing to stand up for them.

Chapter Twenty
....

Simon recognized Daniel immediately and reined in his horse, though he didn't bother to dismount. The hunter smirked down at him. "Fine day for a meetin.'"

Daniel didn't even nod in return. "What are you doing back in Liberty?"

"Just passing through."

"The woman you're searching for isn't here."

"You're one smart Yank to figure that out." Simon dug into his pouch and pinched tobacco in his grimy fingers. He stuffed the black chaw into his cheek until the skin bulged like an ugly wart. "We done caught up with her near Richmond last night."

Daniel wanted to jump on the horse and wring the man's neck. There wasn't a hint of remorse in his words. He was proud of his catch, prouder than an animal hunter who had hauled in a bear or a cougar.

It took everything within Daniel to keep his voice calm. "I'm sorry to hear that."

Simon leaned his head back. His raucous laugh echoed down the street, grating Daniel's skin. "I bet you are."

Daniel could feel eyes on his back. They were watching him from the hotel's patio and through the windows. Before he'd joined the Society of Friends, he wouldn't have hesitated to punch this guy, even if he'd gotten pummeled in return. Now he kept his fists at his side, choosing peace over violence, although he desperately wanted to plant one of his fists on the guy's nose.

"You got what you came for," he said as he stepped toward him. "Now you can ride on out of Liberty."

The man clutched the saddle horn and leaned down toward Daniel like he was letting him in on a secret. "The problem is, our little Marie left somethin' behind."

Daniel shoved his fists into his pockets. He didn't want to be his confidant, yet the reporter in him wondered what the man was talking about.

"Marie had her a kid someplace between here and Knoxville. Told her master she lost the baby, but lyin' ain't her thing. Somebody already seen them together out on Silver Creek."

"So her master is looking for the child?"

"Nope." The man spit a stream of tobacco juice toward Daniel's boots. "Owens posted a reward for the kid and then rode on home to his wife."

Daniel ignored the tobacco puddled on his toe. "What's the baby worth to Owens?"

"Five hundred dollars."

Daniel whistled. "He must like babies."

Simon leaned back into his saddle. "Somethin' like that."

"What happened to Marie?"

A laugh erupted from the man's gut, and even when he kicked his spurs against the horse's ribs and began trotting away, he didn't stop laughing.

Standing out in the middle of the smoky street, Daniel didn't move. Frustration and compassion collided inside him. He wanted to act, to do something to stop this girl from getting hurt, but there was nothing he could do. A battle was waging around him, and he couldn't stop the attack.

Where was Marie now? Her master must have dragged her back to Tennessee with him—or worse. No court of law in Indiana would penalize him for harming his property. Even if he was tried for homicide, who was going to speak against him? Colored people weren't allowed to testify in court, and if a white man had witnessed the act, he probably wouldn't volunteer the truth.

Dejected, Daniel scuffed his foot, but he didn't leave the street. He didn't want to go inside and talk about weddings and the weather and the autumn harvest. He wanted to scour the countryside for Marie and her child in case the man was lying and they were still on the run.

But he could spend weeks searching from here to Canada and never find her. There was nothing he could do except pray.

His brother-in-law was suddenly at his side. "You all right?"

Nothing was right, but Joseph wouldn't understand. Only a handful of people at this party would understand why. "Where's Esther?" he asked.

"She's already inside, getting the scoop on the latest gossip."

"Like nothing else matters..."

Joseph clapped him on the back. "You can't rescue everyone, Daniel."

"Maybe not." He straightened his shoulders. "But if God drops someone in my path, I better well try."

* * * * *

Topping each table inside the hotel were jars filled with sunflowers. Each jar was a different color and size, but the room radiated the hearty yellow of their contents.

In spite of the beauty around her, Anna's eyes weren't on the flowers. The jar on her table had been nudged aside so she and Charlotte could see out the picture window in front of them. She didn't want to appear too interested in Daniel or the man on the horse, but no one noticed that she was watching. Her father had stayed on the patio with several other men, and the people inside were either socializing with the newly married couple at one end of the room or they were beside the window with her, watching Daniel, too.

Matthew was neither watching nor talking at the moment. Instead of bothering with the events on the street, he had announced that they all needed something hot to drink. Anna had acknowledged his declaration with a quick nod before he left the table. Then her eyes went back out toward the street.

The silence didn't last long. A loud swish resounded beside her, and a large bundle of ribbons and lace plopped into the chair. Under the light blue hat dressed with feathers and a giant bow, Anna recognized Esther Cooley.

Esther sighed like she had walked ten miles before propping her chin on her hands. Then she leaned toward Anna's ear. "You remember when I told you I had a brother?"

"I do."

Esther untied her hat, and when she removed it, she waved the feathers toward the man who'd been left standing alone on the street. "There he is, in all his glory."

Anna caught her breath and looked back out at the man who had been joined by Joseph Cooley. Esther's brother? Daniel seemed nothing like this woman. First of all, he was a Quaker, and while Esther had been kind to her, she was quite worldly. Daniel was a fighter, both in words and deeds. Esther, on the other hand, seemed to concern herself with material things.

"What is he doing out there?" Anna asked, trying to sound more polite than intrigued.

"Who knows...." Esther sighed again like she had to carry the burden for him. "He's always chasing trouble and is quite adept at finding it." She glanced over her shoulder as if she had just realized that Joseph had left her side. "Thank God, I married a man who has a level head on his shoulders."

Daniel and Joseph turned toward the hotel together, and Anna forced herself to stop watching him. "You are blessed to find a husband like that."

"Indeed." Esther set the hat in her lap and caressed the white feathers on top. "Even if my brother wanted to marry, he never will. No woman wants to marry a fanatic."

There were plenty of women who admired courage and compassion in a man...or at least Anna thought there were. She was no expert on the subject, nor did she want to continue talking about it with Daniel Stanton's sister.

Matthew sat down across from Anna and slid two mugs of melted chocolate and milk toward her and Charlotte. Esther held out her hand and shook his. "You're the Nelson boy, aren't you?"

Matthew gave her a grand smile. "One of two."

Esther leaned toward him like she was conspiring. "Anna here was telling me the other day that she would never marry."

Heat burned across Anna's face like she'd been singed. She reached for the mug of chocolate but didn't take a sip.

Matthew set his elbows on the table and folded his hands. "Did she now?"

Anna looked back toward the window, but Daniel was no longer in sight. She had wanted to change the conversation from Daniel's fanaticism, but she certainly did not want to discuss her own aversion to matrimony, especially with Matthew at the table.

"I don't believe her for a second." Esther waved her hand and then placed it on her stomach. "Someone has caught her eye."

Anna didn't dare look at Matthew. She had done everything she could to discourage him already, and he didn't need someone like Esther to either give him hope that maybe she'd been hiding her feelings for him or that she'd fallen for someone else. Instead of retreating like she'd asked him to do, a competitor would only make him push harder.

"Did she mention any names?" Matthew asked.

Esther sighed like Anna was a fiend for depriving her of such valuable information. "Not a one."

Anna sat up straight. "That's because there's no one to mention."

Esther didn't even glance at her. "But I intend to find out who she fancies."

Two hands seemed to come out of nowhere and set squarely down upon Esther's shoulders. Anna looked up to see Daniel Stanton towering over his sister. She glanced back at Esther and then over at Matthew, who was watching Daniel as well. She wanted to run far, far away, but there was no place for her to go.

"I am sure that you won't rest again, Essie, until you can extract whatever secrets this poor woman is keeping from you."

Daniel looked over at her, and even though she wanted to crawl under the table and hide, she had no choice but to acknowledge him. His eyes bore into hers. "Are you good at keeping secrets?"

She could feel Charlotte's eyes on her. And Matthew's.

"Terrible," she said, forcing a nervous laugh even though it really wasn't funny. She wasn't nearly as clever as her father when it came to sidestepping the truth.

"Then you are in trouble."

Esther slapped at one of Daniel's hands. "Don't listen to him, Anna. I am the model of discrepancy."

Matthew chuckled first, and the rest of them joined in with his laughter. Anna took a sip of the hot chocolate.

Esther crossed her arms. "Why are you all laughing?"

Daniel leaned down to kiss her cheek. "You and your discrepancies amuse us all, dear sister."

Esther's smile turned to a pout, though she didn't allow their teasing to dampen her spirits for long. She patted Anna's arm. "I told you my brother was ridiculous, didn't I?"

"I believe you said fanatical."

"Ridiculous and fanatical, then." She motioned toward Daniel. "Daniel, I'd like you to meet Anna Brent and company."

Instead of reaching out her hand, Anna introduced him quickly to Charlotte and Matthew. She wanted to excuse herself to find her father, but leaving so abruptly would only make Esther wonder even more. She had to focus on what was important instead of the silly butterflies that had embedded themselves in her belly.

Daniel was the only one who had spoken to the slave hunter. He was perhaps the only one who knew if something had happened to Peter and Marie.

"Was the man on that horse a friend of yours?" she asked casually.

"Hardly." His eyes seemed to question her back, wondering why she was interested. "He was searching for a runaway slave."

"Did he find her?" She swallowed hard and reached for her mug again. "Or him?"

"He was actually looking for a baby."

Esther took the glass of blackberry cordial that Joseph handed her. "Must we talk about this?"

"A baby?" Anna interjected, trying to calm her racing heart. "What happened to the mother?"

"He wouldn't say exactly. Only that her master caught her near Richmond."

Esther shook her head. "He probably took her right back home where she belonged."

"That's funny," Matthew said, and they all turned toward him. "Terrance Platt found something strange in a creek up north of Richmond when he was traveling home last night."

Anna tried to force herself not to seem too interested, but the butterflies in her stomach had tightened into knots. Matthew looked at each one of them as they waited, like he was relishing the moment.

"What did he find?" she finally asked.

"The body of a Negro girl."

Anna didn't think it was funny at all.

Chapter Twenty-one

....

Matthew pushed his chair back a few inches after delivering his news, but Anna couldn't move. Sorrow drowned her heart and spilled out into her veins as Matthew described the girl's wounds and the long scar that ran up the back of her neck like the fugitive slave's that had been advertised on billboards across town.

Noah Owens had found the servant girl that he and his wife loved so much. And he'd killed her.

Her hands began trembling and then her feet. When the sunflowers in front of her started spinning, Charlotte reached for her hand under the table. She had to stay strong, at least until she got outside.

Charlotte was the one who asked the question that raced through Anna's mind. "Where is her baby?"

Daniel collapsed into a chair beside Matthew, like he was also gasping for air. "No idea," he said, staring outside the window. "Simon was searching for him, though."

An ashen shade blended with the ivory tones on Esther's cheeks. Her eyes wandered among the small group until they stopped on Matthew. "I don't want to talk about this anymore."

He lifted his snifter of brandy in a mock salute. "Me neither."

Esther patted her damp forehead with her handkerchief and then she patted her hair with her hands. "When do you suspect we'll get our first snow?"

Anna glared at the woman. Who wanted to talk about snow right now? She wanted to lash out at Esther and Matthew, railing them both for their total lack of compassion about this young woman's death—a woman who had been killed solely because she desired freedom for herself and her son.

Her stomach reeled. She couldn't mourn Marie's death right now. The only option she had was to join Matthew and Esther in their indifference.

She took a deep breath. "The almanac said it's supposed to snow the first of October."

The gray color faded slightly from Esther's cheeks. "Oh, I hope it will wait a few more weeks this year. I'm not ready to hibernate yet."

The loud grating of a chair across the wood floor made Anna jump. Daniel stood back up in front of them, his voice filled with disgust. "How can you talk about snow when you just found out that a young woman was murdered? It's like none of you even care."

"Oh, I care." Anna sniffed lightly, her eyes on the jar of sunflowers so she didn't have to meet his gaze. "I care about the child, and I dearly hope he doesn't suffer for his mother's choice."

The words shot out of Daniel's mouth. "Her choice?"

"Yes, her choice." Anna almost choked on her response, but she continued talking as fast as she could, afraid she might stumble on the lies that poured from her mouth. "She risked the life of her child when she chose to leave the safety and provisions of her home in the South. It seems like a selfish decision to me, don't you think?"

She fiddled with her hands in her lap. No one responded to her statement, though she could almost feel the heat seething from Daniel's skin. She wondered if she'd pushed too hard to sound supportive of slavery. None of them would believe she meant it.

Finally, Esther spoke. "You're exactly right, Anna. It was a terrible choice for this mother to run away with a baby. Now she's dead, and the Lord only knows where her poor child is."

A sense of urgency gripped Anna. Peter could still be alive, either at the home of one of the stationmasters or someplace in the wilderness.

She had to find him before the slave hunters or a wild animal did.

Daniel ignored Esther, but his voice was as bitter as quinine when he spoke to Anna. "I'm sure glad that not everyone agrees with your tragic take on slavery." He squeezed the back of his chair, and she watched the knuckles on his strong hands turn white. "The question no one seems to be asking is why a loving mother would risk her life and that of her child's to run. I don't think it's because her home in Tennessee was safe."

"I'm not saying slavery is right," she replied. "I only think that slaves who have been sold to a master should stay and adhere to them as the scriptures say."

Daniel leaned closer to her, his eyes aflame. "And views like yours and my sister's are why so many people are still in bondage to other humans instead of being equal with them like the scriptures command."

Daniel's gaze drifted toward Charlotte, and Anna knew what was next. He was going to ask her colored housekeeper and friend what she thought about slavery. She couldn't bear to hear Charlotte expound on the positive attributes of the institution that had abused her mind and body. Charlotte squeezed her hand, and Anna prepared to scoot her chair back. Before Daniel could ask Charlotte a question, though, Matthew interjected his support of Anna's view.

"Most slave owners care well for their workers, and all they ask for in return is obedience," he said.

Daniel swiveled his head toward Matthew. "And a fourteen-hour workday without pay."

Matthew shrugged. "I'm not saying it's easy work, but the owners do provide shelter and clothing and food for people who probably wouldn't be able to provide it for themselves."

Charlotte lurched beside her like she'd been scalded, and Anna knew it was time to leave. Neither of them needed to hear anything more about slaves, especially the insinuation that they were perhaps too lazy or stupid to care for themselves. She would get Charlotte away from this table and then go in search of Peter before the hour passed.

"So give them the option," Daniel continued, oblivious to the thoughts racing in Anna's mind.

Matthew swirled the brandy in his glass. "What do you mean?"

"Let those who are now working as slaves decide if they'd prefer to provide for themselves or let their masters provide for them."

Anna leaped to her feet and dragged Charlotte up with her. "Here we are gabbing away at our own little table, and we haven't even greeted Luke and Rachel yet."

Esther frowned. "There's plenty of time to speak with them."

"I want to see if there's anything I can do to help."

Esther glanced at Daniel and then looked back at her. "You and your father must come to dinner at our house this week."

"Perhaps that would work."

"Please don't forget to bring your poetry."

Anna nodded, but her mind wasn't on her writing right now. She had to deliver the envelope in her pocket, find her father, and then leave this building so she could ride to the Sutters' before it started to get dark.

"I suggest you return to the topic of snow." Anna nodded toward Esther and then Matthew before she walked away from the table. She avoided looking at Daniel, not wanting to see disappointment on the face of someone whom she admired so. "It's been a pleasure talking with you."

"Yes," Charlotte muttered beside her. "A pleasure."

Chapter Twenty-two
....

Even after Anna left the table, Matthew kept talking to Esther, although he changed the topic to the gold that people were finding in California's streams and riverbeds. As Daniel strolled toward the window, he heard Matthew tell her about his plans to go west in the next few months. His parents frowned on his idea, but he was leaving Liberty the instant he had enough money for supplies.

Good riddance! Daniel thought and then raked his hands through his hair as he searched the street for Simon Mathers. Bells chimed from the tower at the Methodist church and rang through town. The street was crowded with more buggies and more horses, but he didn't see any sign of the man who had delivered his news about Marie and then laughed at her fate. Simon had known that Marie was dead, maybe had even killed her himself. It was a travesty to think that a man could do that to any woman, especially one as vulnerable as a slave girl.

On the wall beside the front door of the hotel were ten or eleven posters, many of them advertisements for missing slaves. At the top was a handbill that matched the advertisement he'd read in the *Union County News* for Marie and her baby. How much had Simon already made for helping track them down?

Daniel turned away from the posters and glanced across the room until he found Anna. What kind of woman didn't understand a mother's compulsion to seek out freedom for her child?

She and Charlotte were talking with an older man, though the wide smile he'd seen at the debate had been erased from her face. She was still pretty, but she looked older and a bit sadder.

Even Esther seemed to understand the horror of selling a young slave child away from his parents, but not Anna. She had said that Marie was being selfish for running away with her child.

His head ached from the confusion that tangled itself in his mind. Who was this woman? Out on the courthouse lawn, he had thought she was supporting his words. Her smile and gentle nods helped carry him through the fight. Yet here she was speaking not only against abolition but against the slaves themselves.

He leaned back against the wall but couldn't take his eyes off Anna. He had to stop fooling himself. He may not think he would ever marry, but he had been attracted to Anna from the day he saw her at the courthouse. Today, though, she had summarily doused any illusions he had about her or a possible future.

Even if she was a beautiful Quaker woman, there was no hope that something might happen between them. God had clearly spoken the answer today through Anna herself. No matter how he felt about her, the issue of slavery divided them as clearly as the Ohio divided the North from the South.

"There you are, Daniel." Isaac Barnes reached for his hand and shook it. "There's someone I've been wanting you to meet from the Salem Meeting."

A Quaker girl stepped from behind Isaac, fluttering her eyelashes up at him. She was about nineteen or twenty, with a petite face dappled with light freckles. Her hair was black and her eyes a stunning green.

"This is Charity Penner," Isaac explained with an outrageously large smile.

Daniel managed to smile back. "It's a pleasure to meet you."

As Isaac rambled about Charity's talents in gardening and quilting, Daniel watched Anna out of the corner of his eyes. She hastily came up behind his employer, handed something to him, and then blew past Daniel in such a hurry that he doubted she even knew that the hem of her skirt had brushed over his feet.

He nodded at Charity, trying to listen to her talk about her quilting project, but his mind was on the girl who had just swung open the hotel's front doors and run outside.

* * * * *

Anna flicked the reins over Samara's back, and the horse rushed her out of town. She hadn't told her father her destination nor did she tell Charlotte, although her friend knew exactly where she was going. This time Charlotte didn't try to argue with her—neither of them wanted Peter to be hurt.

When the wedding reception was over, Charlotte and her father would walk home and she could quietly tell him why Anna needed to leave before they'd even begun to serve the food.

There was no reason for her to stay at the party anyway. She would have to spend the afternoon avoiding Daniel Stanton so he couldn't read the truth in her eyes. And she didn't want to be around Matthew, either. After hearing his views on slavery, she had never been more certain that she couldn't marry him.

Even though she longed to speak with Daniel and tell him what she really thought, there was no chance that the two of them could even be friends. As long as he thought she believed as Matthew, he'd despise her. She'd never be able to let him think otherwise.

The road to Connersville was fairly clear, so she pressed Samara ahead as hard as she could until they came to the turnoff toward the Sutters' home. At the creek where she had left Marie and the others over a week ago, she parked the buggy and pushed the brake down over the wheel. After taking the harness off Samara, she pulled up her skirts to mount.

She'd never actually been to the Sutters' home, but she knew the directions well. Two miles up the creek she turned right at the large beech tree with the S carved deep into its pale gray bark. Ducking under the low canopy of yellow and red leaves, she and Samara galloped up the path.

A sigh of relief slipped from her mouth when she saw the blue trim on the farmhouse ahead. The dozens of fugitives she'd brought this way had probably felt the same sense of relief, or more, at the sight of the stately home with the cupola.

There was no light in the cupola, but it was also early afternoon on the Sabbath. The Sutters weren't Quakers, but they attended church in Connersville. On this beautiful day, she hoped that one of them had needed to stay home from the service.

She pounded on the door and then rang the bell. A middle-aged woman finally answered, her green eyes streaked with red. Either she'd been crying or sleeping when Anna arrived.

"I'm sorry to bother you," she said. "Are you Betsy Sutter?"

The woman looked over Anna's shoulder and then back at her, studying her plain gray dress and bonnet but not saying anything.

"I'm alone," Anna assured her.

The woman waved her into the house and motioned for her to sit down on a chair in the formal parlor while she spread herself across the settee. Propping a pillow under her head, the woman studied her for a moment before she spoke.

"I'm sorry I can't offer you anything to drink." The woman closed her eyes and took a deep breath. "I've been struck with a terrible headache this morning."

Anna folded her hands together. "I don't need anything to drink."

"I'm Betsy Sutter." She pressed hard on her temples like she could squeeze the pain out of her head. "Who are you?"

"Anna Brent. Edwin Brent's daughter."

Betsy opened her eyes and stared aghast at her. Stationmasters weren't supposed to have any contact, especially not a visit like this.

All communication was done through their elusive agent, Ben, and his contacts. Anything else could upset the precarious system they'd developed to help rush runaways up the line.

Betsy propped herself up on her elbows. "And why are you here, Miss Brent?"

"I'm looking for a friend of a friend."

Fear flashed across Betsy's face. "I don't know any of your friends."

"Usually I bring them to the creek and let them walk to your house. I tell them to look for the light in the cupola before they knock."

Betsy shook her head and then groaned at the pain. "What are you talking about?"

"I know this isn't the way we're supposed to do things, Betsy, but I need your help."

"I'm always glad to help, Miss Brent, but my husband and I are law-abiding citizens. I can't speak to this notion of lights and secret knocks."

Anna hesitated. It was a risk to talk to this woman about specific runaways, yet she didn't have a choice. Peter may have been left alone for days. She prayed he was alive, but even if he weren't, she still had to find his body. For Marie's sake.

Betsy closed her eyes again, a sharp end to their conversation.

Anna understood why Betsy was scared. An hour ago, she'd done the same thing as Betsy, denying herself the opportunity to say exactly what she thought about slavery to protect the runaway slaves. Without the woman's help, though, she would never find Peter. She had to convince Betsy that she wasn't part of a scam to expose her safe house.

"A little over a week ago, I brought a young runaway girl to your house named Marie. She had a light-skinned baby with her named Peter."

Betsy opened her eyes again, recognition dawning in them, though she didn't open her mouth to reply.

Anna paused. "I believe that Marie has been murdered."

"What?" Betsy exclaimed.

Anna quickly told her the story about Daniel and the slave hunter and what Terrance Platt had found.

Betsy's red eyes turned teary. "That explains my headache."

Anna blinked. "What do you mean?"

"I never get headaches." Betsy pushed herself up on the settee. "And I never stay home from church."

Anna leaned forward and spoke gently. "I need you to tell me where you took Marie and Peter."

Betsy sat still for a moment, and Anna was afraid the woman wouldn't divulge the next station on the line.

"East of here is an apple orchard," Betsy whispered, and Anna listened intently as Betsy gave her directions to the next house, ten miles northeast.

Anna stood and thanked her.

"It will take a miracle to find him," Betsy said.

"Yes, it will."

The woman smiled softly. "But I believe in miracles."

Anna stepped toward the door. "So do I."

Chapter Twenty-three
....

At the small farmhouse of Adeline Hampshire, Anna sat in the parlor and repeated her story. Her hostess's shoulders shook as Anna spoke, and then she began crying. Anna felt terrible delivering such bad news to an elderly woman who cared deeply for Marie and her baby.

Adeline dabbed at her cheeks with a handkerchief. "They left here late last night."

Anna caught her breath. Maybe there was hope. "Where did they go next?"

Adeline shook her head. "I'm not privy to that information."

Anna squeezed her hands together in her lap. "But you must know someone who could find out where they went."

When Adeline didn't reply, Anna collapsed back against her seat, deflated. She was so close to finding Peter, but to search the miles of forest and fields around here would take days. If she ever did find Peter, it would probably be too late.

"It's dreadful, isn't it?" Adeline's voice cracked, and her gaze wandered to the crackling fireplace behind Anna. "What they do to these slaves."

"Yes, it is."

"I'm only doing a small part to help them, but then look what happens to one of these precious children that have rested here."

Anna reached over and took the woman's hands. "That very same child who rested in your house is resting today in the arms of Jesus."

"Thank God," Adeline sniffed. "Thank God she is finally home."

Anna stood up to warm her hands by the fire. "Did Marie take Peter with her when she left?"

"Yes, she had him bundled in blankets and a flannel gown." Adeline paused as she remembered something. "She had split her foot on a nail or something else sharp before she arrived here, so she could barely walk as it was. I begged her to stay until she healed, but she said she had to keep going."

Anna could feel the woman's anguish deep in her own heart. "It's not your fault, Adeline. Her master would have shown up here to look for her, and when he found her, you and any other runaways in your home would have been in danger."

Adeline's eyes met hers, pleading for an answer. "How did he find her?"

Anna stepped even closer to the fire. The secret network they'd developed to move slaves north was known only to a few, but those who supported the slave owner's rights would have a network as well, with eyes and ears in the farmlands and the forests and the main roads.

"I don't know," Anna said as she reached for the cloak over the back of her chair. "But I'm not going to let them find Peter as well."

"I don't know where she went." Adeline hesitated. "But my farmhand can tell you."

She silently thanked God that Adeline was willing to trust her.

Adeline escorted her to the door and called out toward the barn. "Earl?"

A short man wearing denim overalls and a straw hat moved toward the house. His arms bulged under his shirt, and his nose was bent to the left— good signs that he wouldn't hesitate to throw a punch if someone crossed him.

Struggling through another round of tears, Adeline explained the urgency of Anna's story to Earl. The man eyed her warily at first, but then his expression turned to alarm when Adeline said they'd found the body of a colored girl nearby.

He stiffened. "I heard the dogs."

Anna took a step toward him. "What dogs?" she pressed.

"I heard 'em when I left my passengers by the cornfield. I told myself the dogs were barking from a nearby farmhouse, but I knew better."

"You couldn't have known," Anna said.

His face clouded with guilt. "I should have turned back."

"You can't go back," Anna spoke softly. "But you can help me find Marie's baby."

When Earl nodded slowly, Adeline grasped Anna's hand. "I shouldn't hear this."

Anna thanked her, but before she left the kitchen, Adeline turned back to her. "Can you let me know...?"

"I'll try."

Adeline wiped another tear off her cheek. "Thank you."

* * * * *

With Samara at her side, Anna trekked through the forest north of Adeline's house for hours, searching under logs and in the depths of matted brush along the path. She called out Peter's name over and over like he could call back to her. All she needed to hear was one cry in the dense forest—but except for the faint rustle of dry leaves dancing with the breeze, the forest around her was silent.

Please God, she prayed again and again. Help me find him. And then she dared to ask, *And please help me find him alive.*

As she walked through the trees, she could see Marie clutching her baby close to her chest, snuggling with him like he was all she had in this world. She had wanted freedom for this child of hers, and if God in His mercy helped her find Peter, Anna would do everything she could to get him to freedom—even if it meant traveling to Canada herself and placing him safely on free soil.

"C'mon, Samara," she coaxed her tired horse.

Earl's directions led them out of the trees and toward an abandoned homestead along the river. The blue sky above the old cabin was slowly darkening, and in another hour the sunlight would be gone. Before the sun disappeared, she had to get back through the woods, or she and Samara would be spending the night lost out here in the frigid air.

There were five outbuildings around the cabin in front of her, still intact in spite of the harsh Indiana winters. As she passed by the chicken coops, she glanced inside each of the wiry cages, and then she checked inside the outhouse.

The moment she closed the door to the empty root cellar, she heard a muffled cry. Or she thought she did. She glanced around quickly, praying that the sound wasn't just a door batting in the wind.

Then she heard the cry again, coming from the smokehouse, and she sprang forward. There, centered in the small brick room, was a shivering bundle of skin and blankets. The instant Peter's eyes met hers, he let out a loud wail.

She grabbed him and pulled him into her arms until his cries were broken by a deep cough that erupted from his chest. The blankets were soaked, and she quickly unwrapped him from the soggy mess sticking to his skin.

"It's going to be okay," she whispered as he continued to cough. Cradling him in one arm, she opened Marie's knapsack, pulled out a clean gown and diaper, and folded his body into the dry clothes. Then she wrapped her shawl around him and pulled him to her chest.

Thank You, she whispered.

As she held him close, his cough turned into a terrible wheeze that made him labor for his next breath. He was ill, but thank God, she had found him with some breath still in his body. After doing a miracle to keep Peter alive, surely God wouldn't let him pass now.

"I know you miss your mama," she said gently as she opened Marie's pack again. "I understand—I miss my mama, too.

"Your mama would want you to hold on just a little bit longer. She wants you to grow up into a man before you see her again."

At the bottom of the pack, she found a bottle filled with milk and twisted off the cap. She had no idea if she should feed a sick baby cold milk, but the alternative seemed even more deadly to her. She wouldn't let him starve to death.

She propped the nipple in his mouth, and he sucked hungrily. "You have a good life ahead of you, my friend."

He shivered again, and with her cheek placed against his forehead, she felt his burning skin. She had to get Peter home right away.

Chapter Twenty-four

....

"We can't keep him here." Her father's voice cracked when he said it, but his words still infuriated her. What were they supposed to do? She couldn't travel with Peter to Canada now, not while he was so sick. And there was no place else to take him. Did he want her to put Peter back inside that frigid smokehouse and leave him there to die?

Charlotte lifted the kettle of water out of the fire and poured it slowly into the other end of the tub to mix with the cooling bath water. Anna cradled Peter's shivering head with one hand and scooped the warm water over his flushed skin, hoping that it would help relieve the chill.

"He needs to see a doctor," Anna insisted.

Her father's look was filled with sadness. "We can't take him to a doctor, Anna. It would put his life in jeopardy as well as ours."

"But he's a white baby!"

"There are handbills posted all over town for a light-skinned baby," Edwin said. "It wouldn't take long for someone to guess."

Anna poured warm water over him again. "I'm not going to let him die."

"I don't want him to die either."

At the table beside them, Charlotte crushed a clove of garlic and mixed it into a small bowl of lard. "This will help."

Anna pointed for her father to get a towel that had been warmed by the fire. After he opened it, she lifted Peter out of the water and swathed him in the cotton. As Anna held him to her chest, he rested his head on her bosom, and she knew she would do anything to keep this baby alive.

"Lay him down on the table," Charlotte said, and Anna did as she instructed.

Charlotte uncovered his feet and plastered them with the mixture of lard and garlic before she smeared the mixture on his neck. Anna tucked the blanket over him again and then held him against her chest once more.

"He'll need castor oil," Edwin said, and Charlotte nodded her head. Anna turned away from them and sat with Peter in the rocking chair her father had brought downstairs. Peter's cough sounded worse than when she had taken him from the smokehouse five or six hours ago, but he wasn't shivering anymore.

Charlotte brought over a bottle with a few teaspoons of castor oil and molasses. Anna thought Peter might spit out the potent mixture, but he was so hungry he slurped it up. God help her, if Noah Owens were around, she would want to hurt him like he'd hurt this baby, stealing away his mother and then stripping him of his health.

"I have an idea," Charlotte said as she took the bottle.

Anna patted Peter on the back and rocked him. "What is it?"

"There is a free couple who live in the colored settlement near Salem," Charlotte began to explain. "The husband was hurt a few months ago at the grist mill, so he's home all day, chomping at the bit to do some work, until he goes back to the mill at the first of the year. He's a fine man, Anna. Loves God and all the people in the settlement. If you could supply him and his wife with food and clothing and medicine for Peter, they may be willing to take him in for a spell."

Anna clutched Peter even closer to her, not wanting to let him go. "What are their names?"

Charlotte paused. "We'll call them the Palmer family."

Anna nodded. It would be an answer to prayer if the Palmers could nurse him back to health, but the entire six weeks of his life had been spent going from one house to the next, with different faces and arms rocking him to sleep at night. The only consistent face and voice had been Marie.

Why couldn't she keep him here and care for him herself? She couldn't replace his mother, but she could care for him consistently until he was well.

"When can we take him?" Edwin asked.

"I can go visit them first thing in the morning and take Peter with me."

"Not yet," Anna insisted. "He's not ready to travel again."

Her father sat down on a bench. "The hunters will return, Anna, and if they find him here, he may suffer the same fate as Marie."

"We'll hide him in the attic."

"One cry is all it will take for them to find the room."

Peter sighed against her, the lard and garlic and castor oil relieving his cough for the moment. Marie had chosen the selfless path for her life, risking everything to get Peter away from slavery. Anna had to let him go from her, as well.

"Charlotte," she said, her eyes on Peter, "could you send a message up the line through Ben?"

"Of course."

"Please have him tell Adeline Hampshire that I was mistaken about the cargo I misplaced." She kissed the top of Peter's head. "Tell her I found the package this afternoon, and we'll ship it north again very soon."

* * * * *

Daniel sat at Joseph's wide secretary, trying to lob the scattered thoughts in his head onto a sheet of paper. How could a respectable society allow a slave owner to come into its fold, kill one of his slaves, and not suffer the slightest repercussion? They should all rally against Noah Owens and let him and his cohorts know that no matter what the federal government says, no one could tromp into Indiana and murder a colored girl.

A person wasn't property, to do with what another man pleased. It was inane, the absurd wording used to justify an evil act. In the government's wording of the new law, they'd demoralized a human and then criminalized those helping a slave by saying they were stealing property. Apparently there was nothing wrong with damaging your own property.

Daniel dropped his pen on the desk. How could someone like Anna Brent speak in support of slavery?

The question had haunted him for two days. Since the wedding, he hadn't been able to write anything decent for the paper. His thoughts were all jumbled in his head, and they looked even more jumbled on paper.

The *Liberty Era* went to press tonight whether or not this final article was completed, so he'd escaped his room and his office to try to finish it in Joseph and Esther's parlor, hoping the words would flow better here.

Joseph had left an hour ago to care for a patient, and the only thing that flowed through Daniel's head right now was his agitation toward Anna and his sister. Esther sat near him on a cushioned chair. She had just finished writing a letter, and now she was reading the latest *Godey's Lady's Book* more earnestly than most Christians read their Bibles.

He picked up his pen and began to write feverishly again, but even he wasn't swayed by his own words.

Esther groaned, and he swung around. "What's wrong?"

Her face was flushed, but she smiled at him. "Just a small pain."

"Is it time?"

"Oh no." She laughed, but even that sounded painful. "Not for two more months."

He stared at her. "Do you want me to find Joseph?"

"It's nothing to worry about." She fanned her face with the magazine, but he could see the sweat beading on her forehead. "All women have pains here and there."

He faced the secretary again, picked up his pen, but even the jumble of words in his mind had disappeared.

* * * * *

The instant Charlotte walked down into the kitchen after visiting Peter, Anna knew that something was wrong. "Is he still sick?"

Charlotte hung her cape on a peg. "Gravely."

A shiver went through Anna's body. Peter was dying, and she wasn't doing a thing to help him recover. "I need to go to him."

Charlotte reached for her arm. "There's nothing you can do."

"I can hold him."

"The Palmers are holding him, Anna."

"But I can still go…."

"No, you can't."

The Palmers may be caring for him, but there had to be something she could do to help. It was wrong—being here in the security of her home while he was so ill. Not being able to relieve his pain. She swung open a cabinet and rummaged through it quickly until she found another bottle of castor oil. "Take this to him."

Charlotte set the bottle on the table.

"What are you doing?" Anna pointed to the oil. "Take it to him right now."

"They've given him castor oil and onion tea and rhubarb tea to fight the croup," Charlotte said. "They've given him warm baths and kept flannel wraps around his neck since he arrived. He was exposed to the cold for too long."

She leaned her head back against the wall. "He needs a doctor."

Charlotte nodded sadly, and then changed the topic. "Ben left me a message today."

"Any news?"

"He personally delivered your note to Mrs. Hampshire, and he wanted me to tell you that she was grateful for it."

Anna nodded. If something bad happened to Peter, she would never tell the woman.

"Ben also said he should be delivering two more packages here tomorrow night," she explained. "And our new signal is a large pot of flowers by the front door instead of a quilt."

The bell rang upstairs, and Anna caught her breath at the sound, worried that Simon or another one of the slave hunters could have found Peter's tracks after all. Even if he had, he could search all he wanted tonight. There was nothing for him to find.

She asked Charlotte to tend to the fire and walked up the stairs by herself. Out the front window she saw a boy about nine or ten waiting at her door, but she'd learned not to trust anyone no matter how small.

She slowly opened the door.

"Are you Miss Brent?" the boy asked.

She nodded.

He dug in his pocket and pulled out an ivory envelope. "Doctor and Mrs. Cooley sent you a letter."

"Indeed," she said as she opened it. It was a formal invitation from Esther inviting her and her father to dinner tomorrow night.

She clutched the letter in her hands. Maybe God had sent an answer for Peter after all.

Chapter Twenty-five

....

Anna heard Matthew's voice that evening before she saw him.

"Good evening, Edwin," he greeted her father at the front door. "Is Anna home?"

"Why, Matthew! Please come in."

When Anna stepped out of the parlor, Matthew's smile made her nervous. He had come for a purpose, and she didn't think she wanted to know what it was. She motioned to take his hat, but he kept it in his hands. "Something smells wonderful," he said.

"Charlotte's stewing oyster sauce for the veal."

Matthew licked the side of his lips. "Are you expecting company?"

"We were hoping that some company might come right along," Edwin told him, though he didn't expound upon whom they were expecting later that night.

He looked at her instead of her father. "Is that an invitation?"

"We'd love to have you join us," she said and held out her hand again to take his coat and hat. He didn't give either of them to her.

"I'd like to speak with you first, Anna, if I may."

"Okay." She removed her shawl from a peg and wrapped it around her shoulders so they could talk outside. If their guests should arrive in the next hour, they wouldn't approach the house with two strangers conversing on the front porch.

Edwin opened the door for him and knelt to pull the jar filled with flowers back into the entryway. Matthew didn't seem to notice Edwin move the flowers or shut the door. Instead he sat down on the porch swing and patted the seat. Anna joined his side.

She didn't feel nervous beside Matthew, not like she felt when she was near Daniel. Matthew was comfortable, and she always thought she would want "comfortable" in a husband. Yet there was something missing between her and Matthew, and she'd known it for a long time.

He removed his hat and put it in his lap. "I need an answer, Anna."

"To what?" she asked. She didn't want to sound coy, but she'd already given him an answer to his question about marriage. Twice.

"I need to know if it's more important for you to risk being disowned or more important for you to marry me."

"I can't be disowned, Matthew."

"Yes, you can." The charm he'd displayed at the wedding reception had been replaced with irritation. "God doesn't care where you attend church."

She gazed up at the sun slowly passing over the sky. She was certain that God would still love her no matter where she attended Meeting, but in her heart, she was a Quaker. She desired to listen to the Spirit daily and resist the temptation to stray from His Light. No one, especially Matthew Nelson, would force her to change her mind.

He faced her. "You don't want to marry me, do you?"

She glanced down at her hands and then looked into his eyes. "I'm sorry, Matthew."

He stopped rocking the swing, but he didn't face her. "I thought I could either convert or convince you to leave behind Quakerism and be happy as my wife, but all along you've been hiding behind your religion because you didn't want to marry me."

She stiffened. "I haven't been hiding."

"I've been up-front with you for the past year about my intentions, Anna, but you haven't been honest about yours."

"Both times you've asked, I told you I couldn't marry you."

"Because you're a Quaker."

"Because I'm a Quaker...." She swallowed hard. She hated hurting a friend like Matthew. It went against her very being as a woman who loved God and was called to show His love to other people.

But no matter how much she cared about Matthew, she still couldn't marry him. In her attempt to minimize his pain, she was hurting Matthew even more.

"I can't marry you because I love you like a brother, Matthew, not a husband."

When she turned her head toward his in the fading sunlight, the fury that filled his face devastated and frightened her. He didn't speak, but she didn't need words to know that he was livid.

She looked away quickly toward the far end of the porch. She was the one to blame for his anger. From the beginning, she should have told him that she could never marry him, but a small part of her had once hoped that maybe Matthew would be convinced in the ways of Quakerism and that spark of love Rachel so clearly had for her husband would one day burn inside her own heart as well.

"I'm sorry," she whispered. "I haven't been fair to you."

His silence was even more poignant than his words.

The stillness was broken abruptly by a shuffling noise behind them. She jumped but forced herself to stay facing forward, hoping Matthew hadn't heard the sound in the bushes.

Light footsteps ran away from them, toward the back of the house.

Matthew stood quickly and marched to the side of the porch. He listened, and she prayed that no one would move again. Or speak out. She thought about how Marie had hid in her trees until her baby cried, almost three weeks ago.

Please don't let it be a child.

"It must be an animal," Anna said.

His eyes narrowed. "Probably a wolf again."

Did Matthew know who was in the bushes? The thought scared her. "I hope not."

He took a quick step toward her and lowered his voice. "A group of runaway slaves were spotted near Silver Creek recently."

Her eyes widened. "Really?"

"One of them hurt a white woman just south of here." He looked back toward the yard and scanned it as he spoke. "She still hasn't recovered."

"That's horrible." She shivered, wondering if his words were true. She'd yet to feel threatened by a runaway, though she'd heard a few stories about people who had been hurt. Those rumors, she figured, were propelled by the same people trying to frighten those who helped slaves.

"They haven't caught them yet, but the sheriff is closing in," he said. "You've got to be careful."

"I will."

He shoved his hat back on his head. "I'll look around a little before I leave."

She stood up and motioned him toward the door. "Would you like to eat dinner first?"

He shook his head. "I'm not hungry anymore."

* * * * *

Brown. Gray. Green.

Anna unhooked the moss-colored dress, stared at it, and then hung it back on the peg. It was ridiculous, really. She rarely thought about the color of her clothes. All she had were four choices to wear, and she wouldn't wear the copper-colored dress because that was her finest attire. She didn't want to appear as if she were dressing up tonight in case Esther's brother was joining them for dinner. But she wanted to look nice.

She collapsed back on her bed. She was hopeless.

After their discussion at the hotel, Daniel wouldn't be interested in her no matter what color she wore. And it was good that he was angry with her. If he felt the same spark she did when she was near him, he may want to court her, and that would be a disaster. The entire Meeting, if not the whole town, would wonder why an outspoken abolitionist was courting Edwin Brent's daughter.

Anna finally selected the brown dress even though she'd been told by a few worldly friends that the green looked better on her. Vanity was a sin, and she refused to succumb to it in the hopes of attracting a man like Daniel.

She shook her head. She had to stop wondering if Daniel Stanton had some sort of interest in her. He didn't. Wouldn't. He was focused on his work, and she should be focused on hers.

She finished dressing quickly and rushed downstairs to the kitchen to help Charlotte. Two runaways had arrived last night after Matthew left, a teenaged boy and his nine-year-old brother. The older boy hadn't talked much since he'd walked through the door, and his brother hadn't spoken at all, though the pain in his brown eyes was heartbreaking. She didn't want to imagine what those young eyes had seen.

Charlotte scooped another serving of chicken stew into their bowls, and Anna sliced more bread for them. The older boy muttered a thank-you when she put the bread on his plate, but the younger one didn't acknowledge her.

Last night, Anna had told Charlotte and her father that she thought Matthew suspected them, but the realization made them even more afraid to move these brothers. If Matthew had alerted a hunter, it would mean that someone was watching the house. And they were all hoping that whoever was watching would follow Anna and her father into town tonight when they went to dinner.

"Are you sure you don't want me to stay?" Anna asked Charlotte, hoping the woman would insist she needed Anna at home.

"You and your father never go visiting anymore."

"That's because..." Anna glanced at the two boys cramming stew and bread into their mouths like it was their last meal. She pulled Charlotte to the side of the room. "What if someone comes looking?"

"They won't find them."

"But you'll be by yourself."

"I've faced a lot worse, Anna."

Anna nodded. Charlotte didn't like to talk about her days in slavery, but even when she hinted at them, Anna cringed.

She ran her hands across the brick wall. She may want to stay home tonight, but she couldn't do it. She hadn't told Charlotte or her father, but she was hoping to talk Joseph into visiting Peter...or at least into giving her advice on how to help him heal. Joseph was a kindhearted man. How could he resist caring for a child who might die without medical assistance, even if his mother had been a slave? Anna had sought the Light, and she was certain Joseph was the one to help Peter. It was just a matter of trying to convince him without Esther or anyone else hearing.

"I'll take them up to the attic right after you leave," Charlotte said.

Edwin opened the door at the top of the steps. "The buggy's ready for us."

"I'll be there in a moment."

"There's no reason for you to be afraid for us." When her father walked away, Charlotte leaned in to whisper in her ear. "Or be afraid of Esther's brother."

Chapter Twenty-six

....

Greta answered Edwin and Anna's knock, and when the Brents stepped into the Cooleys' home, the hallway glowed from the lights of a candelabrum. Esther didn't wait for them to be formally announced by her housemaid. Bobbling into the hall, she took one of Anna's hands and squeezed it. "I'm so glad you came."

"Me, too," Anna replied.

Esther glanced down at the papers in Anna's hand. "Are those your poems?"

"A few of them."

Esther took the papers from her. "I will read every one."

"Please wait until after I leave...."

Esther placed them on the cherry sideboard and declared, "I like you, Anna Brent."

She glanced toward the silent parlor, and her disappointment surprised her. She couldn't blame Daniel for avoiding her, but she thought Esther might convince him to come to dinner. Or maybe Esther hadn't bothered to invite him, afraid he would disrupt their dinner with discussion about slavery.

Joseph stomped into the hallway from a back room and took off his coat.

"You barely made it," Esther said.

He hung his coat before he shook Edwin's hand and then Anna's. "I'm sorry I'm late. Last-minute house call."

"There's no reason to apologize," Edwin said. "Many things are more important than dinner guests."

"Not so many." Esther sniffed before she took Edwin's arm and escorted him toward the parlor. "I wanted to talk to you about making a special blanket for my baby."

Joseph directed her toward the dining room, but before they entered the room, he stopped and turned toward her. "Have you been well, Anna?"

She paused. "Very well."

"Glad to hear it," he replied. "The season for pneumonia and croup is upon us."

She paused, grateful for the open door. "Have you had many patients with croup?"

"A dozen or so this season. A baby just north of here died of it last week."

She rubbed her arms to stop her sudden shiver. If Peter died, she would be responsible.

"How exactly do you cure croup?" she asked, trying not to sound as desperate as she felt.

"Keeping the patient in warm water helps, along with garlic wraps around the throat, but lobelia is the only thing that will stop a bad case of it."

Finally, an answer. "Where do you get lobelia?"

"Most physicians have it, though I've just run out of mine since I've been treating so many children. Should have more by the first of the week."

Anna's heart sank. She didn't know if Peter could wait that long.

A slight movement in the dining room distracted her, and Anna glanced over Joseph's shoulder. There was Daniel Stanton at the table, turning the page of the latest *Independent Weekly*. She caught her breath.

Daniel looked up at her, his eyes wary. "You thinking about going into medicine?"

Joseph laughed and ushered her into the room. "You've met my fine brother-in-law, haven't you?"

A muscle twitched in her face. "I have."

Joseph gave her a quick wink. "You'll have to excuse his bad manners. He worked all night finishing his paper, so we're pretending that his exhaustion is the reason he's in a foul mood."

"I'll just ignore him."

"Very good."

An uncomfortable silence settled over the room as she and Joseph waited for him to respond, but instead of talking, Daniel focused again on the paper in his hands. Remembering Charlotte's words, she refused to be afraid of this man.

"What are you reading?" she asked.

"A columnist by the name of Adam Frye." His eyes didn't leave the type. "You've probably never heard of him."

Her shoulders stiffened. "I do know how to read."

"This article is about a slave girl trying to get her child away from a master who wants to kill him."

"Now, Daniel," Joseph said. "You don't insult a lady just because she doesn't agree with you on social issues."

"She doesn't agree with me. You don't agree with me." He lifted his hands in frustration. "No one seems to comprehend that slavery isn't an economic or social issue. It's a moral one."

Anna raised one eyebrow. She was very familiar with those words. "That's a bold statement."

"Those are words of Adam Frye's." He finally closed the paper and thumped his hand on it. "He's a writer with a soul."

Joseph pulled back a seat for Anna, and she sat down beside Daniel. "Only God can see into a man or woman's soul."

"When God looks deep into your soul, Anna Brent, what does He see?"

She sat up straight and glanced around for Joseph, but he had slipped out of the room.

No one had asked her about her soul before, and it didn't seem right to have that type of discussion with a man she hardly knew. A man she wanted to be honest with but couldn't risk divulging her heart to.

He was watching her closely, waiting for a response. How was she supposed to answer that question?

"God doesn't have to search my soul," she replied quietly. "I hide nothing from Him."

He leaned back in his chair and continued to watch her as if he might be able to read what she was thinking. "You were there when I debated Milton Kent at the courthouse."

"I was."

"Were you there when Enoch Gardner was questioned about whether he wanted to be a slave?"

She nodded slowly. "I heard him."

"Why do you think he lied when I asked him if he wanted to get out of slavery?"

"What else could he say, Daniel?" His name slipped off her tongue. "You backed him into a corner."

"So you condone lying?"

She cocked her head. "You like to ask a lot of questions, but I don't think you are so fond of giving answers."

His mouth dropped, and then he clamped it shut. She counted to twenty before he opened it again. "No one listens to my answers."

"That doesn't mean you should stop giving them."

He smiled slightly. "Are you avoiding my question, Anna Brent?"

Esther and her father entered the room, Esther explaining how she wanted lavender and pink flowers on the blanket like daffodils blooming in the sun.

Daniel leaned so close to her that she could feel the heat from his skin. How was she supposed to continue this ruse when he wouldn't leave her alone?

"Should we continue this discussion later?" he whispered.

She scooted away from him. "I don't think so."

* * * * *

For the next hour, Anna and Edwin indulged in roasted turkey and cherry toast while tiptoeing around the topic of slavery with their hosts. The only time it was mentioned was when Anna asked about Simon and Daniel said the man was still hunting for Marie's child. Joseph joked that a five-hundred-dollar reward would buy him the buggy and new horses he'd been eyeing, but not even Esther laughed.

Whether or not it was meant to be a joke, Anna knew the moment he mentioned the reward that she couldn't ask him about tending to Peter.

When the night finished, Anna tied her cape and reached for her poems on the sideboard. If she had known that Daniel was an avid reader of the *Independent Weekly*, she never would have brought them.

Esther smacked her hand away from the papers before she even touched them. "Those are for me to read later."

She tried to smile. "I don't think they're ready for public reading after all."

"Don't be silly." Esther laughed. "I know I'll love them."

Esther's laugh froze on her lips and then faded so fast that the men stopped and looked at her. Joseph reached for her arm. "Are you all right?"

She nodded, though she didn't speak for a moment. When she finally talked again, she told them she was fine.

Joseph pointed her toward the parlor. "You need to rest, Esther."

Before she stepped toward the door, she reached for Anna's papers. "Please let me read them."

Anna looked back at Daniel by the steps, but he was watching his sister. It wasn't like he would look at them anyway. He only read writers who had a soul.

* * * * *

As she climbed up into the buggy, Anna scolded herself. She had kept her word. She had brought her poems to Esther. But she never should have left them with her.

Even if Esther didn't read the abolitionist papers, Daniel did. And some of her writings in the *Independent* stemmed from her poetry.

He will never read them, Anna told herself over and over as Samara trotted toward their home. And even if for some odd reason he decided to read her prose, he would never equate her with his esteemed Adam Frye.

A small part of her relished the fact that he read her work—and liked it. She wished she could tell him the truth, but the only person she needed to concern herself with pleasing was God. It didn't matter what men, including a man like Daniel Stanton, thought of her.

Her father interrupted her thoughts. "You're just like your mother."

She smiled in the darkness. There was no one else she'd rather be like than the woman she had adored. She wanted nothing more than to carry on her legacy. "You mean I'm handsome and headstrong?"

Edwin chuckled, and it was nice to hear her father laugh. It was a rarity these days to even see him smile. "I mean you'd give up your very life to care for other people just like she used to do."

Ahead of them was the covered bridge, and Samara's hooves clicked over the wooden planks when they entered. She glanced out the windows of the bridge, but it was too dark to see the water below. "So would you, Father. That's what God has called us both to do."

"Yes, He has," he said. "And I'm an honored man to have a daughter who serves Him."

Whatever else he had to say, he was taking his time. "But...?" she prodded him.

He sighed. "As a father, He has also called me to protect and care for you."

She reached for his arm. "You've spent your entire life caring for me."

He hesitated as they exited the bridge with a bump. The branches beside the buggy danced in the wind, and she pulled the woolen blanket closer to her.

"I loved your mother the first time I saw her in Meeting."

She liked remembering her mother's gentle words and strong heart, but her father rarely talked about her. Why did he suddenly feel compelled to speak about her now?

"She never seemed to question God's purpose for her life. She never even questioned Him when it was time for her to leave this life behind." She could feel the hurt in his tone. Surely he had questioned why God took his wife home so early, but he had never shared his doubts about God's will with her.

"She loved you as much as you loved her."

He nodded slowly. "She would want me to protect you, Anna."

"You do care for me, Father. Very much."

The wind sprayed water off the creek beside them, and it sprinkled over their legs. "Lydia would want you to marry a Quaker man who would care for you, as well."

"Father—"

He turned the buggy away from the water and up the path toward their home. "Daniel Stanton is fond of you, you know."

"No, I don't...."

"I like him, Anna. He would take care of you long after I'm gone."

She faced her father. "You aren't going anywhere."

And if he did, she could care for herself.

"You pretend to ignore him." He laughed. "He pretends to ignore you."

"He's not interested in me."

"You can try to scare him off all you want, but he doesn't seem like the kind of man who frightens easily."

Anna heard the neighing of a horse ahead. "Father?"

The path up to their house was too treacherous for Samara to run, but her father stopped talking about Daniel and pushed the mare as fast as she could move. When they crested the hill, Anna jumped out of the buggy.

A horse was tied to the hitching post by the porch with chains dangling over its flanks. Their front door was wide open and swinging in the breeze.

Chapter Twenty-seven
....

"Charlotte!" Anna yelled as she ran through the front door. Two chairs in the parlor lay toppled, and glass shards covered the floor. Her father grabbed her arm and put his finger over his lips, his eyes showing the fear that must be in her eyes as well. He quickly picked up an overturned chair in the parlor and retrieved the flintlock above the fireplace.

Moving in front of her, with the gun in his hands, he whispered, "We're going to move slowly."

She nodded with confidence, but her arms trembled as they crept up the staircase.

They found Charlotte in the back bedchamber, Simon the slave hunter behind her. He was holding a knife to her back, and Charlotte's eyes grew even wider when she saw them, seemingly more frightened than grateful that they'd arrived home.

Simon snorted when he saw the gun in Edwin's hands. "You're a Quaker," he said like it was a curse.

Edwin lifted the gun. "Let her go."

The man's laugh sounded nervous this time. "You ain't gonna shoot me, 'specially not over some colored woman."

When Edwin cocked the gun, Simon shoved Charlotte, and she collapsed on the floor. "I coulda got a pretty penny for her down in Louisville, but she ain't the one I come for anyway."

Anna reached for Charlotte's arm and helped her friend stand.

Edwin lowered the gun a few inches. "You need a warrant to be in our house."

"Funny thing about that." He reached into his pocket and pulled out a paper. "The judge issued me one this mornin'. I've got just as much a right to be here as you do."

Anna glanced at the paper before throwing it on the floor. The law was on his side. "What are you looking for?"

"A slave baby, Miss Brent. Worth five hundred bucks if I get him back to Tennessee alive. Two-fifty if he's dead."

Maybe God, in His mercy, would let Peter slip away to heaven tonight. Being with his mama would be much better than being in the hands of this man. Or in the hands of Noah Owens's wife.

Simon stomped on the floor behind them. Shoved furniture. Kicked at the walls. The two young brothers were hiding right above them, hearing it all.

"Where's the attic?" the man demanded. Edwin escorted him out of the room.

"I'd already put the dishes away when he arrived," Charlotte whispered.

"Are you okay?"

"Better than they are."

"It used to be safe for you in Indiana."

Charlotte lowered her head. "The free states aren't so free anymore."

Anna heard something crash into the ceiling above her, and she rushed toward the attic stairs. By the lantern light, she watched Simon hack through the wooden planks on the floor, searching for slaves hiding underneath the boards. Her father stood to the side of the room, his hands still on the gun. She didn't know what he would do if Simon found the two runaways behind the wall.

A barrel of flour tipped and shot white powder across Simon's dark face and clothes. He swore but didn't stop. He chopped down the dry sprigs of rosemary and basil hanging from the ceiling and aimed toward the wall on his right side. The one without windows.

He heaved the ax over his shoulder and swore again when it hit the brick. He glared at her father. "I can smell 'em up here."

Edwin sniffed the air. "The only thing I smell are onions and garlic."

The man leaped toward him, the ax clenched in both his hands, but her father didn't flinch. "I know you're hiding slaves," Simon growled.

"There are no slaves in my house," Edwin said, and even in the midst of her fear, Anna smiled. Her father hadn't lied. In his mind, every person under his roof was free.

The man spat in his face. "I've got it from a good source that you stole a couple of 'em."

Edwin calmly wiped off his face with his sleeve. "I hope you didn't pay someone for this information."

The man shoved the ax handle back down into the leather carrier on his waist. "I ain't leavin' your county till I find the baby."

A trail of flour shadowed Simon as he stamped down the stairs and out the front door.

Even when he hopped on his horse and turned south, Anna knew he hadn't gone far. It would take weeks for them to clean up and repair his damage, but they could start later. Right now, they had to decide what to do about the boys.

Edwin turned toward her and bolted the door, his face grim. "We have to move them tonight."

Anna nodded. "I'll help get the wagon ready."

Charlotte stepped into the hallway. "And I'll get our guests."

Edwin lowered his voice. "Tell Ben it's not safe for him to bring runaways right now."

"We're supposed to have two more arriving tomorrow," Charlotte said.

Edwin paused. "We can hide them in the mill."

Anna faced him. "But all the workers?"

"We'll take them there at night, after almost everyone is gone." He took his hat off the peg and put it on his head. "I'll hide them in the basement."

"The hunters will find them there," Anna insisted—but when they asked her for a better idea, she didn't have one. The mill, she finally agreed, was safer than their house. For now.

* * * * *

Someone pounded on Daniel's door before the sun rose. He groaned and pulled his pillow over his head, thinking a drunk from the tavern must be searching for a place to sleep. But the knock grew more and more persistent.

"I'm coming!" Daniel shouted as he rolled out of bed and struggled to pull on his pants and button his shirt in the darkness. He no longer drank alcohol, but he felt like he'd drunk a bottle of whiskey last night. Stumbling toward the door, he tripped over one of the many stacks of newspapers and scattered them across the small room.

Someone knocked again, and when he opened the door, the haggard face of his brother-in-law looked back at him. Daniel's own exhaustion vanished. His mind cleared.

"What is it?" he demanded.

"Esther's having cramps."

"Labor?"

Joseph shook his head. "Not yet, but I've told her she has to stay in bed until the baby is born."

"For two months!"

"That's exactly how Esther said it."

Daniel buttoned the top of his shirt. "I bet she wasn't too happy to hear that from you."

"She thinks I'm being unreasonable, but I want this baby in our family as much as she does."

Joseph may be making demands of his wife that he wouldn't of his other patients, but Daniel understood. "I know you do."

"I have an urgent call to make this morning." He clasped his hands together and begged. "Could you come sit with her while I'm gone?"

"I can't promise to make her stay in bed."

"She'll stay there," Joseph replied. "I told her that if she kept moving around at this pace, she might lose the child."

"Is that true?"

When Joseph nodded, Daniel reached for his jacket. "I'll come right away."

* * * * *

Esther had propped herself up on the lace-swathed pillows and bedding. She was awake and staring out the window when Daniel sat down in the chair beside her. Slowly she turned her head toward him.

"He said I'd have to stay here until the baby is born."

"I heard."

"I'm going to go crazy."

"Joseph and Greta and I will take turns entertaining you," he said. "That baby will be here before you know it, and I bet she'll be as fiery as you were as a newborn."

Her lips turned down. "I wasn't fiery."

Daniel smiled at the memories of the newborn girl who'd arrived into their family the year he'd started first grade. He used to hold his hands over his ears to block out her cries while he attempted to sound out the words in his primer. When she turned four, he began reading to her, though she resisted learning to read herself. She always said she'd rather play with her dolls.

"You never enter or leave a room unnoticed, Essie."

She pouted. "Are you saying I'm insufferable?"

He couldn't help but laugh. "You've been full of life from the day you were born, and that's why it's nearly impossible for you to stay still."

"For eight weeks," she sighed.

"And in eight weeks, you will be holding your own fiery newborn in your arms."

The thought made her smile.

"Will you read to me?" she asked.

The last thing he wanted to do was pick up a copy of *Godey's Lady's Book*, but he had promised to care for her. He took a magazine from the top of her nightstand and opened it to an article about furnishing a fashionable home. The two women in the story were shopping to decorate their new homes, and he read about rosewood sofas and papier-mâché tables and damask satin chairs of crimson and black. Once the women had indulged themselves with expensive new furnishings, they visited a crowded shop called Miss Waters's to search for new hats.

Daniel glanced up at his sister.

"Go on," she urged him, like she couldn't wait to discover what type of hats the girls would choose.

Daniel forced out the words. "Marsha picked out a white hat, and Abigail exclaimed, 'What? That plain Quaker-like affair? Oh, do have some yellow flowers, at least.' "

When he choked, Esther giggled. "You can't stand it, can you?"

He slammed the magazine pages together. "There has got to be something else around here that we can read."

She pulled a blanket around her shoulders. "You can read me Anna's poems."

His groan was louder than he'd expected. He didn't want to think about Anna Brent today, and he certainly didn't want to read any of her writing. He stood up. "Why don't I get a book from Joseph's library?"

She shook her head. "Just the poems."

"I'm not very interested in poetry."

"Well, I am," she said as she shooed him away with her hand.

He found the papers on top of the piano in the parlor. Picking them up, he eyed the smooth strokes of Anna's handwriting and wondered what she would write about. The joys of slavery? The benefits of the institution? He would read them for Esther, though he wasn't particularly interested in her work…only a bit curious was all.

When he returned to Esther's room, he sat down beside the bed with Anna's poems in hand. At least he didn't have to read about damask chairs or white bonnets anymore.

Her first poem was descriptive verse about falling leaves that shimmered to her toes. She reveled in autumn's light and described nature wrapping itself into a cocoon for winter days until the rebirth of its beauty in spring.

As he read her words, Daniel felt oddly disappointed. She was a good writer, but he'd expected more passion in her content. Deeper subject matter than the seasons.

Esther didn't share his sentiments. When he was finished, she sighed with delight. "That was beautiful."

He dropped the paper onto the nightstand. "I suppose it was."

She turned toward him. "Why don't you like Anna?"

He slapped the remaining pages against his hand. "It's not that I don't like her. I just don't agree with her views on slavery."

"You disagree with me, too, but you manage to be cordial."

How could he explain to his sister that it was complicated?

She would only say that he was the one making things difficult. He couldn't allow himself to become interested in a woman like Anna Brent. Couldn't keep his mind from wondering if there might be something more.

"You're my sister," he said dryly. "I have to be nice to you."

She rolled her eyes. "What's her next poem?"

He lifted the next piece and scanned it. "It's about contentment."

Esther leaned back against the pillows, and Daniel dove into the words. " 'Above all things my longing heart strives to be content. Though bitterness looms in darkness. Though trials glean torment.' "

He read on, but his mind was still on the first stanza. Where had he heard those words before? Maybe he'd read something similar in the stack of materials that Isaac hauled in each week and plopped beside his desk.

" 'Many suffer so much more than I, souls begging me to pray,' " he read. " ' "Help me," they cry out in pain, but I look the other way.

" 'How can I listen to their cries and still ignore their pleas? My heart will never find contentment until those prisoners are set free.' "

He looked up at his sister, and her eyes were closed, pondering Anna's words. "That's what I want," she whispered. "To be content."

He stared at the last stanza. "By helping other people?"

She glanced sideways. "Of course I want to help people."

They were poignant words, even he would agree, and much more thoughtful than her poem about the fallen leaves. But how could Esther and Anna talk about helping people when they ignored those who passed through Liberty? Those who needed help the most?

Church bells rang out on the street, and he waited for them to stop before he picked up another poem. They chimed seven times. Eight times. Nine times.

And they didn't stop.

Hurrying to the window, he looked down and saw a crowd of men running toward Main Street with buckets in their hands.

He pushed the window open and shouted down. "What is it?"

One of them looked up and shouted back at him. "The newspaper office is on fire!"

Chapter Twenty-eight

Daniel collapsed on the stoop of the blacksmith shop, exhausted. His clothes were coated with soot and soaked from the buckets of water he'd passed along on the brigade. Smoke hovered in the street, clinging to the buildings and crowds of people who'd come to gawk at the burned remains of his office. No one said anything to him. Either they didn't recognize him or they were ignoring him.

He, along with dozens of Liberty's mill workers and farmers and businessmen, had dumped hundreds—perhaps thousands—of buckets of water on the blaze, trying to save the printing press and his tools inside, but everything was ruined. All the wood and paper had gone up in flames.

The fire had been no accident. Someone had come and destroyed the press before dousing the room with oil. What hadn't been chopped or pried apart had melted or was warped beyond use.

He'd known that the article about Noah Owens terrorizing Liberty's citizens would anger Milton Kent and his pals, but he'd never guessed they would resort to arson. He leaned his head against a post and stared at the charred skeleton of wood and nails across the street.

The same people who had stolen away the innate freedom from those in slavery had also stolen away his freedom to speak out against it. They'd stripped him and Isaac of their press and everything they needed to publish a newspaper.

Whoever had set the blaze must have known that Isaac was in Cincinnati for the week. Maybe they even knew Daniel was over at Esther and Joseph's house that morning.

He took off his hat and raked his streaked hands through his hair. All he had wanted to do was tell the truth. He'd only wanted to help those who weren't being heard.

He kicked a tin pail in front of him, and it rolled into the street. He'd worked so hard these past two months, and now all his work was for naught. He'd spoken the plain truth as loud as he could, but no one wanted to listen.

"Action is a thousand times more powerful than words."

Daniel blinked as he watched the people crossing in front of him.

"Christ used more than words to demonstrate His love for people. He died for them. There is no greater demonstration of love than to sacrifice your life for another."

Daniel thought about the stacks of newspapers in his room and wondered where he had read those words.

He sat up straight on the edge of the porch when he finally remembered. It was in the same place he'd read Adam Frye's column on contentment.

* * * * *

Anna poured Charlotte a mug of hot coffee and handed it to her. The shock from Simon's appearance last night clung to Anna like smoke that wouldn't wash away. She knew that aiding slaves was a dangerous job, but she'd never wanted a slave hunter to threaten her dear friend.

She lifted the fireplace poker off a nail above the hearth and stirred the blaze in front of her.

What would happen if Simon did catch Charlotte while she was going to town? Free papers didn't matter to a man like him. Even if she carried the papers with her, he could burn them and whisk her away before Anna even realized she was gone.

Then he might do what he threatened and sell her on an auction block in Kentucky.

"What's wrong?" Charlotte asked.

"Joseph said Peter needs lobelia, but I don't know where to get some."

Charlotte reached into her pocket and pulled out a vial filled with a deep wine-colored liquid and passed it along to her.

"How—?"

"Best not to ask."

Anna clutched the vial. "Do you know how much he's supposed to take?"

"Five drops every half hour until his fever breaks."

She prayed it would work.

Charlotte took the medication from her hand and stuffed it back into her pocket. "The Palmers have neighbors whose son disappeared a few nights ago. They think a hunter might have kidnapped him."

She stirred the fire. "His poor parents."

"They're worried, Anna," Charlotte said. "I'm not sure how much longer they'll be able to care for Peter."

She almost dropped the fire stick. "Why not?"

"They're thinking about going to Canada."

"But they're already free!" she insisted.

Charlotte's head hung. "They're free, but they're scared."

Anna hung the poker back on the nail. Charlotte had been purchased and freed a decade ago, but she was beginning to think that Indiana was no longer a safe place for her friend, either.

* * * * *

Daniel shuffled through the stacks of newspapers on the floor of his room. When he found an *Independently Weekly*, he opened it and scanned Adam Frye's column quickly until he found the words he was searching for.

"How can we listen to the cries of these slaves without acting? How can we ignore their pleas? The only way for each of us to find contentment is to set those prisoners free."

Either Anna Brent had been lifting words from Adam Frye's column or...

Or what? he pondered. Anna didn't talk like the type of person who would be reading a column by an abolitionist, but her pro-slavery rhetoric had been so harsh that they almost hadn't seemed like her words, either.

He flipped through the pages until he found another column by Adam Frye, this one written days before Congress passed the Fugitive Slave Act.

"Neither fear nor intimidation will force me to flee this fight. Some of us must be silent as we battle. Others must speak out. But none of us will stop fighting until the war is won."

He tossed the paper onto his bed and tore off his shirt. The acrid smell of smoke permeated his clothes and his skin, but he'd take a full bath later. Instead he scrubbed his hair and face and arms in the basin on his chest of drawers.

Eyeing the trunk at the end of the bed, he felt the sudden desire to pack it up and run back to Cincinnati. He could rent an office. Hang up a sign saying he'd returned to lawyering. Plenty of people in Cincinnati liked to sue each other. He would have more than enough work.

He buttoned up a clean shirt. No matter what he desired at that moment, he wouldn't return to the city. Adam Frye was right. No matter what happened, God had called him to fight. A burned building would not force him to stop.

He picked up the latest *Independent,* the one he'd started to read before dinner last night, before Anna Brent had interrupted him.

Adam Frye's column was about a slave girl named Tessa and her baby that had stayed at the Fryes' home. Adam described the traumatic life of the young girl, who had been abused by her master and forced to run away before her baby was even born. He portrayed the trials of the runaway slave, not only birthing a child in secret but confronting the anger of other runaways as she attempted to keep her baby quiet on their journey north.

At the end of the column, Adam wrote that the story was true but the names of Tessa and her child had been changed to protect their identities.

He dropped the paper, and it fluttered to the floor.

Adam Frye's story wasn't about some unknown slave named Tessa. His story was about Marie and her baby.

Daniel reached for his clean coat by the door. No wonder Adam Frye wrote with so much emotion and description.

The writer of the "Liberty Line" was a woman, and Daniel knew exactly where to find her.

Chapter Twenty-nine
....

A lantern swung gently in front of Anna and spilled shadows across the bank of Silver Creek. Clutched to her chest was a bouquet of brightly colored irises and chrysanthemum, and she inhaled their sweet aromas as she hiked past the loud hum of Father's woolen mill and into the refuge of the trees.

About a quarter of a mile past the mill, she stopped at a brick wall that encircled fourteen graves. There was no fence or iron gate like the cemetery by the meetinghouse, but it was a peaceful place. When her mother died, she and her father had decided to bury her here so they could visit her grave in private instead of having to look out at her stone whenever they went to Meeting, remembering that she was gone.

Her light flickered across the small stones and wooden markers until she stopped at Lydia Brent's grave in the second row. She placed the flowers on the grave and then, with the edge of her skirt, she brushed away the three crosses that had been drawn into the loose dirt in front of the headstone. She kissed her fingers and touched the cold marker before she crept away.

In a tone so subdued that only the creatures nearby could hear, she began to hum her mother's favorite song. The tune to "Amazing Grace" traveled softly on the breeze, and by the time she reached the second verse, someone had joined her side.

Anna didn't look up until she'd finished the stanza, and when she did, she saw a dark-skinned man towering above her. She stood up quickly, afraid for the first time since she'd left the house. Matthew had said that runaways along the creek had hurt other women, but she hadn't believed him. Maybe she should have listened.

She thrust out her foot to run when, behind the giant of a man, a girl emerged. She was about eight years old, and her long hair had been woven into braids. Even with the many stains on her white dress, Anna could tell that her torn clothing had once been quite fancy.

"I'm Reginald." The man's voice was as daunting as his stature. "And this is my daughter, Sarah."

The girl curtsied. "Pleased to meet you."

Anna held out her hand to the girl first and then to the father. "I'm pleased to meet both of you, as well." Anna picked up her lantern. "Who sent you to me?"

"A friend of a friend," Reginald replied.

"Very good." She looked over at the creek rushing by them. "We've had some unsavory characters patrolling the creek as of late."

The man nodded. "Ben told us."

"We'll move quickly, but you should walk thirty paces or so behind me. If you hear horses, there's a cave just south of here where you can hide."

She gave them directions to the cave and explained that she would meet them back here tomorrow night if they were separated.

The girl reached up and took her father's hand like they were going on an evening stroll. "We're ready," she declared.

* * * * *

After locking Reginald and his daughter into a small basement room, Anna secured the side door to the mill and hiked back up the hill toward her house. Her father and several workers were running the loom on the main floor until late, but she never saw them. Reginald and Sarah had food and water and plenty of wool blankets to keep them warm for the night. Her father had assured her that no one would find them before he delivered them to the next station tomorrow night.

She'd wanted to stay with them, to hear the story of where they were from and how they'd found themselves running away, but after learning so much of Marie's story, she realized that the less she knew was probably better for all of them.

Opening the back door, she slipped inside the house and headed down into the kitchen to tell Charlotte that her trip had been a success, but she stopped short on the last step. Sitting at the table was Daniel Stanton, mug in hand, chatting with Charlotte like they had known each other for years.

He stood when he saw her, and she watched as his eyes traveled to her muddy skirt and hands. "I was visiting my mother's grave," she stated simply.

He cocked his head, and she saw dirt smeared on his neck and forehead. "That's what Charlotte said."

Charlotte handed her a mug filled with coffee, and when she did, Anna realized that her teeth were chattering. Had it started while she was outside or after she came in?

She wrapped her fingers around the ceramic cup and let it warm her hands. "Do you always call on people this late?"

"Seems like I was a bit early."

She sipped the coffee, refusing to let him rattle her, as she sat on the bench across from him. "Are you looking for another debate?"

"No." He paused, and she watched the smile on his lips disappear. "I wanted you to know that someone torched the newspaper office today."

Her hands started and coffee splashed out of the mug and onto her fingers. "Milton?"

He reached for a cloth rag by the fireplace and walked toward her. "Possibly, but I doubt we'll ever be able to prove it."

"What's going to happen to the paper?"

He handed her the towel, and she began to wipe up the spilled coffee with it. " 'Neither fear nor intimidation will force me to flee this fight.' "

Her head popped up. "Did you make that up, too?"

He leaned so close to her that she could smell the smoke on his neck. "No, but I know who did."

She backed away from him, searching for Charlotte, but her friend had somehow gone up the staircase unnoticed.

Daniel was clearly mocking her, but why? Isaac and Hannah were the only ones who knew about her column, and they had both said they would keep it a secret. A Quaker's word was more binding than an oath.

For the first time, she noticed a copy of the *Independent Weekly* on the table beside Daniel, opened to her column. He picked up the paper and read aloud the first three paragraphs about Marie.

"Adam Frye writes about honesty and liberty," he said, "but there's a problem."

"What's that?" she murmured.

"Adam Frye isn't an honest man."

She tried to meet his stare but couldn't. The bricks lining the fireplace suddenly caught her attention, and she stared at those instead. "That's a harsh accusation."

"I thought Quakers weren't supposed to lie."

"I believe that Quakers should guard the truth."

As he closed the paper, she could feel his gaze on her face. "The truth is what I'm after."

"What do you want?" she asked. Her voice sounded smaller than she'd hoped. Scared.

"Isaac won't let a fire stop us from printing the *Liberty Era*," he said. "Until we get a new press, we'll send the paper over to a printer in Oxford."

"I'm glad to hear of it."

"I'll be needing to make at least one trip a week to Oxford, which means I'll need someone to help me from here." His hands brushed over the newspaper. "Someone to help me write."

She couldn't help herself. She looked right at him. "What?"

"Write articles. Write stories." His smile unnerved her. "You could write whatever you want as long as you tell the people in our county what's really in your heart."

"I don't know what you're talking about—"

"Under a pseudonym, of course," he interjected. "No one around here would ever know that you run a station on the Underground."

With both hands she slapped the top of the table, and she wished she could reach over and smack the smile off his face, as well. How dare he come into her home and talk about the Underground in such casual terms, like they were discussing the state of the corn crop or the weather! Secrecy was vital to the success of their network. Secrecy saved lives.

She turned her back to him, dumping the rest of her coffee into the fire. "You're crazy!"

The fire hissed back at them. "Are you saying you're not Adam Frye?"

She whirled around and faced him. This time she was no longer scared.

Chapter Thirty

....

Daniel's head was in his hands, his back against the hard cane chair in Joseph and Esther's parlor. For three hours he'd been pacing and praying and wondering what he could do to help his sister. Even though he knew that God's will would be done no matter what happened, he'd still asked God to strengthen Esther during her early labor. And to give health to her little one.

The stillness of the afternoon was punctuated with another scream from the chamber above, and he prayed harder. He'd never heard his sister cry out like this. Not when she broke her arm after falling from a horse, nor when her hem caught on fire at their home in Cincinnati and she'd burned her legs. Today she was in even more pain, and he was helpless.

Joseph and Greta were by her side, delivering the child, and for that he was thankful. But he wished there was more he could do.

Footsteps plodded down the stairs, and he leaped to his feet. Maybe that final scream welcomed their baby into the world.

Joseph's entry into the room wasn't one of a proud new father. Instead his face was stark as his lips struggled to form the word: "Stillborn."

Daniel fell back down into the chair. Esther had longed for a child since she was a child herself. The brutality of it angered him, and he was afraid. This dashing of her heart's desire might plunge her into the darkness from which so few returned.

He wrung his hands together. "Does she know?"

"Not yet." Joseph patted his front pocket, searching for his watch. "I gave her something to make her rest a few hours first."

"Was it a girl?"

The slight nod turned his anger into sadness. When Esther woke up, her heart would break.

"Do you have the time?" Joseph asked.

Daniel glanced up at the clock on the wall. "Four o'clock."

Joseph mumbled something and began to pace in front of the fire.

Daniel sat and watched for a moment, not knowing what to do. Perhaps Joseph needed to take something to help him rest, as well.

Joseph stopped abruptly. "I need you to do something for me."

Daniel stood to his feet, ready to do anything that would help Joseph or his sister. "What do you need?"

"I need you to swear to secrecy."

Daniel didn't hesitate. "Anything you tell me will be kept secret, Joseph."

Joseph walked toward him, and when he stood by Daniel, his voice was so low that Daniel could barely make out the words. "I am supposed to meet a canal boat near Brookville in two hours."

"Why?" Daniel asked.

Joseph began pacing again, and Daniel started to wonder. Was his brother-in-law involved in something illegal? He never would have imagined it, but he had also never seen Joseph so nervous before. Maybe he shouldn't have agreed to keeping the secret.

Joseph stopped. "The Talbourne family boat will travel through the final lock between five and six o'clock." Daniel waited for him to finish. "A mile north of the lock, they will let out four runaway slaves."

Daniel struggled to repeat the words. "Runaway slaves?"

"Hush," Joseph insisted and then asked what time it was again.

* * * * *

Sitting by her bed, Anna unpinned her long hair and brushed through it. They hadn't had any guests in almost a week, but late tonight she was supposed to meet four more runaways at the graveyard. She planned to rest until Charlotte returned from the Palmer home, and then she would leave for the cemetery.

Henry Nelson had received a big order from Cincinnati for blankets, so her father was staying at the mill night and day to work the looms except when he had to take a small shipment north. Her job was to make sure the runaways arrived safely at the mill and had plenty to eat and drink.

A fire burned at the foot of her bed, but the room was still frigid. She tugged her comforter over her and tried to get settled on the pillows. It was tiring, hiking down to the cemetery late at night and then waking a few hours later to begin her chores, but she couldn't complain. Her exhaustion was nothing compared to the brave men and women who walked twenty or thirty miles a day with little sleep and food.

No one had seen Simon Mathers for days, but neither she nor her father were willing to endanger any more runaways by bringing them to their house, not until the fervor over finding Marie's baby had ended. She'd heard that there were more hunters in the area and they'd obtained warrants to search a number of homes. Thankfully, they had yet to visit the Palmers. She closed her eyes, but sleep evaded her. For a week now, every time she tried to sleep, Daniel's handsome face haunted her. Never would she have guessed that he'd read her work and compare it to Adam Frye—at least not until he sat in the Cooleys' dining room and lauded the words of his favorite columnist.

She didn't lie to him last week, but she had tried to assure him that he had the wrong person. He'd have to ask Adam Frye to write for him, not her.

She earnestly hoped he wouldn't expose her secret. She could imagine him writing an article in the *Liberty Era* about Adam Frye living near Liberty, though she didn't think he would intentionally tell people about their station. In the heat of a debate, though, he might spew it out. *Covert* wasn't exactly his style.

Her door creaked open, and Anna sat up in bed. "Charlotte?"

"It's me." Charlotte scooted through the doorway. "I'm sorry to wake you."

In the firelight, Anna could see the bundle in her arms.

Charlotte handed Peter over to her, and Anna quickly took him and looked into his face. His gray skin had been replaced by a milky white, and his cough seemed to be gone. "Did his fever break?"

"Three nights ago."

She pulled him close to her chest. "Thank God."

Anna looked back at Charlotte as two questions pressed against her. Why was Charlotte home so early? And why did she bring Peter back with her?

Neither question needed to be asked. Charlotte sat down in the rocking chair beside her bed and answered them both at once. "The Palmers are moving to Canada."

Anna nodded slowly. She was glad to have Peter back with her. Grateful he was healthy again. She couldn't bear to think about him going to Canada, but Simon or another hunter would find him if he stayed here. She had no choice but to send him along.

"I will miss him."

Charlotte wrung her hands together but didn't say anything.

"When will they take him north?" she asked.

"They aren't taking him, Anna."

She pushed herself up farther on the bed. "What do you mean they're not taking him?"

"They're afraid."

Anna's gaze went back down to the beautiful baby in her arms. She didn't understand. "They don't want him?"

"It's not that." Charlotte stood and warmed her hands by the fire. "They don't know what to expect on their way to Canada or once they get there. What if Peter gets sick again? Or what if they can't find work?

Or what if someone catches them stealing a slave? Their punishment might be death."

"They would do whatever any other parent would do for their child."

Charlotte turned again toward her. "Except he's not their son."

Anna's heart sank.

"They're good people," Charlotte said softly. "This is a tough choice they have to make."

Anna wanted to say they were making the wrong choice, but she couldn't. She could never understand what they faced.

"When are they leaving?" she asked.

"In the morning."

"I'll keep Peter here for now." She hesitated before she spoke again. "Charlotte?"

Her friend turned.

"I think you should go to Canada with them."

"I'm not leaving you, Anna."

"Just until they overturn the Fugitive Slave Act. Then you can come back home."

Charlotte looked down at the baby. "You want me to take him to Canada?"

Anna shook her head. "You'll have to find work, too."

Charlotte reached for the poker and stirred the fire. "I'm not leaving you here with a newborn."

"He's not staying with me, Charlotte." Anna kissed his forehead, confidence swelling within her. "God will find him the perfect home."

Chapter Thirty-one

....

A mule plodded up the towpath, pulling a boat not ten feet in front of Daniel. A boy walked slowly behind the mule, and Daniel waited for him to begin singing "Coming Home"—Daniel's cue—but the boy didn't even hum the popular tune. As hard as it was for him to wait in the thicket, Daniel didn't move.

He'd never had any reason to come down to Brookville to visit the canal, but he'd read that family boats often transported coffee, molasses, and mail from the border of Kentucky up to Hagerstown. Now he was privy to what else some of these families carried up from Kentucky with them.

The boat floated past, but he stayed in place, one knee on the ground.

He still couldn't fathom that his brother-in-law was an agent on the Underground Railroad. All the time he'd known Joseph, even in the months Daniel had lived in Liberty, he had never even guessed that Joseph was sympathetic toward those who decided to run.

Once the shock began to wear off, he started to understand why Joseph frequently left at night or in the early morning hours to make urgent house calls. Some of the visits were probably to attend those who were ill, but how many were to ride down to Brookville to escort runaway slaves?

All the times he'd condemned Joseph for his views, Joseph had never blinked. He had never even tried to defend himself. He'd kept silent and continued his work.

Daniel realized he might never know more about Joseph's work than he did at this moment, but he felt privileged to know even a bit.

Joseph had sworn him to secrecy and then said they would never speak of it again.

On his ride down tonight he had been frustrated, both at Anna and at Joseph, for opposing him in public while helping slaves in private. But he'd come to understand their need for secrecy. He wouldn't tell anyone about either of their work.

He only wished that Anna Brent would tell him the truth. Maybe if he were right about tonight, she wouldn't be able to hide from him anymore. He would know for certain about her.

In the distance, he saw the lantern lights of another canal boat rounding the bend, moving slowly toward him. This time Daniel didn't have to strain his ears. The man on the towpath belted out the lyrics to the parlor song Daniel was expecting, and with every step, the man's singing grew louder.

Daniel's heart raced with excitement. He was about to help the escaping slaves.

When the mule was almost in front of him, Daniel joined in the song. He didn't know the words well, but he'd heard "Coming Home" sung plenty of times before he'd become a Quaker.

His singing was enough for the man to stop his horse.

Quickly Daniel lit a candle. The driver didn't call out to him, but moments later four runaways emerged from the boat. Daniel hummed the lyrics again until they found him in the brush.

He could hardly believe it worked.

The driver clicked his tongue, and the mule lumbered forward again. With his hands, Daniel directed the three middle-aged men and one woman toward his horse. Joseph had told him to move swiftly and only speak when necessary. Right now Daniel felt the profound urge to get away from the canal.

When they got to the horse, Daniel introduced himself to them as Ben.

"The closest safe house is four hours north of here," he said. "We'll follow the river until we get to Silver Creek. You'll find shelter and food with friends there."

He motioned for the woman to climb on the horse, but she resisted, saying she could walk with the men. He refused to ride while she walked, so he waited until she mounted.

Adrenaline pumping, Daniel escorted them up the east fork of the Whitewater. The minutes and then the hours passed slowly as they trudged ahead in the darkness. Joseph had told him not to light a candle unless it was absolutely necessary, so the stars and sounds of the river were their only guides.

Finally they reached the swift-moving creek that dumped into the Whitewater, and Daniel pointed them east. He listened for horses or dogs, but no one interrupted their journey. They traveled past a small settlement of houses and up Silver Creek. When they came to a rope bridge, Daniel stopped and asked one of the men to help the woman dismount.

Joseph had told him to stop at the bridge and give directions for the runaways to journey to the graveyard alone. But he had already decided to deviate from Joseph's instructions.

They were less than a half-mile from Anna Brent's house, and he wanted to wait in the shadows to see who was meeting them. If Anna weren't meeting them, no one but the runaways would even know he was there.

He tied Joseph's horse to a tree and crept forward with the others in the starlight. His legs were cramped from their long trek, but he wouldn't stop now. They passed by the waterwheel at the woolen mill steadily churning through the creek, and then another quarter-mile ahead, he saw the wall of the cemetery. The people around him moved into the shadows of trees and brush, and he slid behind a large rock.

He didn't see anyone arrive at the cemetery, but after about twenty minutes, he heard the soft hum of "Amazing Grace" drift through the forest.

It was Anna.

The runaways moved toward her, but he waited, reconsidering his decision to surprise her like this. Joseph had made it clear that this was the only time he would ask Daniel to direct a group up the line. If he didn't talk to her now, she would forever pretend that she was oblivious to the runaways. And to him.

As she shook the hands of the men and woman, he stepped out of his hiding place, toward her. She turned quickly, but she didn't gasp like he supposed she would. Instead she glared at him.

It was too late to turn back, but it was very clear at that moment that he should have listened to all of Joseph's instructions.

"Please wait here," she told the runaways. Then she grabbed his arm and pulled him to the side.

"What are you doing here?" she asked, though her words sounded more like a growl.

"Joseph asked me to escort the runaways tonight."

Her eyes widened, and then she hissed, "You mean Ben."

He groaned when he saw her surprise—so much for keeping everyone's identity a secret. She didn't even know who was bringing the runaways to her house.

She let go of his arm and shook her finger in his face. "Lesson one—you don't *ever* give away names on the line. And lesson two—the agent is never allowed to have contact with stationmasters unless *absolutely* necessary."

"But how do you know—"

Her voice escalated. "You have got to stop asking questions!"

"I'm not the enemy, Anna."

She glanced over her shoulder as if she had forgotten that hunters were probably searching the forest tonight. "We have to leave here right away."

He stepped back toward the gravestones beside her. "I'm terrible at this, aren't I?"

Her voice softened. "At least you got them here safely."

If Joseph would let him, he'd do it again. And again.

* * * * *

Anna may have told him to leave, but she didn't tell him where to go. The boardinghouse seemed rather lonely after his exhilarating walk north, so instead of going home, Daniel mounted the horse, crossed the creek, and rode up the hill toward Anna's home. He wouldn't jeopardize her or the runaways in her care. Nor was he done talking to her.

She may not have directly lied to him about her work or her writing, but she was running from the truth. Maybe she couldn't tell anyone else what she was doing, but he wanted her to trust him. Even if she wouldn't acknowledge it, Anna understood why he fought so hard with his pen.

A lantern glowed inside the front parlor, but neither Edwin nor Charlotte answered his knock. He sighed as he walked toward the porch swing. Was the whole family avoiding him now? Even if he had to sit here all night, he would wait for Anna to return.

The front door cracked open behind him, and he spun around.

"Come on, Daniel," Charlotte whispered.

He slipped through the door—into the parlor—and saw the reason Charlotte was whispering. A fair-skinned baby lay on the rug, wrapped in a blue-and-black afghan. Daniel watched as the boy's fists batted the gum ring that jutted from his mouth. He watched, and he began to wonder.

"Whose child is this?" he asked, his voice more severe than he meant for it to sound.

Charlotte picked up the baby and motioned toward the hall. "Come have coffee with me."

Daniel followed her, his mind racing to solve a puzzle that held few pieces.

The baby obviously wasn't Charlotte's child, and Anna had told them at dinner that she didn't have any nieces or nephews. Or brothers and sisters.

Marie had been killed, and as far as he knew, they had never found her baby. But this baby's skin was too light to be a colored child.

Did the baby belong to Anna?

He had thought she was avoiding him to cover up the secret of her work on the Underground, but maybe she was hiding something else from him.

Chapter Thirty-two
....

Even after she locked her wards into the mill, Anna couldn't stop trembling. Never had she suspected that Daniel Stanton would show up at the Silver Creek cemetery. There was a reason they had to keep things separated on the line. She only knew that Charlotte communicated with Ben; she wasn't supposed to know who brought the slaves to their home or who communicated with the next station.

Or who gave Charlotte the lobelia for Peter.

Daniel never should have mentioned Joseph. She would act differently around him and Esther now. How could she not?

She brushed the hair off her face and hiked up her skirts to climb the hill.

Did this mean Esther was fronting for her husband? She didn't seem like the type of person who could be entrusted with a vital secret, but there were so many of them who worked undercover. It didn't really matter either way. Anna could never talk to her or Joseph about it. Nor would she would tell anyone about their work.

Daniel, however, kept cornering her, trying to extract her secrets. He demanded that she talk to him, like he had a right to the private details. How could she begin to trust him with the truth? He may have led those four runaways to her tonight, but then he'd offered up Joseph's name in such a loud voice that anyone hiding nearby could have heard.

She pushed a branch out of her face and ducked under it.

Why did he have to push so hard?

When she walked down into the kitchen, Anna wasn't surprised to find him there again, talking with Charlotte. It was like he was trying to hunt her down, and she couldn't understand it. Did it matter if she liked to write or her pseudonym was Adam Frye? She didn't have to tell him a thing.

He spun toward her, his smile wary. "Hi, Anna."

She crossed her arms and glared back at him. "I told you to leave."

He shrugged. "But you didn't tell me where to go."

She marched to the fire and pulled out the coffeepot. He was more than aggravating. He was appalling. It wasn't hard for her to revise her earlier statement. "You need to go home, Daniel."

"And I plan to do that...right after you talk to me."

Anna poured a cup of coffee, but she didn't talk to Daniel. She flung her next question to Charlotte instead. "Why did you let him in?"

"The poor man needed some coffee." Charlotte glanced over at the bassinet sitting a few feet back from the fire, and Anna followed her gaze to see Peter inside, sleeping. "And I thought it would be good to have him on the inside of the house this evening."

Fantastic. Now Daniel knew that secret, too.

Anna shivered and took a sip of the hot coffee. "Are you ready to leave in the morning?"

Charlotte shook her head. "I'm not going to Canada."

"You may not get another chance...."

Charlotte closed her mouth and nodded her head toward Daniel.

"He already knows." Anna sighed loud enough to demonstrate that she didn't approve of his knowledge. "Too much."

"You need me to be able to communicate with...him."

"You can say his name, Charlotte. Daniel even knows about Ben."

Charlotte turned sharply. "How do you—?"

Daniel hung his head. "He needed me to go down to the canal tonight to help some runaways."

Anna didn't bother to look at him, pretending instead that he wasn't in the room. "And Daniel felt compelled to tell me exactly who Ben is."

Charlotte fell back onto the bench, and when Anna stole a glance toward Daniel, he looked like he was sorry for exposing his brother-in-law. "He didn't tell me to keep it a secret from you," Daniel tried to explain.

"Did he tell you to approach me at the cemetery?"

"No. That was my decision."

"So you were never supposed to talk to me." Anna set down her mug when Daniel didn't reply and reached for Charlotte's hands. "Do you want to go to Canada?"

"No." She paused. "But I probably should."

Anna nodded, but her heart felt heavy. For her own protection, Charlotte needed to leave. "It will only be temporary."

"I hope so."

Peter murmured in his sleep, and Charlotte reached over and rocked the bassinet. "But I can't leave you without an outside contact for...Ben."

Daniel didn't hesitate. "I can be your contact."

Anna wanted to shake him. He couldn't even keep Joseph's name a secret. How could he be trusted with their communication?

Charlotte wrapped the afghan across Peter's chest and stood up. "It might work."

"I don't know...."

"He practically lives at Joseph's house already. It wouldn't be hard for us to think of a good reason for him to come visit here."

"I could think of a reason," he said.

At Daniel's smile, Anna felt her stomach tumble. It was for that very reason that she had to keep her distance from him. Charlotte and even her father may have guessed how she felt, but no one else could know. Especially not Daniel.

Charlotte clapped her hands. "Then it's perfect."

"No, it's not!" Anna insisted. "People will wonder what he's doing here."

"Oh, Anna..."

She wasn't even going to consider what Charlotte was about to propose. "Besides, we can't trust him."

Daniel wrapped his coat over his arm. "I'd like to prove to you that you can."

Anna shoved her coffee away from her. She usually trusted Charlotte's instincts—it was her own instincts that sometimes got her into trouble. But trust Daniel Stanton? She had no qualms about his passion to end slavery, but that didn't mean he could keep his mouth shut about their operations. What if he exposed their station by accident? Her life, as well as the lives of the runaways she was harboring, would be at his mercy.

If she dismissed him right now, Charlotte would refuse to go with the Palmers tomorrow. It wasn't fair to make Charlotte stay because Daniel disarmed her. She may be afraid to have him around, but she wouldn't let her own selfishness and fear get in the way of protecting the woman who had been her friend for so many years. She could learn to control her heart.

"It won't be permanent," Anna told him. "Just until we can find someone else."

Charlotte sighed in relief, and then she warned them, "Esther doesn't know anything."

"I won't be the one to tell her," he said.

"Very good." Charlotte glanced back down at the bassinet. "Now we have to figure out what to do about Peter."

* * * * *

It was well past midnight when Charlotte went upstairs to pack, but Daniel wasn't tired. The coffee had revived him...or maybe it was the thought of seeing Anna more often.

She was sitting across from him in silence, her foot gently rocking the bassinet at her side. She didn't volunteer conversation, so he finally asked, "Where's your father?"

"Working on a large order for Henry Nelson," she replied. "He sleeps at the mill more often than not these days."

He wanted to ask her more about the Nelsons, specifically about Matthew Nelson, but she started to yawn. "It's far past my bedtime."

"Mine, too," he said, but he didn't move. He didn't want to go back to his cramped boarding room that still smelled like smoke and soot. He wanted to sit here all night, across from Anna. He motioned to the bassinet. "Tell me about this baby."

She lifted the boy out of the cradle, and though he didn't wake, he snuggled close to Anna's breast. Her face softened with love and wonder. The moment she kissed the baby's skin, Daniel didn't want to fight it anymore.

He cared about Anna no matter what had happened in her past, no matter what secrets she still kept from him. He didn't want to just talk all night. He wanted to gather her into his arms and hold her as close to his chest as she held that baby. And he didn't want to let go.

She walked around the table and sat down beside him. Had she already given herself to Matthew or one of the bachelors at Silver Creek? Or somewhere, in the depths of her heart, was she still waiting to find love?

He didn't trust himself to touch her hand, but he inched closer to her. "I'm tired of the secrets."

Her gaze was still on the baby. "Me, too."

"Is this baby yours?"

Her head jerked up, and a cloud settled over her eyes. "Would it matter?"

Yes. No. He wanted to be honest with her, but he knew he would wrestle with jealousy, knowing that she'd been with another man. "I've sinned countless times," he finally said. "And God has forgiven every one of my trespasses."

She leaned toward him. "What if I wasn't the one who sinned?"

"I'm learning how to forgive," he said, his voice strained. "Though it would be very hard for me to forgive the man who took advantage of you."

The cloud had lifted, and her blue eyes implored him. He didn't want to stumble over his words yet again and say something he didn't mean.

"But you could forgive him?" she asked.

"Only by God's grace."

"You're a better Quaker than me, Daniel."

He shook his head. "Hardly."

Her fingers rolled gently over the quilt in her arms. "No one took advantage of me."

He paused and reluctantly digested her words. Maybe it would be harder to forgive the man she'd given herself to willingly.

Her eyes locked with his. "But someone did take advantage of this child's mother."

"Who...?" he started but choked on the word.

She held the baby out, and it felt awkward for him to hold such a small child. One hand supported the back of the child's head, and he wrapped his other hand around the baby's legs so he wouldn't accidently drop him on the floor.

He looked down at the child and then back up at Anna for answers.

"His name is Peter," she whispered. "He is a colored baby."

Daniel glanced back down at the baby's face. His skin was whiter than most of the children's in Liberty. "There's not a trace of African in him."

"His father is a plantation owner in Tennessee," Anna said. "And his mother was a light-skinned slave."

"Marie?"

Anna reached for Peter and cuddled him close to her again. "If Simon or one of the other hunters find her baby....."

He didn't want to consider Simon stealing away Marie's child. "What will you do with him?"

Anna explained about the Palmer family and how they had cared for him. "They are leaving in the morning...and I don't know what I'm going to do." Her voice trailed off, and he felt her sadness.

Almost as much as he had felt for Esther earlier that day.

The thought came to him quickly, and he scoffed at himself for even considering it. Anna would never trust Esther with this child. And Esther would never let a Negro baby replace the child she lost.

He opened his mouth and shut it. Would Esther even consider it? Certainly not if she knew the child was colored. He glanced back at Peter's face.

Perhaps she would never have to know.

Chapter Thirty-three

....

Esther shoved the pile of goose feathers off her bed and searched for another pillow to destroy. Her fingernails dug into the seam, ripping the threads apart. Feathers exploded onto her face and stuck to her tears. She pulled the feathers off her eyes and tore them in her hands.

God had given her the gift of a baby girl and then snatched her very breath away. Her baby was no longer inside her. Nor was her baby in her arms, where she belonged.

She'd never even seen Lilith's pretty face. Joseph stole her baby away from her and then forced her to sleep.

Her very heart had been ripped apart, and nothing could stop the pain. Joseph kept spooning laudanum into her mouth, but she always woke up hours later with the pain fresh again.

She almost wished she wouldn't wake.

She banged her head back against the wooden headboard, willing the pain to expunge the gaping wound inside her.

It was her fault she'd lost the baby. She should have crawled into bed the first day she found out she was expecting and not moved again until her daughter was born. It was ridiculous, all her busyness around the house...like any of it mattered. Nothing mattered anymore.

She reached for the last pillow on her bed and tore it open.

How could God do this to her? How could He take away the only thing in life that she wanted? He could have her fancy home and her clothes. All she had ever desired was to be a mother.

She had wanted more children than just one. Four, at least. Maybe more. But it had taken her five years to get pregnant the first time. She was almost too old to have so many children.

She shoved the empty pillowcase and feathers off the side of the bed. What if she never even had one?

Her hands clutched the back of her neck, and she rolled into a ball. Sorrow poured out of her, but the grief never emptied from her heart. How was she supposed to live like this?

Joseph came into the room, hovering over her, but even then, she couldn't stop her sobs.

He placed his cold hand on her forehead. "Do you want some more laudanum?"

She rolled away from him. Didn't he understand? Medicine couldn't heal what was hurting her. Nothing could.

He sat down on her bed, pulling her into his arms. "I'm sorry," he whispered into her hair.

Why was he apologizing? She was the one who'd lost their baby.

"Why did He take her away?" she asked.

His shoulders shook, and she felt his tears on her head. "I don't know."

She sank her head into his chest. "I want my baby back."

On the bed, with his arms around her, Joseph's tears mixed with hers. God have mercy on them. She didn't know what they were going to do.

* * * * *

A chorus of bullfrogs croaked in sequence along the swampy path toward Liberty. The buggy's lantern illuminated the trail, but they wouldn't need its light for long. Within the hour, the sun would begin its slow creep over the horizon.

Anna glanced over her shoulder and saw Daniel wrapped up in the black blanket. He was ready, if necessary, to hide on the floor with Peter, but she doubted that even Simon would be out hunting at this early morning hour.

"I'm still here," Daniel whispered.

She smiled at his voice. Even though she had told him to sleep, it was a comfort to have him awake and somewhat alert. "And Peter?"

"I don't think he's felt a single bump."

"It's the medicine we gave him."

"Let's hope it doesn't wear off."

She ran her stockinged toes over the soapstone to warm them. "You need to get some sleep."

"Not until we get to my sister's house."

Anna wasn't ready to leave Peter with Joseph and Esther quite yet. Life was changing too quickly around her, and she couldn't make it stop. Only a half hour ago, she had hugged Charlotte and watched her trek toward the Palmer home. The good-bye had been harder than she'd imagined.

A tear blurred her vision, and she blinked it back. She couldn't think about losing Charlotte right now. She had to think about Peter.

It wouldn't be safe to care for him at her house, and Daniel felt certain that Esther would take him. She wasn't sure about the idea, but there was no better alternative.

Daniel had asked for her to trust him, and she was trying. She only hoped she was making the right decision.

* * * * *

Daniel's confidence began to crumble when Anna parked her buggy beside Joseph's barn. Perhaps it was because he hadn't slept for twenty-four hours. Or perhaps it was because this was one of the most absurd ideas he had ever had. Even in her grief, Esther would wonder at his bringing her a baby.

What would she do if she realized it was a Negro child?

He slowly unwrapped himself and Peter from the wool blanket.

Anna slid out of the driver's seat and reached up to take the sleeping baby, but he almost didn't give him to her. He wanted to tell her to take Peter back to her home until they developed a better plan, but that would only put her life at risk. It was dangerous to proceed, but it was even more dangerous not to.

He reluctantly handed Peter down to her.

The parlor was quiet when they walked inside. And cold. Either Greta hadn't arrived yet or Joseph had told her to stay home.

Anna placed Peter in the wicker cradle that Esther had ordered from New York and turned to him. "I'll build the fire."

Her clothes were rumpled and her eyes streaked with red, but she had never looked more beautiful to him. He wanted to pull her to him and tell her they didn't need to leave Peter with his sister. He could whisk them away to Ohio or Michigan and care for them both.

Without asking, he knew she would never agree to run away. This was her home, and even if she did go with him, she would have to leave without the letters to join a new Meeting. The Friends would disown both of them; her reputation would be ruined. Or Simon might track them down and still steal Peter away.

Anna might leave Liberty with him, for Peter's sake, but Daniel wouldn't force her to make the choice. Joseph and Esther would have to take this child.

Ascending the stairs two at a time, he knocked on the door to Joseph and Esther's chamber. No one answered his knock, so he slowly opened the door and found them both sleeping on a mound of white feathers.

Joseph jumped when Daniel shook his shoulder. Wrapping a blanket around himself, he slipped on his glasses and followed Daniel out into the frigid hallway.

Joseph didn't bother with pleasantries. "You should have been back hours ago."

"I had an unexpected stop to make."

Joseph's eyes narrowed. "Did something go wrong?"

"The order arrived safely at its destination."

"Intact?"

"Completely."

"Very good." Joseph pushed his glasses back up his nose and turned. "Now we will forget we even talked about this."

Daniel stopped him. "I'm afraid we can't."

Concern flooded Joseph's face as Daniel told him that Charlotte had left for Canada that morning. Then he told him he'd volunteered to be the messenger between Joseph and Anna.

Joseph walked to the window at the end of the hallway before he faced Daniel again. "I suppose it could work."

"It will work," Daniel insisted.

"You could say you're traveling out to interview different people in the county."

Daniel's lips curled up. "Or I could say I'm courting Anna Brent."

"An even better idea."

"It would be a ruse, of course."

"Of course."

Daniel nodded toward the open doorway. "How is she?"

"Not well," he muttered. "Not well at all."

"There's one other thing...."

Joseph waved him away. "Later."

"I'm sorry, Joseph." Daniel thought about the baby downstairs—and the courageous woman holding him in her arms. "It can't wait until later."

Chapter Thirty-four
....

Ice! The room felt like it had frozen overnight; even her bed was covered in a feathery snow. Shivering, Esther tugged at the blanket and pulled it up to her chin.

How was she supposed to keep her baby warm in such a cold place? Greta and Joseph were supposed to take care of her and Lilith, not let them freeze in bed.

She reached for her abdomen, to feel Lilith moving inside her, but she couldn't feel her baby.

Then she remembered.

Lilith was gone.

She opened her eyes, but tears didn't wet her face this morning. Even they seemed to have frozen in the cold. She balled the quilt in her hands and squeezed it.

Nothing would be the same again.

Someone knocked on the door, and the sound hurt her ears. She didn't want to see anyone. Not Greta or Daniel or even Joseph. Their very presence would remind her that Lilith was gone, but in the quiet she could still pretend.

The door opened in spite of her, but instead of Joseph or Greta walking into the room, Anna Brent entered. Anna usually made her smile, but today Esther didn't want to smile. Nor did she want a Quaker telling her to trust in God's will.

How could God will the death of her child?

She pushed her hair back from her forehead, and for the first time in two days, she realized she must look appalling. Joseph should have at least let her clean up before he showed a visitor to her door.

Anna brushed the feathers from the chair beside her bed and sat.

"Did you hear what happened?" Esther asked.

Anna took both of her hands and nodded.

Esther closed her eyes. "She would have been beautiful."

"The prettiest girl in Indiana," Anna agreed.

Anna's simple words comforted her. Most people would think of Lilith as another unknown who'd died during childbirth, but Anna would help her remember Lilith as a baby girl.

"I spent so many hours talking to her and reading to her and singing to her. She knew my voice, but I never got to hear hers."

"One day you will see her again."

Esther crushed the quilt again in her hands. "I can't wait that long."

Her tears dried up, Esther poured out her dreams to Anna and told her what she wanted for Lilith—for all of her children—until she exhausted herself. She leaned back against the headboard, and Anna took the afghan off the back of the chair and tucked it behind her head.

"Thank you," she whispered.

Anna squeezed her hands again. "There's something I'd like to talk to you about."

She nodded her head though she barely heard Anna's words.

"A baby boy was born near here a few weeks ago, Esther. A baby that needs a family."

She scrunched her eyes shut. She didn't want to talk about another mother's baby. She only wanted to talk about *her* baby.

"We thought maybe..." Anna's voice trailed off, and Esther opened her eyes.

Daniel was at the doorway with something small in his arms. She squinted at him and realized he was holding a baby.

Her heart lifted. Maybe Lilith wasn't stillborn! Joseph had only taken her out for a while, until her mother was rested. She sat up and reached out her arms. "Lilith?"

Anna patted her. "It's not Lilith."

The room spun around her. She tried to focus on Anna's blurry face. "But who, then?"

Daniel was beside her bed now, holding a sleeping baby out to her. It was a boy, dressed in a plum-colored gown. He was older than her Lilith by a few weeks. And he was beautiful.

Her arms ached for the child, but she pushed him away. Why were they teasing her? It was torture, looking at someone else's perfect baby when hers was already in the grave. Didn't they understand how much it hurt?

Her fingers twitched on the blanket. "What's his name?"

"Peter."

Her arms twitched. "How old is he?"

"Eight weeks," Daniel said.

"His father?"

Daniel hesitated before he spoke again. "He doesn't want him."

"Where is his mother?"

He paused. "She's deceased...and he desperately needs a mother to care for him."

His words slowly registered in her mind and then rooted into her heart. She couldn't care for another woman's baby, could she? She wanted her daughter. Her little girl.

She looked down at his light eyelashes and listened to the soft breath on his lips. Joseph walked into the room, over to her bed, and her voice shook when her eyes left the baby and looked up at her husband. "He's not Lilith...."

Joseph kissed her forehead and stepped back. "No baby could ever replace her."

She nodded, the sadness for this child pushing a bit of her own sadness away. Lilith wouldn't mind if she cared for him, for just a little while. Her baby would want her to help another child.

"Many suffer so much more than I, souls begging me to pray. 'Help me,' they cry out in pain, but I look the other way."

The words to Anna's poem washed over her in a gentle wave. She could never love this baby like she had loved Lilith, but that didn't mean she should look the other way.

She glanced at Daniel and then at Anna, trembling as she spoke. "I want to care for him."

Daniel stepped even closer to her. "We were hoping you might."

Joseph put his hand on Daniel's shoulder, and her brother backed away. "It's your decision, Esther. You don't have to do this."

Her arms reached for the baby, and she pulled him close to her. Poor thing. He probably missed his mama as much as she missed her Lilith.

Peter's eyes opened, and when he looked up at her, she saw the brightest color of blue. Her lips trembled, and tears flowed again from her eyes. She didn't want to frighten him, yet she couldn't help it. He needed her as much as she needed him.

"Who else knows he is an orphan?"

"No one in this town," Daniel replied.

"I'm going to keep him."

"Now, Esther...," Joseph started, but she had already made up her mind.

No one spoke, and she looked up at the three people over her bed to make sure they understood. "His name will be Joseph Benjamin, after his father."

Daniel cleared his throat. "That's a good name, Essie."

She kissed his forehead. "I will call him Ben."

* * * * *

Gray clouds plastered the sky, but Anna's heart felt light as Daniel escorted her to the buggy they'd parked behind the Cooleys' home. She could still scarcely believe that Esther had kept Peter, but the instant the woman had taken him into her arms, Anna knew he would be secure.

Daniel had told Joseph that Negro blood ran through Peter's veins. Joseph had asked them not to tell Esther.

Seeing her with the child, Anna didn't think it would matter. He would never replace the memories of Esther's birth child—no one expected him to—but he would be much loved as Joseph Benjamin Cooley II.

"God has been good to us this morning," she said.

Daniel nodded. "That He has."

She petted Samara and turned to the man at her side. His eyes would disarm her if she weren't careful. "She'll take good care of him, won't she?"

"No one will be able to take that baby away from her."

Esther would probably fight off Simon himself with her fingernails if he appeared at her door.

For a moment, Anna didn't know what else to say. She had said some cruel words about Daniel's character hours before, but he had proven himself more than trustworthy. He had proven himself to be an honest and true friend.

"Thank you," she said softly.

He looked away, embarrassed. "It was only a small thing, Anna."

"It wasn't small to Peter...or to me."

He stepped close to her, his shoulders inches from her face. Her heart pounded.

Some of the farmers in Liberty might have bulkier arms than Daniel, but she'd bet money there wasn't a man in their county stronger in spirit. He'd fought Milton Kent with his words and won. He'd tracked down slaves and shared their stories with the community. Even when someone burned down his office, he didn't stop his pursuit of justice.

Yesterday he'd walked twelve miles to guide the runaways to her station, and then he'd found Peter the perfect home.

Daniel Stanton reminded her of King David in the Bible, a strong and passionate man. A man after God's own heart.

He took her hand and helped her climb up to the seat.

"Let me drive you home," he said, his voice husky.

She didn't want to say good-bye, but there was nothing more to say. After today, they couldn't even pretend to be friends. "We can't be seen together, Daniel."

"But I'm taking over…"

"You can write me," she said, her words tumbling together. "With Esther's stationery. You can send a note when Ben has a delivery to make."

"I don't want to write you." He stepped up on the running board, and the pounding in her heart stopped when his eyes met hers. Heat rushed to her face. "I want to come see you."

When he brushed a strand of hair out of her face, she could scarcely breathe. He was so close, and she wanted to stay right here. With him.

But she couldn't. They couldn't.

She reached for the reins. "I'll have my father bring Joseph's horse back to town."

"Anna…"

She stared ahead, not trusting herself to look over at him. "Our entire network is built on secrecy, Daniel. Too many people depend on us."

The soft click from her tongue urged Samara forward, and Daniel hopped off the buggy. She didn't turn her head. She couldn't bear to see him standing there, alone.

As she rode out of town, she scarcely noticed the flock of geese overhead or heard cornstalks banging against boards in the fields around her. The tension between her and Daniel was palpable. He had almost kissed her; she saw it in his eyes. Heaven help her if he had. She wouldn't have been able to resist.

If she weren't careful, her weakness would ruin everything.

"C'mon, Samara," she pressed.

Daniel couldn't come visit her on Silver Creek. For the safety of the people they were trying to help, they mustn't let their relationship get personal. What she desired was nothing compared to the needs of those who were staying in their home.

Nothing could come between her and her station. Not even someone strong and handsome and kind.

Chapter Thirty-five

Sitting at Joseph's secretary, Daniel scribbled down the words to his next article, not particularly concerned about the quality of his work. The story was potent enough on its own.

It was about Isaac's friend Zack Haviland who had been an agent down in Jeffersonville. Haviland had helped hundreds of slaves flee across the Ohio and run up to places similar to Liberty, but last week he was found dead, drowned in the river.

A mob had caught him helping a slave woman and her four children escape, and they'd decided that justice for this incorrigible act was to beat him and bind him and dump him into the very water from which he'd rescued so many.

Even more appalling to Daniel was that not a single man was being penalized for Haviland's death.

Daniel pressed his palm into his forehead. How could people in Indiana sleep while good men like Haviland were being murdered? What more could he do to wake them up?

His contribution was piddling compared to people like Zack and Joseph...and Anna.

Anna would understand why he grieved for someone like Zack Haviland even though he had never met the man.

He looked out the window of Joseph and Esther's parlor and searched the street again for her. For the past three weeks he had watched, thinking she might come to Lyle Trumble's mercantile or stop by the Cooleys to visit Esther and Ben. He even dared to hope that she might seek him out and explain her abrupt departure so many days ago.

But she hadn't appeared.

She'd written him five short notes, responding to the instructions he'd sent her about purchasing and delivering the materials for Esther's baby blanket. All her responses were curt. Formal. None of them hinted at anything other than a thoroughly professional relationship, nor did they hint that she might care for him as he did her.

Footsteps padded across the floor behind him, and he turned to see Joseph holding Benjamin in his arms. "I didn't hear you arrive."

"I let myself in the back door an hour ago."

Joseph nodded at the desk. "Are you working on an article?"

He nodded. "It kept me up most of the night."

He supposed he would have told Joseph about Haviland if he asked, but he was glad when Joseph changed the subject.

"I received a message yesterday," Joseph said as he tucked the afghan around Ben's shoulders. "I have three new patients with consumption that I need to visit."

He stepped back toward the secretary. "Will you be transporting them?"

Joseph lowered his voice. "To Silver Creek, around ten tonight."

Daniel sat down on the chair and picked up his pen. His letter-writing seemed minuscule in importance to what Joseph and Anna did on the Underground, but he did what Joseph bid. "I'll send a messenger out right now."

* * * * *

Anna took the envelope from Ruth's hands and ran her fingers over Esther's return address. Daniel wrote to her about once a week, his notes as short as hers. She had hoped, when she didn't see him, that she would begin to forget about him, but as of yet, it hadn't worked.

"Esther Cooley sure likes to write to you," Ruth said.

Her new housekeeper was barely eighteen, and quite adept at cooking and cleaning, but Anna didn't know her sentiments on slavery—nor did she dare ask. Ruth's father worked at the mill, and her father said he trusted both him and his daughter, although he wasn't certain what her father's stance was on slavery or abolition, either. Ruth worked only five days a week, walking the two miles home to her husband every evening. When she needed to visit the graveyard, Anna left after Ruth went home.

She ran her fingers over the letter again. Every time a message arrived, she wished she could see Daniel again. "That's what friends do when they don't see each other often," she said.

"I hardly ever see my best friend anymore, but neither of us particularly like to write."

Anna sat in a chair by the fire, not bothering to correct the notion that she and Esther were the best of friends.

"Course you probably know my friend, Charity Penner?"

Anna shook her head. "Not really."

"Here I thought that Esther would have told you all about her." Ruth sat down beside her. "Her brother has had his eye on Charity for weeks."

Anna's fingers froze on the envelope. "Daniel?"

The curls bounced on Ruth's head. "Charity's playing hard to get, of course, but she says they'll probably be married in the spring."

Anna turned toward the fire. Daniel, getting married? Here she had thought... They had almost...

She shook her head. She shouldn't be thinking about any of this. She should be happy—for Daniel and for Charity.

But she wasn't happy at all.

She dismissed Ruth to finish baking bread and ripped open the envelope. His message was coded—about shipping three parcels out to Silver Creek at ten o'clock with instructions to deliver them to Newport on the morrow. Nothing about Charity Penner or weddings.

She held the note up to her cheek and then threw it into the parlor fire. The edges curled and blackened in the flames. She would be there early, waiting for the delivery, but tonight she wouldn't let herself wonder if Daniel would sneak to the graveyard again to see her.

She had told him they couldn't even be friends, and she had meant it, but she thought he might at least come visit again. Now she knew why he didn't come. He had been busy courting another girl in town.

Her father entered the parlor, and as she turned from the fire, she determined to force herself to stop thinking about Daniel Stanton. She was the one who had said they couldn't be friends. It wasn't fair for her to expect anything else.

Her father's face looked haggard when he smiled at her; even the lines on his forehead seemed to have grown in the last few weeks.

"How much longer are you going to have to work like this?" she asked.

"I don't know." He kissed her on the cheek. "It seems like everyone chasing gold to California needs an extra blanket or two to take with them."

She worried about him. He rarely slept at home anymore, or ate there, either. And at least once a week he was delivering valuable cargo to Newport or Connersville. The mill was the perfect front for their work on the Underground, and the perfect reason for him to stay away from the home that reminded him of his deceased wife, but if he wasn't careful, he was going to work himself into the grave.

She whispered so Ruth wouldn't hear her words. "We're expecting three parcels tonight."

"When does he want me to deliver them?"

"He asked that we take them to Newport tomorrow."

He put his hat on his head. "I'll leave the moment the sun goes down."

She put her arms around his shoulders and hugged him. "Why don't you let me deliver them?"

He kissed her cheek. "Not while I'm here, Anna. I already worry about you too much."

"Surely they aren't searching for..." She stopped herself. "For our friend anymore."

"Isaac told me that Noah Owens upped the reward to seven hundred dollars."

She groaned. As long as there was money to be had, Simon and the other hunters wouldn't go away.

Edwin placed his hat on his head. "I saw Isaac in town a few days ago. He asked about your next column."

Isaac had asked her about it after Meeting, too, but she didn't know what to tell him. Every time she sat down to start the article, the only story she wanted to tell was Daniel's, and she couldn't tell that one.

"I think I'll have to wait until next month."

Edwin stopped by the front door. "Are you ill?"

She shook her head. "I'm perfectly fine."

He gave her a curious look and then left for the mill.

Chapter Thirty-six

....

Esther tied the white taffeta ribbons of her bonnet under her chin and then pushed the perambulator toward Liberty's town center. The sky was clear and temperatures were unseasonably warm for the last week in October.

Ben was awake for their walk, shaking his rattle and relishing the ride. Joseph had insisted that they both needed fresh air, before the snow came, and she finally relented. Though even more than the air, she hoped their little stroll would qualm some of the gossip that had surely been clambering across town during her confinement.

It had been over a month since Joseph had sent her to bed, and she had refused to venture outside until Ben was a bit older. People had been talking, she was sure of it. Probably wondering what was wrong with her and her new baby.

Today she would show them that there was nothing wrong with either of them. He was wonderfully healthy, and so was she.

Her head high, she strolled toward Trumble's.

The first person she recognized was Gertrude Gunther, who was slipping out of the milliner's shop. The woman gave an exclamation when she saw her; then she pecked her on the cheeks and bent toward the carriage. "I heard you had your baby."

Esther smiled, her voice light. "And I haven't slept since."

Mrs. Gunther poked Ben's arm. "Trudy had her girl almost two months ago, and she's still not sleeping."

Esther had no real complaints about the sleep. She and Ben rested during the day together, and they were both content.

Mrs. Gunther studied Ben like she was trying to find something wrong with him. "We thought he might be ill or something."

"Joseph has declared him perfectly fit."

The woman tickled his chin. "You are going to be one spoiled fella."

Esther's gaze traveled to the handbill behind Mrs. Gunther's head, and for a moment she couldn't move. In big letters, the poster advertised a reward of seven hundred dollars for a light-skinned slave baby that had been abandoned in Indiana. His owner lived in Tennessee.

Her fingers curled tighter over the handle of the perambulator.

A slave baby? Surely not.

Still, she wanted to turn the carriage and run back home to hide both herself and her baby.

Mrs. Gunther glanced behind her at the bill. "It's tragic, isn't it?"

"Yes, it is."

"A slave leaving her child like that in the wilds. No white woman would ever put her baby in such danger."

Esther muttered something unintelligible, but Mrs. Gunther didn't seem to notice. She was watching Ben. "How old did you say he was?"

"Almost five weeks."

"He looks older than Trudy's baby."

Esther straightened her bonnet. "All the children on Joseph's side are big."

"Well, maybe he'll be a doctor, too," Mrs. Gunther said. "He's quite a handsome boy."

The door to the tavern opened next to them, and when Esther saw who was walking outside, she took a step backward.

"I don't see Joseph's features in him at all," Mrs. Gunther said matter-of-factly.

Esther's heart started to sink. "I think he looks a little like Joseph."

"I don't believe so," the woman continued. "But he definitely has your eyes."

She held her breath as Matthew Nelson moved around Mrs. Gunther and tipped his hat toward her. Seeing Matthew didn't bother her. It was the black man beside him she didn't want to see, the slave hunter who'd scuffled with her brother outside Rachel's wedding celebration about a Negro girl and her baby.

"Who has her eyes?" Matthew asked with a smile.

Mrs. Gunther swept her arm across the top of the perambulator. "This adorable new baby of hers."

Particles of food clung to Simon's coarse whiskers, and he smelled like he hadn't bathed in months. He didn't look like he was in much of a congratulatory mood, although Matthew congratulated her with flair. "Motherhood seems to have agreed very well with you."

"I've never been happier."

"I'm sure you are a fine mother," he said, and she hoped to God it was true.

"I thought you would be off to California by now."

"I'm working on it."

"Still gathering supplies?"

"And a little extra cash," Matthew said, as he buttoned the top two buttons on his jacket. "Have you seen Anna Brent recently?"

She shook her head. "Not in ages. Why?"

"I'd like to talk to her."

"Why don't you pay her a visit?"

Matthew's eyes traveled up to the handbill behind them and then he looked away. "I may do that."

Simon didn't look at the bill or down at her son, but his hand crushed the carriage top as he stomped around both her and Ben. Esther almost slapped his hand away, but she kept her hands clutched over the handle. If he dared to question her about her child, she would show him exactly how a mama bear responds to threats on her cub.

Simon didn't glance back, though. Instead he called for Matthew to join him.

"You'll have to excuse my friend," Matthew said as he slipped by her. "He doesn't know what it means to be happy."

Esther reached down and pulled Ben out of the carriage. She knew what it was like to feel miserable, and thank God she knew happiness now.

She wouldn't let anyone take that away from her again.

* * * * *

The moon was almost full when Anna tromped back toward the cemetery. None of them liked escorting runaways under a lit sky, but the mill was the first stop after their friends arrived from the canal. They had no choice but to keep them here for the night.

Still, she'd sent a message back to Daniel this afternoon, asking him to try to wait until the moon faded again before forwarding the next delivery to their station. He didn't need to know that she was concerned about her father. Only that she was worried about the light.

There were no *X*'s by the gravesite when she arrived tonight, but she was a half hour early. Perhaps she had arrived before them. Kneeling at the grave, she began to hum "Amazing Grace."

The song had become a sign for the escaped slaves to join her, but each time she hummed it, it reminded her of her mother's beauty and courage. And it reminded her that the grace that covered both her and her mother also covered every soul she met in the night.

A man and a woman crept toward her, their heads down. Clothes tattered. It looked like they had walked hundreds of miles since they'd rested last.

"Who sent you?" she asked quietly.

It was the woman who spoke first, her voice surprisingly strong. "A friend of a friend."

Anna's eyes searched the trees behind them. "Is there another?"

The woman shook her head. "There are only two of us."

Anna thought of the message she'd burned in the parlor. Daniel had said there were three runaways coming tonight, hadn't he? Or had she read it wrong?

No, she was certain he had said three. He must have written the wrong number. She sighed inwardly, disappointed that he'd failed her again.

She turned toward her mother's grave.

How could she make him understand that it was details like this that had to be precise or someone might lose their life? Occasionally someone would arrive unannounced—like Marie—but Charlotte had never once given her a wrong count on the number of expected runaways.

Anna twisted the candle in her hand. Charlotte had been gone for a month now, but she still missed her friend. Charlotte knew how important the particulars were.

Something shuffled in the trees behind her, and Anna listened. Were those footsteps?

The realization dawned on her slowly. Frightfully.

What if Daniel hadn't been wrong? What if there really were supposed to be three?

In the moonlight, she could see the thick arms of the man waiting for her. Even the woman appeared to be strong. The two of them could overpower her in an instant if they wanted.

She directed them toward the side of the graveyard, her mind scrambling to determine a way to extract the truth.

"Did Henry escort you here?" she finally asked.

"Yes," the colored woman said, too quickly, and the man nodded with her. "At least he said his name was Henry."

Instinct sparked her to turn—flee—but she held steady. She didn't know who they were or how many others were around them.

"Very good," she quipped. "Did he tell you where we are going next?"

The woman shook her head. "Just said it was someplace safe."

"We've been having trouble out this way with slave hunters," Anna whispered. "You need to follow me about forty or so paces behind, in case we need to scatter and hide."

She didn't tell them about the mill. Nor did she tell them about the cave.

Instead of going west, Anna walked east for a half mile and then she turned right. If Ben hadn't brought this man and woman to her, how did they find her? Had they been waiting out there all week for her to show?

A tremor shot up her spine.

Who had sent them to trap her?

Something rustled the leaves near her again, and she quickened her pace until the man joined her side. "Excuse me, Miss."

She hushed him. "You have to stay behind me."

"But ain't we travelin' south?"

She steadied herself on a branch and faced him. "What is your name?"

"Eli."

"Of course we're traveling south, Eli. How else are we supposed to throw off the hunters?"

He nodded quickly, almost like he was afraid to make her angry.

She walked another quarter mile, and then she stopped abruptly.

"Are you okay?" she asked them when they joined her side.

They nodded vigorously to let her know they were fine.

"We're almost to the safe house," she explained. "But I need to go first and make sure it's clear."

Eli stood tall. "I'll go with you."

She shook her head. "You'll be trapped if the hunters are there."

Distrust was evident in their eyes, but she waited until they hid behind a moss-covered cropping of rocks before she crept away.

She walked for a few feet into the trees. And then she ran.

Commotion erupted behind her. Shouting. Running. She didn't dare stop and look back. The path she wanted was dead ahead of her. If she could make it to the cave, maybe they wouldn't find her there.

The moon hid behind the trees, but she didn't need much light. In front of her was Jacob's Knob, and she pulled herself up the steep hill by clinging to tree roots, her feet struggling for holds. A light swung over her, and she ducked under a bush.

"She's over here!" another man yelled not far behind her, and she scrambled faster up the hill.

A waterfall trickled nearby. An owl hooted. She could hear every sound, every stomp of feet.

"This way!" someone else called.

She summited the knob and ran off the path, covering her face from the blows of the pines. The dark mouth of the cave opened in front of her, and she slipped inside. She'd never been here without a lamp, but she crawled back as far as she could—forty or fifty feet— over the sharp stones and mud. She cringed at the thought of finding a bear or panther crouched in the back, but the alternative outside was no better choice.

She only hoped her pursuers didn't know about the cave.

Her shoulders against the rock wall, she clenched her fists. Until this moment, she'd never known what it was like to run away from someone. To be pursued.

She breathed in the cold air and watched the lights flash outside the cave. There was no place left for her to run, but she only had to hold out until daylight and then her father—or maybe even Daniel—would come looking for her.

At least she hadn't led her pursuers to the mill.

"I think she's in here!" someone shouted, and fear snaked through her skin.

Light blinded her, and she covered her eyes though she stood strong on her feet. They may outnumber her, whoever they were, but no matter what happened, she refused to cower.

She would try to stay strong until the end.

"Anna?" she heard, and she squinted into the light.

"Matthew!" she cried in relief. She reached out to him, so glad to see a friend. He wouldn't let the others hurt her.

But Matthew didn't return her embrace. Instead of protecting her, he snapped metal around her wrists like the jaws of a bear trap. She recoiled from him, but it was too late. The handcuffs had been secured.

"What are you doing?" she begged.

"You lied to me, Anna."

"I didn't lie...."

"I've been up-front with you from the beginning, but you...you chose stealing Negroes over marrying me."

Where was the lighthearted voice of the boy she'd known since birth, the one who liked to play with her, tease her? Anger had overcome him. And jealousy.

Nowhere in his eyes did she see Matthew Nelson, her friend.

He jerked her arm, but she wrestled against him and the handcuffs. "I'm not going out there."

Another man ducked into the cave, and Simon Mathers's lips curled into a sneer when he saw her. "Miss Anna Brent. I'm so glad to see you." He stepped toward her, and she could smell alcohol reeking from his pores. "There are a few people I'd like you to meet."

With a quick turn of his head, he shouted back over his shoulder, "We've got her!"

A small crowd of men cheered in response. Until this moment, she'd never realized how much men like Simon hated the Light.

He pushed back her bonnet, and the alcohol on his breath seared her skin. "Tell me where the baby is."

She turned her head and looked him in the eye. "What baby?"

He grabbed her shoulder and shoved her out of the cave.

There were six men on the other side, all of them with pistols or daggers in hand. "Should we string her up, boys?" he asked.

"Nah," one of the men called back, "let's take her down to the river."

She searched the crowd for the woman whom she'd led from the cemetery, but she was gone, probably paid handsomely by Simon to trap her. How much had Matthew and the others earned for their work?

Simon pushed her again, and she fell to the ground. "I want to know where the baby is."

Her knuckles bled from catching her fall on the stony ground. He could hurt her all he wanted—even kill her—but she would not offer up Peter to protect herself.

He yanked back her hair and stared down at her. "Where is he?"

She didn't blink. "I'm not the one to ask."

He cranked back his hand and she closed her eyes, bracing herself for his slap. It never came.

"Evenin', fellas," she heard another man say. "What have you got here?"

Matthew spoke first. "Where did you come from?"

A glimmer of hope fluttered in her. Perhaps God had sent a guardian angel to her after all. She bowed her head so no one would see even a hint of relief cross her face.

"I was riding back from a house call, when all of a sudden I heard this awful commotion over here in these hills." The man paused. "Is that Anna Brent in those cuffs?"

"She's been stealing slaves," Matthew said as he jerked her back up to her feet, like she was the worst of criminals. "Helping them run away."

Joseph Cooley dismounted his horse. "Now that's a shame," he replied. "And a serious crime."

"You bet it is," one of the men said.

"She should be punished to the full extent of the law."

"The law?" Simon snickered. "The law ain't gonna do nothing except fine her."

"Hardly enough of a punishment, is it?" Joseph said, and her hopes began to slip away. Would he sacrifice her completely to protect his identity? "I think you should lynch her."

Someone cheered, and her legs collapsed under her. Matthew pulled her back up by her arm.

"It's too bad, though," Joseph muttered as he stepped back.

Simon edged toward him. "What's too bad?"

"Just think of the money you'd make if she helped you catch a few runaways."

Simon lowered the lantern.

"No offense to Miss Brent here," Joseph said. "But do you think she could survive a few months in jail?"

"She should be in jail," Matthew insisted. "I've seen her stealing slaves with my own eyes."

"I'm not saying she didn't commit a crime, Nelson. I'm only guessing that she'd be willing to bargain a bit for her freedom." Joseph reached for his horse's bridle. "Perhaps even help you find that slave baby with the reward."

Simon glared at her. "She ain't telling us about the baby."

"Shh...," Joseph said. "We have to get her to jail before someone else decides to, shall we say, *opportunize* on her information."

Simon tugged on her cuffs. "I won't let anyone else opportunize."

"Excellent decision." Joseph looked around. "Are all you fellas going to come to town with us?"

Simon mumbled something about paying for nothing and then shouted for them to go on home.

Most of the men scattered, but Matthew and Joseph remained at her side.

"I don't trust you, Doctor," Simon said.

"It's not wise to trust anyone these days."

"Matthew and I will take her in."

"I'm riding back to town." Joseph mounted his horse and turned toward them. "No reason, I suppose, that I can't join you."

Chapter Thirty-seven

....

The jail cell in Liberty was dank and bitterly cold. The floor was made of dirt, and the solitary window along the stone wall was obstructed by iron bars. Night air crept through the wall's many cracks, and Anna shivered under the threadbare blanket. There was a chamber pot in one corner and a fireplace in the other, but there was no wood or even a candle to keep her warm.

Joseph and the others had awakened Randolph Zabel well after midnight, and the man grumbled all the way down to the jail, blaming her and those like her for the iniquities in their community. He replaced Simon's handcuffs with a chain around her ankle and then threw a blanket into her cell.

She closed her eyes. She should have played dumb tonight and told that colored man and woman they had the wrong person—she was just a girl visiting her mother's grave. She should have said she couldn't help them, that they needed to find someone else to assist them on their journey.

Instead of relying on Daniel's message, she had doubted him. And her doubts had gotten her locked into jail.

There was a soft scraping sound by the door, and she sat up ready to fight yet again. Simon could interrogate her all he wanted. She wouldn't give away her secrets.

A key clanged, and Anna braced herself as someone unlocked the door. A flicker of light brightened the room, and in the candlelight, she saw Will Denton's face. She tried to force herself to relax. Surely Will wouldn't try to hurt her, too.

He set the candleholder on the dirt floor. "Are you okay?"

She shivered again as a blast of cold air settled over her. "Better than I was an hour ago."

"I wish I could..."

"There's nothing you can do, Will, but I thank you."

"You were only acting as any Christian should."

"Shh...," she hushed him. "We can't get you into trouble, too."

Will slipped a basket out from behind the door and pushed it toward her. "Lizza wanted to send you a few things."

Anna removed two thick blankets from the top of the stack and a pillow. Under the linens was a plate of corn bread, some cheese, and a few apples. "Your wife is a treasure, Will."

"That she is."

"May God heap blessings upon both of you."

"Anna?" someone called from outside.

Will kicked the door open with his boot, and they saw Daniel Stanton standing on the other side.

"What are you doing here?" she asked.

"I...," he started—and then stopped like he didn't really know why he was there. "I was worried about you."

Will walked forward and slapped Daniel on the shoulder. "Take your time. I'm gonna set up camp for the night outside this door."

Daniel rushed to her, and she wanted to collapse into his arms. Tell him how sorry she was that she hadn't trusted him. Instead of pulling her to him, he knelt down beside her and folded her hands into his. His touch warmed her skin, and when he leaned down close to her, she trembled so slightly that he never would have known except that his hand clasped hers.

"I am so sorry, Anna."

She shook her head. "It wasn't your fault."

"My message—"

"You said there would be three, but there were only two. I should have known."

"You couldn't have known." His voice broke. "If only I had been there...."

She gently squeezed his hand. He didn't need to carry her burden. "They would have hurt us both."

"Joseph feels awful...."

"He shouldn't," she whispered. She didn't know who else was outside or in one of the cells on the other side of the rock wall. "I'm fairly certain he saved my life."

"I'm not going to let Simon or his men threaten you again."

Anna shook her hands free from his. What was she thinking? She had wanted so badly to be close to him that she'd almost forgotten what Ruth had told her. Daniel was almost engaged to marry another woman.

She couldn't allow herself to believe that there was more between him and her. Or force him to care more than he did.

"I'm not your responsibility," she insisted.

"That's not how I see it."

She straightened her skirt and inwardly reprimanded herself for her vanity. And then she reprimanded herself again. While she'd been thinking about herself and her desires, there were three runaways still wandering the forest without a safe place to spend the night.

She leaned close to Daniel's ear. "What happened to the others?"

"They hid in the trees." His skin brushed against hers when he whispered back. His breath warmed her ear. Her neck. "He's leading them to another station for the night."

She fell back against the cold wall, relieved at his words, unnerved by his touch.

She reached for one of the blankets that Lizza had sent and flung it over her. She didn't want to be alone, yet Daniel couldn't be here with her.

"What can I do?" he asked.

She didn't hesitate. "Could you go tell my father what happened?"

He stood quickly.

She lowered her voice again. "He will want to say that he is the stationmaster so I can go free, but he can't."

"I don't think anyone will be able to convince him not to, Anna."

"You have to talk to him," she pleaded. "If he's quiet, we can continue our work, but if not, Randolph Zabel will lock us both up."

Daniel took the corn bread out of the basket and broke a piece off for her. She took it but didn't eat. "And what shall I tell him about you?"

Moonlight streamed through the window bars, spilling onto the floor. She thought about the padlock on the jail cell. Will Denton guarding the door. "You can tell him that I'm safe for the night."

He hesitated before he pushed open the door. "I'll be back to visit in the morning."

She turned her face toward his. "You can't come visit me. It will destroy the secrecy of our work."

"Anna..." His smile was gentle. Sad.

"What?"

"Your work is no longer a secret."

* * * * *

Daniel flung off his covers at first light, his head throbbing. He hadn't bothered to put on his nightclothes when he collapsed into bed three hours ago. It hadn't seemed worth his time to change since he knew he was going back to see Anna at dawn.

He'd been up for most of the night, trying to convince Edwin Brent that the sheriff wouldn't let him take his daughter's place in jail. Edwin blamed himself for Anna's arrest, said he never should have let her act as a conductor. Daniel didn't tell him that he probably couldn't have stopped his daughter even if he wanted to. Nor did he tell him how close Anna had been to becoming another victim in the fight for abolition.

Sentiments were out of control on both sides of their country. It was contemptible to think that the men in their community could gang up and threaten a godly woman like Anna. It didn't matter what Anna said. He wasn't going to let it happen again.

He washed off in the basin and dried his hands and face on a towel.

Anna was about to find out how strong she really was. She wouldn't wilt in prison, he was sure of it, but she still didn't deserve to be locked away. Just weeks ago he had told Isaac that he was willing to go to prison for his stand against slavery. He was the one who should be in jail this morning, not Anna. She should never have had to spend even one night in that dirty, cramped cell.

Downstairs in the kitchen, he snatched six muffins from a basket and tied them along with a few apples into a napkin. Then he reached for the coffeepot and filled up tin cups for both him and Anna.

As he left the boardinghouse, he saw a new handbill tacked by the door—Noah Owens was now offering eight hundred dollars for Marie's baby. He set the mugs on the sideboard and ripped the poster down.

Hadn't Noah Owens and the others already done enough?

He crumpled the paper in his hands and threw it on the ground. Thank God for people like Marie and Anna who risked their lives to save someone else. Anna was the last person who deserved to be in a dark jail cell alone, especially while men like Simon and Noah Owens and even Matthew Nelson roamed free.

Will Denton was folding up his blankets by the doorstep when Daniel arrived. He handed Will one of the tin cups, and the man gulped it gratefully.

"You reckon she'll be okay for a few hours?" Will asked.

"I'll stay with her."

Will pushed open the door for him. "You've got company."

Sunlight poured into the room, and Daniel saw Edwin blink and push himself up the stone wall. Anna was asleep on the pillow, her hair still covered with her gray bonnet.

"Did you get yourself arrested, too?" Daniel asked him.

The man shook his head. "Not yet."

An hour passed, the men waiting for Anna to awake. Finally her eyes opened slowly, and when she saw Daniel, she sprang up. Her teeth chattering, she glanced at him again and then at Edwin before she looked at the dark stone and smeared window.

She sighed and straightened her bonnet. "I was hoping it was all a nightmare."

Daniel handed her the tin of cold coffee. "It was a nightmare."

He unwrapped the muffins and apples from his pack and handed them to both Edwin and Anna. Anna thanked him several times, but Edwin wouldn't touch the food. "I need to talk to the judge about bail," Edwin insisted.

Anna reached for her father's hand and clung to it. "He'll want information."

"I'm only going to tell him about my role."

"Don't tell them, Father."

"They will guess."

"But they don't know…," she said. "I was the one who aided those slaves last night. They don't know where I was going to take them or who else is involved."

"Anna…"

"I knew what I was getting myself into," she whispered. "Now that they've stopped me, they will think they've stopped our entire line. You and Ben need to figure out how to get the next group through."

Edwin picked up his hat off the dirt floor and placed it on his head. "Your mother would be proud of you, Anna."

Anna's cheeks glowed pink, and Daniel watched her, mesmerized, as she lowered her head.

Anna Brent deserved someone so much better than him.

Chapter Thirty-eight

Anna twirled her ankle under Isaac and Hannah's dining table, glad to be free from the chain. After two nights of accumulating dirt in the jail cell, her skin had been scrubbed clean again, and she wore the formal copper dress her father had brought out from Silver Creek for her appearance in court this morning.

When the judge had refused to release her on bail, Daniel volunteered to be her attorney. He was at the courthouse this morning, pleading for the judge to lighten her sentence today.

She wouldn't face trial. The court had enough evidence from witnesses, including Joseph Cooley's testimony, to penalize her for her work on the Underground. Her only hope was that Daniel would be able to talk them out of more jail time.

Hannah leaned over her and filled her glass with milk. "Are you feeling better?"

"I am."

"Daniel will do his best—"

Anna stopped her. "I know."

The older woman sat down beside her, and Isaac joined them at the end of the table. Hannah scooped corned beef out of a dish and spooned it onto their plates. The meat was salty and hot and soothed the pangs in her stomach.

Isaac cut his beef into minuscule pieces, but he didn't take a bite. Instead, with fork and knife in hand, he turned to Anna. "My contact at the *Independent Weekly* keeps asking for another column."

Hannah hushed him. "This isn't the time, Isaac."

He waved his fork at both of them. "Why not? She'll have plenty of time to write."

Anna caught the look that Hannah shot him, a look that would silence most men. Either Isaac didn't see his wife or he was ignoring her. Instead he spoke directly to Anna. "And you have plenty to write about."

"Daniel is going to get her out of jail today," Hannah insisted—but Anna knew it wasn't likely. She was the first person in Indiana to test the new Fugitive Slave Act laws. The court would probably make an example out of her. She would have a few months' time to write, and truth be told, she was ready to tell her story.

"I'll need paper...and a pen."

Isaac grinned. "I have both for you."

"If we *must* talk about this," Hannah said, "I think you should stop writing for the abolitionist papers and start writing for a magazine like... something like *Godey's Lady's Book*."

Anna's mouth hung open, and so did Isaac's. Isaac was the one who spoke first, but his voice was garbled. "Hannah!"

Now his wife was the one smiling. "Why not?"

"Because...," Isaac sputtered. "Because it's a worldly paper."

"Aye, that it is. A worldly magazine influencing thousands of women who wouldn't touch a paper like the *Independent*."

Isaac's fork clunked on his plate. "She couldn't..."

Hannah didn't stop. "You could tell a story, Anna, about a fashionable woman who defies the law."

"I don't know anything about fashion."

"Oh, that's the easy part—Esther Cooley or someone else could help you with that."

The idea started to grow. She could write the stories of different men and women who stayed at a station. She could talk about their dreams and their fears and perhaps she could even inspire a few of the readers to work on overturning the Fugitive Slave Act.

"Perhaps under a pseudonym," she said. Hannah clasped her hands together. "It would be perfect."

Isaac stood up, and his chair grated across the floor when he shoved it under the table. "No, it's not!"

Hannah ignored him as he marched out of the room. "Just think of all the women who would read it."

The doorbell clanged behind them, and Hannah rose quickly to answer it.

Anna rubbed her hands together. She was ready to start telling stories again.

"You have a visitor," Hannah said when she returned, and then she slipped out of the room.

Esther Cooley pulled out a chair, pushing down her skirts as she sat. Her gown was a deep red color, and she wore a small red hat with white feathers. Her face shone as she held out her baby, and Anna took Peter... Ben...in her arms.

He wore a long red gown that matched his mother's outfit. Draped over the gown was a blue-and-yellow blanket made at her father's mill, embroidered with his name and birth date lest there be any questions as to exactly when Joseph Benjamin Cooley II was born.

"He looks handsome."

"He's a good baby, Anna. Hardly ever cries at all."

"Is Greta helping you care for him?"

Esther shook her head. "Greta is no longer with us."

"What do you mean?"

"Weeks ago we got a letter from her. She and her husband went to Canada."

"Canada?"

Esther swept her hands over her skirt. "Greta got stopped by a slave hunter in Liberty last month. I think it frightened her."

"It would frighten me, too," Anna replied. "When exactly did she leave?"

Esther pinched her eyes shut for a moment and then reopened them. "The morning Ben was born."

Anna blinked. The morning that Charlotte and her friends had headed north.

Esther scooted her chair closer to Anna. "Do you remember when I saw you at Trumble's that first time? You were buying an outfit for a baby."

Anna held out her finger to Ben, and he clutched it. "I remember."

"You purchased a plum-colored gown for your friend's child."

She nodded very slowly, remembering the gown. And then she remembered that it was the same one Peter had worn when they brought him to Esther.

Esther wrapped her fingers around the edge of her chair. "Where did you find him, Anna?"

Her mouth felt dry, and she reached for a glass of water. "You don't want to know."

"Ben couldn't be more my child if I'd birthed him myself." Esther took him back into her arms. "Nothing is going to make me change my mind about him."

Anna felt her own face flush. "It would change your mind."

"I saw the handbills, Anna. The ones saying that there's a reward for the light-skinned baby of a slave named Marie. I need to know if someone has put a price on my son's head."

Anna stood and walked to the window. Two horses grazed in Isaac and Hannah's yard, and at the far end of their property, she could see the town of Liberty. For a moment she almost wished for the privacy of her prison cell so she wouldn't have to tell Esther Cooley that her baby had been born a slave.

She clasped her hands together. "I found him in a smokehouse."

"A smokehouse?"

She turned and faced Esther. "His mother hid him there before she died."

"Why would she—"

"Ben's mother was a mulatto slave, and his father was her master."

"Noah Owens," Esther said.

Anna nodded. "He has been posting the bills."

Esther sounded scared. "He wants his son back."

"No," Anna lashed out, "he doesn't want him. He wants to punish Marie and perhaps send a signal to his other slaves about what would happen if they tried to run. Or he might even sell off the child in Kentucky. White slave children make a good profit."

"I didn't know." Tears wet Esther's eyelashes and dripped down her cheeks. "His mother was the girl they found...."

Anna wished again that she didn't know the truth. "We believe Noah Owens killed her."

Esther tugged Ben even closer to her. "My poor baby."

Anna knew at that moment that Esther would never tell Ben's secret.

"When you testify today...," Esther began, fidgeting with the bow on Ben's gown.

Anna reached for her cloak from the back of the seat. She had to start walking toward the courthouse.

"They'll offer you a deal to get out of prison."

"Daniel told me."

Esther's tears flowed again. "Please don't tell them about Ben."

Anna reached for her and squeezed both her and Ben in a hug. "I won't give him away, Esther. Not to the courts or to anyone else."

Esther wiped the tears off her cheeks. "Even to Joseph."

Anna looked at her friend. "You haven't told him what you thought?"

"Joseph is a good man, Anna, but he's a good man who supports the rights of slave owners to keep their property."

"Surely he would keep this a secret."

"I think he would, but..."

"But what?"

"He's been eyeing a piece of land north of town for a year now," she said. "They're asking seven hundred and fifty for it."

"I'm sure..."

Esther reached again for her arm, insisting that she hear her. "And I don't think he'd claim a slave child as his own."

Anna knew with certainty that he would, that he already had, but that wasn't her secret to tell.

She tied her cape over her chest. "Not a word to Joseph either."

"Thank you, Anna." Esther paused to wipe her tears on her lacy handkerchief. "For finding Ben...and for giving me a son."

Chapter Thirty-nine
....

Inside the Liberty courthouse, Daniel told Judge Arnold Harper about Anna's love for people, both colored and white. He told the judge that her Christian charity wouldn't allow her to look the other way when she saw someone hurting, and he explained how most of the people she helped had been abused by their masters down South.

He described how the man and woman Anna had helped along the trail two nights ago weren't even really slaves. They had been hired by Simon Mathers out of spite...and to lead him to the place where he thought Anna was hiding a slave baby.

She hadn't taken them to this supposed secret place. Nor had they found the baby. Simon and Matthew and the others had tried to trap her, but none of them had yet to find any evidence that she had been harboring fugitive slaves.

Daniel talked for over an hour, presenting the judge with every argument he could render to keep Anna out of jail. The judge listened to him, and then he pounded his gavel, sentencing Anna with a five-hundred-dollar fine and sixty days in jail.

Arnold Harper offered to bargain with Anna, dissolving her sentence if she revealed who usually brought the fugitive slaves to her and where she took them after she left the graveyard. When she refused, the judge didn't push her to testify on the stand.

For that, Daniel was thankful.

Isaac and Hannah were among the one hundred people crammed inside the courtroom that morning. Rachel and Luke were there along with Charity Penner and the Nelson family. Milton Kent was in the front row, and Joseph and Esther were in the back.

After Anna changed into a plain dress, Daniel led a crowd of supporters across the lawn to Anna's jail cell. Randolph Zabel, obviously enjoying his role as chief lawman in Liberty, snapped the handcuffs back on Anna before they left the courtroom. Daniel insisted that the sheriff remove the cuffs, but Anna whispered that it was all right. He backed off and let the crowd see how Randolph was treating her.

When the sheriff opened the door to her cell, Anna smiled at the crowd behind her. They called out their support for her as the sheriff unlocked her cuffs, and with a brief wave, she walked through the door.

Edwin stepped into the cell behind her and Daniel started to follow, but Randolph stopped him before he could enter the cell. "Anna's the one serving time. Not you or her father."

Daniel met the man's stare. "There's no law against visiting her."

"This isn't a social hour," the sheriff barked. "She's in jail."

"For doing the right thing!"

The sheriff glared at the crowd. "Neither my deputy nor I can sit out here all day long, escorting visitors in and out of this cell." He took his watch out of his pocket and glanced at it. "I'll give you and Edwin— and whoever else wants to visit— thirty minutes, starting at eight each morning. Then I'm locking the door."

It wasn't much time, but Daniel didn't argue. Visiting hours in Liberty were at the sheriff's discretion.

When he walked inside the cell, Anna looked up.

"I'm sorry," he said, afraid that she would be upset at him because he'd let her down.

Instead she held up a letter. "It's from Charlotte."

She ripped open the envelope and scanned the writing. Then she looked up and smiled. "She made it to Canada two weeks ago. She's already found a room and a housekeeping job."

Only Anna could find happiness in a jail cell through the joy of another.

"She doesn't have to worry now," Anna said, and her words seemed to hover over them. She glanced at the locked door and blinked, as if she had just realized that she was back in jail.

Daniel shoved his hands into his pockets and looked at Edwin. "Will you be able to pay the fine?"

"I will."

He turned to Anna. "I didn't want you to have any jail time."

"It could have been six months, Daniel. I can survive for sixty days."

"Still..."

"And I didn't have to testify." She flashed him a smile. "Thank you."

Edwin set a knapsack filled with Anna's things on the floor and shook his hand. "Will you stay with her today?"

"The sheriff has given us a half hour."

"She needs someone to watch over her."

"I'll do my best."

Then Edwin kissed his daughter's cheek and walked out the door.

Daniel glanced down at the dirt floor and then looked back at Anna. She was beautiful. Not just with her dress, but from the glow of peace and strength that radiated from her. It was as if the Spirit bubbled out of her, shining light in the darkest of places.

He wanted to take her in his arms and kiss her—if she would have him. But he didn't want the memory of their first kiss to be in a jail cell.

He sat down on a blanket beside her. "You don't deserve to be in here, Anna."

"Nor does anyone deserve to be trapped in slavery."

"You are an incredible woman, Anna Brent."

Silence settled over them before Anna spoke again, her voice quiet. "Daniel?"

He inched closer to her. "Yes?"

"I heard a rumor."

His mind raced for a moment, wondering what she had heard. Had he said something wrong? Done something? "Rumors can be nasty things."

"This one was about you and—"

The door swung open. "Time's up," the sheriff said.

"And who?" he probed, but she shook her head as Randolph stomped across the floor. He clamped a chain around Anna's leg and locked it.

"She doesn't need a chain!" Daniel insisted.

"She does in my jail."

"It doesn't matter about the chain," she told Daniel. "I'm not going anywhere."

"What will you do today?"

She opened the knapsack and pulled out a pen and a small box of paper. "Write!" she said with a smile.

* * * * *

Anna had thought imprisonment would suck the life out of her, but she had been wrong. She passed her first hours by writing a long letter to Charlotte. Then she passed the days writing articles for both Isaac and Hannah, and she even helped Daniel edit his work. Every morning her father visited—bringing her Charlotte's return letters and baskets filled with new paper and food and clean clothing.

Rachel Barnes came three or four times a week as well as Esther and little Ben. Ruth even stopped by occasionally with fresh bread or cookies.

She was grateful for every person who came to see her, but she wished for a few minutes alone with one man. The man who was waiting outside at eight o'clock every morning for the sheriff to unlock the door.

Even though the cell always seemed crowded, she savored every minute she spent with him. And she waited for the morning when no one except Daniel would come, but as the weeks slowly passed, she never saw him alone.

Matthew Nelson never came to see her, nor did she see him passing by along the street. She asked once about Simon, and Esther told her that he was still in town, determined to make his eight hundred dollars before he left the area. Esther didn't say it, but Anna wondered if he was waiting until she got out of jail. Did he think she would lead him to the baby? Or was he planning to try to force her to talk?

Instead of withering in jail like she had imagined, she thrived in the quiet. Daniel had brought her a Bible and she read the entire book, though every day she reread Colossians—the book Paul had written while he was in prison. Late into the night, when the wind howled outside her door, she did what Paul and Silas had done when they were locked in a cell. She belted out the few songs she knew, certain God would approve while she was in jail.

The evenings grew shorter into November, and snow finally came. The sheriff rationed her firewood, but he gave her enough to keep from freezing. She wrote more letters and stories, but on the days that it snowed, she stood by the window, a blanket wrapped over her shoulders, and watched it come down.

During the nights, when she couldn't see the snow or the people wandering the courthouse lawn, she prayed by the firelight. And she sang. And most of all, she listened.

Chapter Forty

....

Wind rattled the windows of her cell, waking Anna an hour before her father was supposed to drive her away from Liberty on his sleigh. There was at least a foot of snow on the ground, and she could hardly wait to be outside—to feel the sun on her face, the snow on her boots, the breeze in her hair.

Days earlier, she'd watched and listened to the carolers traveling up and down Main Street on Christmas Day, stopping to visit with family and friends along the way. She didn't celebrate holidays like Christmas, but listening to them sing, she had longed even more to be with the people she loved.

She wanted to go home.

God had been faithful to her during the past two months. He had shown her that no matter what happened, no matter how many more days she had to spend in jail, she shouldn't stop helping the runaways. It didn't matter how many people knew about her night escorting that man and woman toward Jacob's Knob. They didn't know about the hiding place at the mill. And they didn't know who helped her with her work.

She only hoped Joseph would bring more people to their station.

Someone rustled the door and Anna stood, expecting to see her father. Instead Daniel walked into the room and smiled at her. "Are you sure you don't want to stay a few more days?"

Her heart leaped at the thought of being alone with him again. "I think I'm ready to go."

Randolph Zabel skulked through the door after Daniel. "I'm ready for you to go!"

She turned to the sheriff. "Thank you for allowing so many people to visit me."

He grumped at her in return and then dug into his coat pocket. "A letter came to my mailbox yesterday, addressed to you."

Usually her letters were delivered to her father, but this one was special. She reached for the envelope and saw Charlotte's return address. Her fingers traveled across the lip, and she felt a tear in the paper. It seemed as if someone had opened it and tried to glue it back together. She hoped it had been the sheriff.

She looked back up again. "Thank you."

She pulled on her gloves. Even though she'd tried to exercise her legs in the cell, they still ached as she lifted her skirt and tromped through the dry snow. The sky was blue, the air an icy cold. It all felt incredible to her.

"It's like your poem about the seasons," Daniel said as he escorted her toward her father's sleigh. "Nature has wrapped itself into a cocoon."

She stopped walking. "You thought that poem was about the seasons?"

"It was the poem you gave to my sister."

"I know which poem, Daniel," she said, disappointed that he didn't understand. "It's the one about rebirth."

She watched as it slowly dawned on him that she hadn't been writing solely about the changing seasons, but about a slave falling away from his old life and the sufferings he must endure before he was reborn.

They reached the sleigh, and Daniel stopped walking. "It's about the journey...."

"Of course it is." She kissed Samara on the nose and then climbed into the seat.

Daniel covered her in blankets, but as they rode toward home, she barely noticed their warmth or the heat of the soapstone at her feet. She listened to every sound around her. Relished every sight. Clumps of snow fell off tree branches and dropped to the forest floor. Smoke billowed up from chimney tops and floated into the air. Every woodpile they passed was dusted in white.

Two deer leaped across their path, and she clutched her hands to her chest. God's creation was everywhere. In the trees and the animals and even the rocks frozen into the river beside them.

Most of all, though, she was aware of the man sitting beside her. It had been two months since he had crept to her cell in the middle of the night, worried about what had happened to her. Two months since he had fought for her rights in court. If he hadn't, she would still be in that jail cell.

It was strange that Esther had never mentioned his engagement during her time in jail, nor anyone else. Perhaps he hadn't proposed yet to Charity. Or he was waiting to tell her when they were alone.

She couldn't wait a moment longer.

She pulled the blanket down from her face. "Daniel, do you know Charity Penner?"

He flashed her a look of surprise. "Is this the rumor you were trying to ask me about?"

She fidgeted on her seat. "Perhaps."

"I do know Charity."

She tried to prepare herself for his words. To prepare herself for the happy news of his engagement.

"The last I heard, she and Matthew Nelson were on their way to California."

Charity and Matthew? That meant...

She pushed the blanket back over her nose so he wouldn't catch her smiling. "They married?"

"According to the Justice of the Peace."

A mixture of emotions collided inside Anna. She was sad that Charity had chosen Matthew over her faith. Glad that Daniel wasn't marrying her. "But I thought..."

He slowed Samara as they neared the covered bridge. "What did you think, Anna?"

"My housekeeper told me you were courting Charity."

He didn't try to hide his grin. "And this bothered you?"

"Well...no." She glanced through the windows of the bridge. She wanted to be honest with him, but how could she tell him that his courting Charity, or anyone else, bothered her very much? "Maybe a little."

"Isaac introduced me to her at Luke and Rachel's wedding, but I don't suppose that's considered courting."

Her reply was muffled. "I don't suppose."

They rode the next mile in silence, past the mill and up the hill to her house. Her heart pounded in her chest, wondering at this man beside her. She was relieved that he didn't love Charity, but did he love someone else? Or could he possibly love her?

As they crested the hill, she saw her father on the porch, waving both hands over his head. She waved back, and when they stopped, she jumped down from the sleigh and ran to him.

The inside of the house was warm and smelled like pine. She needed a bath and a good night's rest, but she was glad to be home—with her father and Daniel.

"Where's Ruth?" she asked when they stepped into the parlor.

"She's not coming today." Her father motioned her away from the fireside. "Daniel and I wanted to show you something by ourselves."

By a large window on the other side of the room was the large mahogany trunk that her mother's family had brought with them when they escaped persecution in England. The trunk her father had hauled to the barn after she died. She brushed her hands over the lid, marveling at its beauty like she had when she was a child. She never thought she would see it inside their home again.

She reached for her father and hugged him.

"Look inside," he said.

And so she opened the lid, and her hand glided over the piles of her mother's handmade treasures. Her father asked her to remove linens, so she lifted her mother's embroidered pillows and tablecloths and other finery and stacked them on the chair beside the trunk.

Her father reached for the lantern on the windowsill and lit it. "I'm sorry to tell you this, Anna, but we can't keep slaves at the mill any longer."

Her eyes broke away from her mother's things. "Why not?"

"One of my workers found the room with food and water in it, and he asked who had been staying there."

She stood to her feet. "But I have to keep helping these people!"

"Anna..."

The Spirit had urged her to continue on with her work. She couldn't fail when He had so clearly led her. "We'll have them stay upstairs again."

"People will be watching our house even closer now," Edwin said, shaking his head. "We can't have runaways knocking on our door."

She glanced over at Daniel, but he didn't look upset at this news. In fact, he was smiling, and his happiness irritated her. How could he smile? She was going to care for runaways no matter what either of them said.

Her father handed her the lantern. "I'm going to build a small house beside the mill, Anna, for myself—I practically live there anyway."

"But where will I go?"

"Nowhere." He smiled. "It's just time for me to step aside and let someone else try to take care of you."

She didn't need anyone to take care of her!

She opened her mouth to refute his words, but before she could speak, she watched in amazement as her father leaned into the trunk and pushed. "Daniel and I and a couple of men from his Meeting devised a little something here...."

The base of the trunk collapsed, and she gaped at the hole. "What is this?"

Her father took the lantern from her hands and nudged her toward the trunk. "Go see."

She untied her bonnet and hung it on a chair. Lifting her skirt, she climbed over the side of the trunk and onto the top rung of a ladder. Her father handed her the lantern, and with it in hand, she climbed down four rungs and hopped into a small room.

There was a stack of blankets along the wall and a basket for food. For a moment, the room reminded her of her jail cell, except the walls were dirt instead of rock. There would be no wind stealing through cracks in the wall.

Dazed, she hardly noticed Daniel descend into the pit beside her. At the other end of the room was a narrow tunnel as high as her waist, and she ducked down to look inside. With the lantern in front of her, she balled up her skirt and crawled back slowly, thirty or forty feet.

When she reached the other end, there was a trapdoor with a lock above her head. She swung it open and pulled herself up into the root cellar with their potatoes and vegetables...and an old rug that covered the floor.

Slave hunters may continue to scrutinize their back door, but no one would think to watch their root cellar, hidden in the trees. Eventually the hunters would move on to another place, searching for runaways, but if they ever came back in the house, Anna would no longer worry that they would find the room and the runaways upstairs. "This is brilliant!" she whispered. She looked down into the hole to thank her father and Daniel, but Daniel was the only one who crawled out of the tunnel.

She opened her mouth to thank him. To tell him how delighted she was. But instead of talking, she fell into his arms.

He kissed her slowly. Her hair. Her nose. Her chin. When his lips met hers, her knees buckled. She didn't want him to ever let her go.

"Anna?" he whispered, and she shuddered slightly, as if it had all been a dream.

When she opened her eyes, Daniel was there in front of her.
And he was kneeling on the cold dirt floor.

From his pocket, he pulled out a heart-shaped silver locket. It was
identical to Esther's piece, the one their grandmother had given to
remind her grandchildren of all who had gone before them and of those
whom they loved today.

He closed his fingers around the necklace.

"I don't deserve you, Anna, but I love you with all my heart." His
voice broke with emotion, and she took his hands in hers. "I would be
most honored..."

Seconds ticked past, and she urged him on. "What is it, Daniel?"

"Would you consider..." His voice trailed off again, and she couldn't
stop the smile that rippled across her lips. *This* was the proposal she had
been waiting for.

He opened his palm and lifted the locket. When she bent toward
him, he clasped it around her neck. She touched her fingers to the silver,
and then he took her hand back and wrapped his fingers around hers
before he tried one last time.

"Will you marry me, Anna Brent?"

She kissed the top of his hand and squeezed it. "I thought you'd
never ask."

Chapter Forty-one
....

Two Months Later

Daniel stepped down into the kitchen, pulling her to him, but Anna brushed him away. "We're expecting company!"

He took her in his arms again. Even though she was standing a few feet from the fire, she shivered. "The only company I want is my wife," he replied.

He kissed her, and for a moment, she forgot about their company and about their plans for the day. She forgot about everything until the doorbell rang overhead.

She jumped. "Now you'll have to stall them," she said as she snatched the bowls of bread and meat off the kitchen table.

He grinned. "Or we could ignore them."

She nudged him with her foot before she scooted around him. "Answer the door."

She rushed up the stairs ahead of him, balancing the two bowls and a pitcher in her arms. The bell rang again, and she set the food and tea on the floor of the parlor beside the trunk. Quickly she opened the lid, removed the linens, and pushed open the bottom.

Light flickered in the room below. "Hello?" she called softly.

Zebediah climbed up, and she passed him the food.

She could hear voices in the entryway. "We're about to have some company, Zebediah."

"Yessum," he replied.

"No one for you to worry about."

He climbed down the ladder, to his wife and two young children, and she grabbed the end of the board and pulled it up while her guests hung their cloaks in the front closet and dried their shoes.

"Anna?" Daniel called out like he didn't know where to find her.

"I'm in the parlor."

She stuffed the last of the linens into the trunk at the same time Daniel walked into the room, followed by Joseph and Esther and their baby son. Esther didn't even look at the trunk. In her hands was a copy of the latest *Godey's Lady's Book*, and she was waving it wildly in her arms.

"Have you seen this?"

Anna took the magazine from her hands. "What is it?"

"There's an article in it called 'Liberty Line' that you simply must read." Esther sat down beside the trunk. "It's about a society woman who hides slaves on the Underground Railroad."

"Really?" Daniel flashed Anna a smile. "In *Godey's*?"

"Can you believe it?" Esther said. "And it was actually good."

"Imagine that."

Esther held out Ben, and Anna took him into her arms. Every time she saw him, she marveled at his health. And she thanked God that he was protected in a loving home.

"Did you hear the latest news about Simon Mathers?" Joseph asked.

She glanced up. "Do I want to hear it?"

"It seems that he has left town."

She sighed. He had left town before, but he always returned. "I'm sure he'll be back."

"I don't think so," Joseph said. "No one's naming names, but it seems like someone intercepted a letter from Canada that said Marie's child had arrived safely."

Anna held on to Ben's tiny fingers. She had hoped the sheriff had read her letter...and wouldn't be able to keep Charlotte's news to himself for much longer.

"I bet Simon was fuming," she said.

"I believe he was."

Esther cocked her head. "Of course I hope you are no longer involved with helping slaves."

She smiled. "I've learned how to be happy at home."

"Your heart doesn't still strive to be content?" Esther asked, pulling the words from her poem.

"I'm content, Esther."

"Good for you." Her sister-in-law turned her head. "And how about my brother?"

Daniel sat down on the trunk and crossed his ankle over his leg. He wrote the *Liberty Era* from their home now and drove their buggy to Oxford once a week to print it. Anna helped him craft his words.

Every day she loved him more for his courage and his passion and, these days, for the strength of his pen and the many secrets he guarded for her.

"Are you finally content, Daniel?"

He drummed his fingers on the lid of the trunk. "I'll never be content, Esther, until the slaves are set free."

Anna sat down on the trunk beside him, and he took her hand in his. She knew it was hard for him to be quiet about their work when everything within him wanted to spout out the truth. He still railed against slavery in his paper and in his frequent debates with Milton, but when they married, Daniel had known he could never say anything about the people they hid in their own home.

She never tried to squelch his passions. His *fanaticism*, as Esther had called it. She loved hearing him speak out for the slaves, and she loved even more when he bridled his tongue to protect those he wanted to defend.

God had woven hers and Daniel's hearts together in a beautiful bond. And in their silence, in their secrets, they had become one.

Author's Note
....

Writing this novel has been an amazing journey for me! The idea for the story was sparked years ago, when I was growing up in a small Ohio town that had once been active on the Underground Railroad. My cousin's home was rumored to have been a stop for runaway slaves, and as we played hide-and-seek in the dark basement and other secret spaces, I wondered who had hidden there before the Civil War and what type of people would risk everything to help runaways.

As I grew older, I began to research the mysterious Underground Railroad and realized that many people in the mid-1800s didn't talk much about their role helping runaway slaves for fear of being caught. Nor did they write about it. Much of this history was recorded by men and women whose parents had been conductors or stationmasters on the Underground, and it was their memories that inspired me to tell Anna's story.

A month or so before I began writing, I discovered *The Pursuit of God* by A. W. Tozer (highly recommended, if you haven't read it). In this powerful book, Tozer gives a potent reminder that we were designed to connect to God—that we need to seek Him, and we need to listen. "The facts are that God is not silent," Tozer writes, "has never been silent. It is the nature of God to speak."

The Religious Society of Friends spent hours each week listening to God's Spirit. When the Quakers in Liberty and across our country actively sought God almost two hundred years ago, many of them were urged to help slaves on their treacherous journey north. Even though the Quakers in Indiana were initially divided over whether or not to support the abolition of slavery, by the late 1850s most Quakers were devout abolitionists. They opened their homes to runaway slaves and risked everything to assist them, because they believed all men and women are equal in God's sight.

Liberty is now a peaceful farming community of almost two thousand people, surrounded by creeks, hills, farmland, and forest. The mills that used to run along these creeks are gone now, but the Salem Society of Friends still gather in the same meetinghouse where they met in 1850, and right down the road from this meetinghouse stands the home of well-known Underground Railroad conductor and stationmaster William Beard. It was an honor for me to learn about the remarkable heritage of this town and climb up hidden stairs and explore secret rooms where runaways used to hide. And it was an honor to remember all those who risked (and sometimes lost) their lives for their friends.

Blessings,
Melanie Dobson
www.melaniedobson.com

Want a peek into local American life—past and present?
The *Love Finds You*™ series published by Summerside Press
features real towns and combines travel, romance,
and faith in one irresistible package!

The novels in the series—uniquely titled after American towns with unusual but intriguing names—inspire romance and fun. Each fictional story draws on the compelling history or the unique character of a real place. Stories center on romances kindled in small towns, old loves lost and found again on the high plains, and new loves discovered at exciting vacation getaways. Summerside Press plans to publish at least one novel set in each of the 50 states. Be sure to catch them all!

COMING SOON

Love Finds You in Revenge, Ohio by Lisa Harris
ISBN: 978-1-934770-81-8

Love Finds You in Poetry, Texas by Janice Hanna
ISBN: 978-1-935416-16-6

Love Finds You in Sisters, Oregon by Melody Carlson
ISBN: 978-1-935416-18-0

Love Finds You in Charm, Ohio by Birdie Etchison
ISBN: 978-1-935416-17-3

Love Finds You in Bethlehem, New Hampshire by Lauralee Bliss
ISBN: 978-1-935416-20-3

Love Finds You in North Pole, Alaska by Loree Lough
ISBN: 978-1-935416-19-7

summerside
PRESS

FALL IN LOVE WITH SUMMERSIDE